WATCHER

THE TRISH VAMPIRE SERIES

BOOK 3

K.T. ROSE

Watcher
The Trish Vampire Series, Book 3

Copyright © 2025 by K.T. Rose

All rights reserved.

The characters and incidents mentioned in this publication are entirely fictional.

The transmission, duplication, or reproduction of any of the following work, including specific information, will be considered an illegal act irrespective of if it is done electronically or in print. This extends to creating a secondary or tertiary copy of the work or a recorded copy and is only allowed with expressed written consent from the Publisher. All additional right reserved.

Written by: K.T. Rose
Cover Design: Cha

A B O U T   T H E   A U T H O R

K.T. Rose is a horror, thriller, supernatural, paranormal, and suspense author based in Detroit, Michigan. She shares her passion for spine-chilling stories with readers through flash fiction on her blog. Her works include *Ordinary Darkness*, *The Haunting of Gallagher Hotel*, the *Netted Series,* and *The Trish Vampire Series.*

ABOUT WATCHER

Trish's worst nightmare has come true—her secrets are unraveling.

After the events at Miller University, Trish thought she had contained the damage and found Victoria, a victim turned ally. But when Trish's toddler son Darwin's babysitter disappears after a routine evening, she discovers that her carefully guarded double life has been under surveillance all along.

Someone has been watching. Waiting. Recording every move she thought was private.

As Victoria struggles with the aftermath of what she witnessed and new threats emerge from unexpected directions, Trish must confront the possibility that the greatest danger to her family isn't from those hunting her—it's from those closest to home.

With Darwin's life hanging in the balance and decades of deception crumbling around her, Trish faces her most dangerous enemy yet: someone who knows exactly how to destroy everything she's fought to protect.

The explosive final installment to the Trish series, where suburban secrets collide with supernatural survival, and the line between protector and predator becomes deadlier than ever.

CONTENTS

PART I

Darwin's Catch

CHAPTER 1

Gone

Darwin's small face reddened as blood dried around his lips and clotted on his tongue. His uvula trembled, drenched in red, coated in Maggie's blood. Trish held him in her hands, turned his toddler body, and positioned his face over the kitchen sink.

"I don't—" she said as she turned on the faucet, fighting to adjust the lever with her free hand. Her fingers shook, threatening to drop the spray hose before she could pull it long enough to rinse Darwin's gums, his teeth…his fangs. They were small but thick, surely going to be replaced with adult ones, a more resilient pair. Her chest thudded. "I got you. I—" She stifled a sob.

Darwin twisted, screaming louder as she moved closer with the hose. She dropped it and used her free hand to collect some of the running water from the faucet. She poured it on his cheek, and it slid past his mouth, collecting blood and carrying it to the drain. Her breath hitched, a cold prickle ran down her spine, and the world shrank around her. Darwin's teeth retracted into his top gums when the warm water hit them, as if knowing it wasn't blood. Snot flowed from Darwin's nose, mixing with his drool. He shrieked, shouted, cried, kicked—*blamed* her.

"No!" he yelled as his small body jerked. He slapped Trish's hand away.

She tried to steady him by pressing him against her belly.

"Darwin, please," she said.

"No!" He twisted and kicked. "Mama, no!"

"I have to—we have to clean you up, baby." She collected more water, willed him to drink. But he didn't. He slapped her hand away. "I—"

She wanted to tell him to gargle and spit it out, to swish it around and dispose of it. But he wouldn't understand. He'd only just started calling her *Mama* and using the word *no*.

Trish held him upright and watched him weep. Fury and sorrow radiated from his shaken form, begging her to make it all stop. But she could only think about herself—how she'd ruined something so beautiful and innocent. The curse in her cells, her blood, her atoms had transferred to her son, bloating his being with a darkness he didn't deserve.

Time slowed, and Darwin's cries grew quieter.

"How?" she whispered to the person who could not answer. "You can't," she said, her throat tight. Darwin had never reacted to the sun. And he loved food—normal food. He was nothing like her—he couldn't be…

But normal babies didn't kill their babysitters. They didn't stick fangs like boning knives into the soft of their necks, square in the jugular. They didn't paralyze them with venom that could take down the biggest of men and indulge in a bloody treat meant for monsters. They didn't leave their caretakers lying dead, blood spread across their necks and wet shirts like a grotesque bib. Dead-eyed with blood clotting in their dark curly hair, pinned in a moment that they'd wished they'd seen coming.

"Being stress-free is a happier way to be. Things have a way of working out for me, so I just leave it to the universe," Maggie had said a few days before, her petite stature and bright smile so full of life when she turned to Darwin and added, "Right, little monster?"

Trish inhaled a short breath, the tears fighting forward. "No…" she answered the phantom question. She shook her head, taken by her son's wet eyes. "I don't care," she said aloud, the declaration breaking through the fog. "Once you rolled into the world and cuddled up to my chest—needed me in a way that no one else ever had—I was devoted."

Trish pulled him close and rocked him. "Shhh," she said. "Mommy will fix it. I promise," she whispered. "It's okay. Shhhh."

He rubbed his face into her neck, his cries tapering.

"You're mine," Trish said. "Randel gave me the best gift I ever had… I will do anything to protect you. It's going to be okay."

She swayed, and he eased, allowing his body to shudder from the fading panic. "I know you couldn't help it, baby. I know. But I will fix this."

As Darwin's cries simmered to small groans and stumbling breaths, Trish closed her eyes and thought about Maggie—no, the body in the living room. There was no doubt that Maggie had been killed by Darwin. The way her head hung, those vacant eyes…

Trish pressed the sides of Darwin's stomach, noticing it wasn't hard, only slightly bloated. Was his stomach big enough to hold a grown woman?

She turned to find Vicky standing in the doorway wearing the clothes Trish had given her the night before: hot pink yoga pants and a now bloodied gray hoodie. The fight at the storage unit— the thought of finding a new one for all of her personal belongings made her heart leap—left Vicky shot in the collarbone and full of her ex-boyfriend's blood, which indeed helped: the bullet slid out of the wound, and Vicky was comfortably standing on her once mangled ankle. Trish took credit for the latter; if Vicky didn't want to be caught in a bear trap, she wouldn't have chosen to be such a pain in the ass to begin with. Regardless, Steve's blood had indeed healed her, and Trish needed to find a new storage unit.

"Vicky," Trish said evenly, hiding the urgency that would disturb Darwin's settling calm. "Check Maggie for a pulse."

Vicky stared at Trish, her once-hazel eyes now dark and exhausted. They flashed with accusation: Darwin was yet another innocent life that Trish had corrupted.

"Victoria," Trish said. "Vic-tor-ia," she growled. She wasn't in the mood to deal with another child.

"I don't want to touch her."

"Check for a pulse," Trish spat.

"I—"

"Remember our deal." Trish swallowed hard, burying the rising fury in her chest. "You listen to me, and I will teach you to go your own way. Now, please," she hissed.

Vicky turned toward the living room just off the kitchen. The bloody scene on the couch was hard to miss. She stopped, then cocked her head. "Where is she?"

Trish huffed, ground her teeth. "On the couch," she said. She wasn't sure if Vicky was committed to playing some sort of game or…

"Uh, this couch? Because—"

"Yeah, I only have one couch!" Trish quipped.

Vicky turned back to the kitchen, her eyes wide. "She's gone!"

CHAPTER 2

Without Pursuit

Vicky's heart hammered in her chest, feeling for the poor kid in Trish's arms, and wondering about Maggie. Vicky hadn't seen her, but she could smell her blood as it seeped into the furniture, becoming one with the couch. It was coppery and unclean, riddled with THC, much like Steve's had been. Vicky had also heard Maggie's sweet voice before—when she lay in the trunk of Trish's car, waiting to see Steve for the last time, listening to voices louder than she had ever heard them.

"What?" Trish asked. Darwin's face was pressed to her chest as he sniffled, coming down from his fit. Her face crumpled as she took in Vicky's announcement.

Vicky leaned against the doorframe. "*Maggie!* She's gone."

Hot anger flashed across Trish's face and her eyes somehow got darker. Darwin had finally calmed down, but he was still bothered. His breaths stumbled over ghost whimpers as he relaxed in her arms; his face moved up to her neck. Vicky imagined Trish had been contemplating next steps, like how she was going to get rid of Maggie and where she was going to store her entire life that was now in the back seat of her car. Vicky wondered if Trish's most recent crime scene clung to the edges of her mind; Steve's bloodless corpse lay on the floor of her abandoned storage unit, a red hole painted in his forehead where her bullet shredded his brain. A gruesome slash carved his neck, hiding Vicky's bite marks.

And now, Maggie was gone.

"Why? How?" Trish asked.

"I don't know," Vicky said. "Go check for yourself."

She looked at her son. "I-I'm not taking him back in there. Are-are you sure?"

Vicky narrowed her eyes. "Why would I make something like that up? What, should I check under the couch? She's gone, okay."

"Well, why didn't you stop her?" Trish asked as she rushed through the kitchen and into the hallway. Vicky followed. They stopped at the top of the steps. The front door was wide open, allowing the night to flush the foyer. They stepped out onto the porch to catch a glimpse of a car's taillights speeding up the street and hanging a left onto the main stretch, leaving the neighborhood. "Why didn't you stop her?" Trish asked again, whispering.

The nerve of this damn lady, Vicky thought. Not only had she ruined Vicky's life, a college student who had been minding her best friend's messy business when Trish decided to steal her blood, but Trish's kid had gone and killed his babysitter, undoubtably turning her like Trish had turned Vicky. Vicky rolled her eyes. "I didn't see her leave. I was in the kitchen with you. How was I supposed to—"

Trish rushed past Vicky, she and Darwin heading back inside. She stopped in the foyer and looked at Vicky, beckoning her inside. Vicky obliged, and Trish shut the door behind them.

"You know what'll happen if anyone finds her?" Trish spoke slowly, calm enough to ease Darwin to sleep, but urgent enough to raise alarm in Vicky's chest. "If the police find her, they will know where to find us, and when they show up here, they will recognize you."

"How will they draw any of this to me? He's *your* kid. Not mine," Vicky said.

"Because the FBI was at the hospital ready to take you away."

Vicky's lips parted, but nothing came out. The FBI was going to take her away and lie to everyone, saying she died from some kind of virus. That very agent was living in the house across the street. It was all the more reason for Vicky to take her leave.

"You don't think that the people at the hospital are talking to the police? Or that the guy across the street…" Trish closed her eyes as if that inconvenient fact snuck up in her memory.

Vicky shook her head. "Don't take this shit out on me!" She pointed at Darwin. "I didn't turn her into whatever the fuck this is." She pointed at her own chest.

"It doesn't matter!" Trish shouted, lying through her teeth. Darwin stirred. She bounced and shushed him. Then she took a deep breath. "I know. Okay. I know. This isn't your fault. But they know who you are and I bet they're looking for you. If they come here and see you, this will be all on you if we don't go find Maggie. Do you get that?"

"And if I'm not here?"

Trish fell silent and her face dropped. Scorned. "I— You can't possibly want to leave *right now*."

"Why not?" Vicky crossed her arms, the pieces to a nonexistent plan refusing to form in her head.

"Steve would have killed you if I—"

"He was after *both* of us," Vicky reminded her. "Not just me. I did you a favor by telling you he was in town. And you repaid me by trapping me in a bear trap. A *bear* trap!"

"And I taught you how to heal from that! And I protected you from Steve. I *killed* him," Trish whispered.

"You used me as bait."

Trish clenched her jaw as if hating to explain herself to someone who she claimed *should have been dead*… "I did not use you as bait. I was trying to figure out the best way to catch Steve off guard. What was I supposed to do? Leave you here? In my house with my son? Leave you here in a neighborhood full of food when you were hungry?"

The words stomped Vicky in the chest. She dropped her arms. "Don't say that."

"Say what? Say that you're not human anymore? Say that we both knew that the racoons you used to destroy my Jeep, embarrass me in front of my neighbors, were not enough to quench that new hunger that you just can't quite ignore?" Trish shook her head.

"Admit it. It's not just food. It's medicine. It's water. Energy. Strength. It's everything that you've been missing for the last couple months. And you'll make sure you never go without it *ever* again. After what we went through this evening, you can't disagree."

Vicky scoffed, flabbergasted, not sure if she was being gas lit or hearing a new truth. Trish talked Vicky into drinking Steve. Trish turned Vicky into a monster. Trish gave birth to another monster. *Trish* was the villain, not Vicky. She didn't ask for her mouth to drown in sweet nectar at the sight of blood, for her nostrils to flare at its meaty scent. Her body didn't need medicine, food, or water. It only required thick, warm blood. Trish had bestowed that craving on someone who didn't want it. But it existed, and it was strong. "No. You're right. I can't disagree." Vicky tilted her head toward Darwin. "And neither can he."

Darwin let out another stuttering sigh, and Trish hugged him a little tighter. "This isn't about him."

"Yes, it is," Vicky said.

Beg

Darwin had settled down in his car seat, which Trish had set on the floor in the kitchen. He seemed curious about Vicky, sneaking small grins whenever his mom wasn't whizzing around the room, snatching things up. Trish grabbed Darwin's diaper bag, some snacks, and a bottle of milk from the fridge. Vicky watched her hesitate for a minute when she glared at the bottle, probably wondering if there was any point in bringing it along. The boy had tasted blood, and if he was anything like Vicky, it was the best thing that he'd ever tasted. It was so good that he fell into a tantrum. Vicky wondered if the tantrum was from the horror of killing or if he was upset that it was all gone. Or maybe he was high like Vicky had been for most of the ride from the storage unit. There was no way Vicky would have seen Maggie or agreed to give any type of chase; Vicky couldn't trust her own eyes. During the entire ride, she floated on air, her mind veering with every lane change, dripping acid memories, fixated on the final colors that painted Steve's last words in the fateful stairwell: *"I can get you some food, and we aren't playing in the shed, I'll let you back into the basement."*

Then he was dead, and she drank him before he went cold.

Maybe Darwin was reliving his last thoughts with his babysitter?

Projection, Vicky thought. Still, she and the baby had a lot in common, not just their blasphemous condition, but the displeasure of knowing Trish. Vicky grunted.

Trish hung the diaper bag on her arm and then grabbed Darwin.

"Dammit," Trish said as she rubbed the black tape on the back of the front door. She headed out and waited on the porch until Vicky stepped out, then slammed the door and locked it.

Once in the driveway, Trish paused and looked at Vicky, who stood in the yard, wondering if her shed was still up for grabs and if Detroit was still a good idea. Wondering if a plan existed anywhere in her mind. Exposed and naked to the world without a foot to stand on.

Trish's white knuckles tightened on the handle of Darwin's car seat. "You can't be serious." She seemed to choke around the words, distressed in a way that Vicky didn't think she was capable of.

Trish was so sure about herself at the storage unit. She *just knew* they were going to raid Steve's mile-long farmland and catch them off guard. But he ended up doing the same thing to Vicky and Trish, and it got him killed. Even when Steve found where Trish had been keeping her secrets, including Vicky, she kept a steady head. Trish only allowed a glimpse of her disdain to show before she stepped confidently into the next phase of her plan: using Vicky as bait to put Steve down once and for all. But the woman holding her son's car seat was different. There was something desperately human about her as her eyes dragged, longing, almost begging. For a second, Vicky wanted to bask in it. Wanted to tell her to set Darwin down and get on her knees, beg for Vicky's help. She wanted to tell Trish to ask nicely and apologize. It was almost funny, but more pathetic. "What?" Vicky asked.

"You *have* to help me. You can't just leave—where are you going to go?"

Embarrassed that Trish may have been reading Vicky's mind— *Can she do that?*—Vicky whispered, "What does it matter to you? Why do people think that they can continue to manipulate me and tell me what I am and am not going to do?" she yelled.

"Stop yelling," Trish said. Darwin was dozing off, his head lulling as he fought sleep. The thick cotton sweater he had been wearing seemed to serve as a comfortable cushion for what looked like an otherwise uncomfortable position.

Even though Darwin was a sweet child, the fact remained that his mother was an asshole. "Why do you think I need to stay here? Why would I help you after what you put me through? After you *ruined* my life."

As if remembering that it was cold out, much too cold for a baby (even if he was a monster), Trish set Darwin in the grass and opened the driver's side door. She hit the garage remote that was attached to the sun visor and opened the garage door. She grabbed some of the bags out of the back seat and put them in the garage. The black garbage bags were full of Trish's raided storage unit: clothes, shoes, papers, accessories…her life upended by Steve and his friends…and Vicky. Then she put Darwin in the back seat behind the driver's seat. As she strapped him in, she finally asked, "Can we talk about this in the car?" She popped the trunk and took two bags from there, and set them in the garage. She pulled a blanket out of one of the bags and put it in the trunk.

"What? No!" Vicky said, bristling at the question.

"Okay, fine. But where else do you need to be, Vicky? Are you going home to your family looking like that? Look at your clothes—*my* clothes. Look at your *mouth*. You're right. You don't have to stay here. You can venture off and figure things out on your own. But you and I both know that it's lonely out there, and that there are people after you. You have no idea what you're doing."

"You managed to do it."

Trish sighed. "I'll tell you everything. Only if you stay. Only if you help me. I promise you will never be scared or get caught again."

Vicky shook her head slowly. "How can you help me? It's your fault that I'm like this!"

"I can help you because I've been this way for a long, long time. I—I was born in the 19th century." A wet, shameful chuckle. "Can you believe it? I turned 150 on May 7th."

Vicky dropped her arms to her sides.

"I'll tell you more. I'll tell you why I look different from the night you saw me. I was pale and bony. Right? I pass as a nineteen-year-old because that's when I was killed. I can tell you how I live a normal life. Why the name on my license is Patricia Elaine Weston and not Patricia Ellen Bixel like it is on my original birth certificate. I'll tell you everything. I'll teach you everything. But you have to help me."

Vicky swiped fresh tears from her face as she listened to this lost woman's story. Trish should be a mummy or in a casket. Vicky should be talking to Trish's great-great-granddaughter about classes and motherhood. About new coffee flavors and new SUVs, not the life of a living dead serial killer prepping a lesson plan. "Sorry," Vicky spat.

"Look, Vicky, I'm not Steve," Trish said. His name sounded wrong coming off of Trish's tongue. Vicky wanted to unhear it. "I know you are not over him, or you found out in the worst way possible that someone you trusted fucked you over. But guess what? That's your existence now. I would say life, but…" Trish flicked her fingers in the air as if to say, *Have you seen yourself lately?* "Now, please, get in."

"I can't," Vicky protested.

Clearly out of patience, Trish stepped close to Vicky, nose to nose. "Okay. Fine. But by the way shit's looking, you need me more than I need you."

Vicky scoffed. "Really? Because—"

"Yeah. Really. I already told you that I can't change you back. No one can. But my offer is still sitting on the table."

"So, what? You teach me and I help you bury bodies? You're insane."

"This life will do that to you. Make you crazy. At least learn to manage it."

"What?"

"Get in the car and find out."

"No! What is this? A ride-along?"

Trish offered a half-smirk. The sadness fell away from her face, making room for despair with a hint of mania. She seemed more menacing than the night she attacked Vicky. "Yeah. What do you think we're going to do once we get Maggie? There is only room for one—" She looked at Darwin— "two in this training program."

"So that's the lesson for the night? You're going to kill Maggie?"

"You damn right."

"No, you can't… She… It wasn't her fault."

"You got Steve killed…and you sucked his blood." Trish raised a brow.

"He was a threat."

"Maggie is too. Now, I need to go deal with her, and if you're smart, you'll come too."

Trish turned her back. Then she stopped. "Or the agent across the street can follow you to wherever the hell you end up going on foot. You said he had pictures of me standing in front of my house. What if he's watching us right now?"

Vicky's eyes widened as she looked around, dizziness wrapping her head as she searched for a shining lens in the evening dark. She was standing in the grass in front of Trish's porch steps, the background of the very picture that Vicky found in Agent Morgan's home office.

CHAPTER 4

Plans

Trish committed the address to memory the moment she ran Maggie's background check after she interviewed for the babysitting position. Her curly brunette hair was glossy and big, her name brand clothes fresh out of a magazine. Pink blush adorned her fair, round face, and her purse cost more than some people's monthly salary. She had sat on the couch and told Randel and Trish all about school and how much she loved kids. Bubbly and chill, she sold herself, getting the job that would change her on that very couch.

The road outside went pitch black, no streetlights. Trish's phone dinged. She didn't dare look at it. Not until they got to their first destination. The car was quiet as Trish drove, and Vicky kept her eyes on the dark night beyond the passenger window. Darwin finally fell asleep, resting in the back seat. She couldn't remember the last time she took him on a night drive. When he was small, she and Randel took him for rides to get him to fall asleep, which he rarely ever did.

She repented bringing Darwin along to the shitshow. Taking him to a kidnapping, murder—she still didn't know what she was driving herself, her son, and Vicky into. But what else could she do? Who else would take him on such short notice? They had already let Maggie get a lead too wide for comfort, and Trish wasn't calling Pita. There was no time to wait for her to grab him and sneak in a few questions.

Thinking of Pita brought on another thought. After she made sure Darwin was clean, getting any rogue blood drops off him, Pita would be getting a call early in the morning, after Trish cleaned up the mess. *Oh, yes. Hi, Pita,* she acted the conversation out in her mind, imagining herself talking into the speaker phone as she scrubbed the blood off the leather couch. *I'm so sorry to bother you, but can you come get Darwin while I take a not-so-quick trip to the marina? You see, he killed that Maggie girl, and I need to dump her. And no, I'm not sure that she will actually be dead, but at least a monster that had been reduced to body parts and sunken into the depths of Lake Michigan can't do much harm. Am I right?* She imagined Pita stumbling over her words, out of things to say for the first time in their lie of a friendship. Trish would interrupt her. *No, you don't have to worry about him biting you, silly. I assure you, he is full.* Her forced jovial tone made her cringe in the present. *Well, you and my husband always bitch about me being guarded, so I wanted to take this opportunity to let you know everything. Are you happy? Does that mean you'll help me by watching my kid while I commit crimes? Huh? Does that mean that I don't have to do this shit alone anymore and I can trust you to take my secrets to your muddy grave? Huh? Does that mean that you'll understand that when Darwin bites you or your kids or your husband, there's nothing I can do but kill you too? Burn you, your house, and your family to the ground?*

Feeling her vision glazing, she slightly shook her head. *I'm losing my fucking mind,* she thought. She sucked in a deep breath and rotated her shoulders. *Pieces,* she thought. *When there are too many moving parts, take it in pieces.*

She entered the parking lot of one of the many parks in the area. It was on the outskirts of town, on the way to where Maggie's super well-off parents lived. Her father, Mark, owned a construction company, and her mother, Bianca, owned four hair salons along the lakeshore, stretching from Holland up to Ludington. Most of the people in Maggie's neighborhood built their own homes that surrounded Bronze Lake, turning the heavily forested area that once teemed with deer, swan, and bears into an alcove for upper middle-class millionaires. It was odd, really. Why did Maggie feel the need to pick up a babysitting gig? Trish wondered that for a while until she smelled the

THC wafting off Maggie as it lay deep in her dyed roots. Her parents probably made her use her own money to pay for the gas to pick up her cheap drugs. She looked at Vicky. "We need to talk about the reality of the situation."

"Why did you leave Steve's body?" Vicky turned her eyes to Trish. "Was it to get me caught?"

"No. That's not it at all." Trish narrowed her eyes, dreading having to explain the obvious. "If you get caught, I get caught," she said.

"Was it because you were afraid? I saw your face when you saw that he'd found your storage unit."

"It was more about timing than fear. There was no telling if he had called for more people…no telling if his reach was wider than you or me could know. No telling where Earl went… If someone stumbles on the storage unit anytime soon, they'd know that Earl was somewhere in a bad way and that the person who had done it was also dead. How and by who? They'll never find out. Hence the purpose of his slit neck." Vicky was baffled when Trish made a point to cut Steve's throat, covering Vicky's bite marks.

"I…I don't think I can do this. I-I know Steve was a terrible person and that he probably deserved what happened. But there was so much blood. So—"

"And you liked the way it tasted, didn't you?"

"I—" Her lips trembled. "I'm going to hell…"

"Y-you think your karma for healing yourself is going to hell?"

Vicky gave a stiff nod.

"So, you think my son is going to hell? Or would you say that he was acting on instinct?"

"I—That's not my place to say."

The silliness of it all made Trish chuckle. Vicky still wasn't getting it. She was not human anymore; there was no need to allow religion to hang around her neck like an albatross, weighing her down with unnecessary guilt. She was beyond that. "Karma," Trish began. "Yeah, another word of advice: all that hocus pocus, be good, do as I say but not as I do bullshit that you thought was real is all a lie. Every bit of it. There's no karma. There's no God. There's just us in the universe. And hell, what if it's all real? It doesn't matter, because you won't die; you'll never find out. We get to live. We get to eat. We get to watch things evolve around us."

"Hm," Vicky said.

"Yeah, so now that that's all squared away, like I was saying, the reality of the current situation is that we don't know Maggie's state when she left the house, and we don't know the state of Maggie when we find her."

"So, you're doubting that your son turned her into…" The statement sounded silly coming from Vicky, but she was right.

"Did Darwin turn her? Did she go to the hospital? Did she make it to her house? All very good questions."

"Okay. But say we make it to her house, and she's there. Then what?"

Trish tilted her head, careful about her next words because she didn't know *then what*. What would she do with Darwin while Maggie was being taken care of?

Trish looked in the rearview as if Darwin would know the answer to that very question. But unlike Vicky, he couldn't respond; he learned to eat before he learned to speak. He figured out his place on the food chain before he knew the difference between fruits and vegetables. He could not convey his thoughts, leaving Vicky to be the closest Trish would get to knowing, remembering, what it was like to change.

Trish's phone rang, filling the car with the sound of chiming bells blown by an easy spring breeze.

She picked up her phone to find Pita's name. She ignored it.

"Let's just get to Maggie's house first and then we'll deal with what's next—"

"If she's there," Vicky said. Her tone was all knowing. Bitchy.

Pita called again, and Trish ignored the call again.

"Yeah, whatever." Trish almost regretted inviting Vicky along, but what choice did she have? Vicky needed to stay in sight until Trish was confident that they would not get caught.

Trish's phone dinged again, and she looked at it, grinding the backs of her teeth. Pita texted in all caps. It looked like a title to an article followed by a link. The heading to the clip said: *Priest Found Dead in Midnight Home Invasion Massacre.*

Trish's eyes widened and her heart leapt to her throat. She knew who it was about, but it was the second message that threw her for a loop.

Pita: *Gosh. I can't believe how crazy this world is. My niece's professor was killed in his house the other day! I mean, what the hell is going on? In Miller of all places? And to a priest? Anyway, call me when you can. Gabby is really torn up about it. She said she saw him with a strange woman that night and the police are asking her all sorts of questions. I really need to talk to someone about it. I am really afraid for her, and so is my brother. Love you, girl!*

CHAPTER 5

Breaking

Someone in Pita's family had a connection to Toby—saw Trish with him, and Pita had a connection to Trish.

And Gabby. The name sounded familiar. Trish didn't know why. She tried to place it in one of the many conversations that she and Pita had. She found many. But the name came across in a different tone. From someone else. But who?

"Gabby," she said. She said the name over and over as she pressed the link in the text, playing the video and turning the volume up.

Two anchors sat behind a desk and in front of a screen, the words *Preacher Murdered in Miller* were yellow across the navy background. *"We have some news out of Miller University today,"* a woman with dark hair started, the name and title *Kathy Reese, Anchor* scrolled across the bottom of the screen. *"A prominent professor and pastor was found dead along with a Miller University student and two other Miller residents. We are joining Tanya for more on this devastating story. Tanya?"*

A short blonde woman wearing a black peacoat stood in the foreground of one of the many university buildings on Miller University's campus. The name and title *Tanya Spar, Field Reporter* pinned to the screen. *"Thanks, Kathy. We are coming to you live from Miller University, where a professor and student were among four individuals who were found dead at the professor's home. The university reported that Dr. Tobias Webb hadn't shown up to classes in two days, and when he didn't show up for the Friday night sermon, people knew something was wrong."*

"I—" The familiar round babyface from the bar. Her once luscious dark hair looked oily, and her face was red with tears. She was standing with a group of people in front of a church house. *Gabby.* The girl who almost took Toby home when Trish had gone to the bathroom. The girl who almost saved his life. *"I don't know who would do this. I saw him the other day in class, and last week at church..."*

"And that night at the bar when you were trying to fuck him..." Trish said aloud, defending herself to no one, and breaking her no cursing rule.

"...and now... He didn't deserve this."

"Gabrielle Sullen is a student and part of the clergy of young people who often went to Dr. Webb for a kind word or advice," Tanya said.

Trish cocked her head. "Of course, Gabby didn't mention the bar—"

"Police went to conduct a welfare check and found a gruesome scene," Tanya went on as the camera cut to the sky-blue colonial that sat on a stony foundation. Yellow tape encompassed the perimeter.

Sheriff Theo Bolton, also known as Steve's uncle, stood at the podium, leading the charge at a press conference. Steve's uncle was much shorter than Trish realized. His fair skin looked pink as he stroked his thick mustache. Lights from flashing cameras flicked off his glistening dome. *"There were four deceased in different parts of the home. It was a difficult scene to decipher, and we are still collecting evidence. We do not have a suspect in custody. We are going to let the coroner do the autopsies and make the information available. Whoever was responsible for this is a monster and should not be on the streets. We do not have any leads, and I cannot answer any questions at this time."*

"What was the cause of death?" a reporter asked.

"We are not at liberty to say at this time."

"Who were the others in the home?"

"Do you know if the priest had been in contact with anyone that night?"

"Sheriff, Sheriff."

Their questions died down; no answers were given.

"Police have no leads, but I am getting word that they believe that the massacre was drug related. Still, the community is searching for answers," Tanya said.

An older man with a clean-shaven ivory face and a balding head looked down at Tanya as he spoke into her microphone. *"Is there a killer on the loose or was this personal?"* Dr. Tate Wilkins, President of Miller University, was close friends with the late preacher and is pushing for the police to find answers. *"The police need to find who did this because this is usually a peaceful town, and to think that something like that could happen to one of our educators and students is chilling."*

"He was a preacher at Hope United Methodist Church. The congregation held a service in his name and is raising money for his burial."

"I don't know how something like that could happen in this community. We are tight knit, always looking out for each other," said a tall priest with a shock of white hair. Trish didn't catch his name.

"Yeah right," Vicky said under her breath.

"Give me a break," Trish said. Danny sure didn't think the town was so tight knit with all the drugs and mysterious disappearances over the years. His pock-marked reddening face was still fresh in her memory. She lay in Toby's bed staring at Danny's blond buzz cut and shotgun barrel for what felt like hours before she headbutted him in his disgusting erection and broke his neck. "Steve owns the entire town," he had said. And after what Steve had done to Vicky and Earl back at the storage facility, Trish believed every word of it.

"Do the police have any idea as to how they were killed?" Kathy asked from the news desk.

"Like the sheriff said, they have to do an autopsy because the manner of death was so gruesome that it isn't easy to make an educated guess. But we just found out that there was no sign of a break-in; the assailant knew the victims. Two of the victims were Dr. Tobias Webb and a student whose name is being withheld until the family is reached, and we are now getting word that the name of another victim was Barbara Webb, Dr. Webb's, uh, cousin."

"Thanks, Tanya. You heard it here first, we have the name of another victim whose body was found at the home of Dr. Tobias Webb,

and she is his cousin, Barbara Webb. We will keep you updated on any further developments on this devastating massacre. Up next—" The video ended there.

Trish sighed. "Go ahead," she said.

"Go ahead and what?" Vicky asked. She sounded tired.

"Ask."

"Ask if you'll finally get yourself caught? Ask if you are sloppier than you led on? You know, you preached to me all damn day about being this and doing that. But it's you. You are the sloppy one. You did that." Vicky pointed at the phone. "And they might catch you because of it."

"How?"

"How what?"

"How are they going to catch me?"

To that, Vicky said nothing.

"Exactly." Trish's throat tightened as a chill crawled up her back.

CHAPTER 6

Bronze Lake

775 Niger Lane.

Maggie's mailbox, a tin monstrosity that someone painted with black blotches on a white background, making it look like a cow, was the only thing on the flat gravel shoulder that lined the narrow road. Vicky understood why they used the gag mailbox: it acted as an indicator, letting anyone know that there was indeed someone's property behind the crowd of trees.

Vicky didn't understand how anyone would live out in the middle of nowhere—did they even have a Wi-Fi signal? Then she decided it didn't matter. Nothing mattered anymore. Vicky had no plans. She didn't know where to go with no way to get there, and she didn't have a phone that was charged—she hadn't checked to see if anyone was still looking for her. Besides Agent Morgan, who lived across the street from Trish, of course. Maybe he did see her standing in Trish's yard, waiting to pounce and drag her to whatever facility in whatever underground bunker. Her heart flickered. Why was she hanging out with someone that the government was so interested in?

Because you don't have anyone else, she thought. She huffed at that.

"Campground, campground," Trish whispered to herself.

The car was quiet, no music or GPS. Trish left everyone, including Darwin, alone with their thoughts as they turned onto another road. The tires climbed, displacing pebbles and crushing dirt as they crept up the entrance way. The sign read, *Bronze Shores Campground*. The deep green letters arched over a painting of a glimmery copper colored lake. They followed the road, taking the light away from the sign, leaving it alone in the dark where they found it. But the road before them did not steal the light; Trish turned the headlights off.

They rounded a shadowy clearing. In the center was a small lime-green tent. Next to it was a table with a lone lantern. Vicky's heart pounded for the brave soul who decided to camp alone. If Trish were alone and hungry, there was no doubt that she would go after them. Trish would walk up to the tent and use her claws to open it. She'd wrap her hands around the unsuspecting person's neck—a middle-aged, gray-bearded man—and suffocate him with a strangle-hold before sinking her teeth into his neck. But the hands around him, holding him tight, crushing his bones, willing him to stay still, were not pale. They were brown. And his phantom blood tasted good on Vicky's tongue as her mouth watered with sweet nectar. She wanted to swim in Crimson Lake Manor. She could sleep in it, inject it directly into her—

"Looks empty," Trish announced as she tilted her head at the building that was coming up on their left. The ranger station, which looked more like a cabin, was empty with all the lights out and no movement inside. There was one car in the parking lot, and it must have belonged to the man of nature who was out there in the grass, alone.

Or at least that's how Vicky imagined him.

They continued along the narrow road that circled the property until they slowed down, nearly coming to a stop.

Trish pointed and said, "Her house is that way."

All Vicky saw was a thick row of trees that kept whatever secrets hidden behind them. From where they sat, they looked like pine trees standing guard, ready to stab and poke whoever dared to defy the perimeter. At least the campground retained some semblance of life that was there before people came along and destroyed things. Or maybe they had not had the chance to tear the trees down to expand or build more shit. Vicky didn't know and... *It doesn't matter.*

Trish threw the car in park and turned it off. Vicky didn't want the woman to ask her to do anything—to go anywhere. She simply wanted to wake up from her fever dream and get on with her day, kissing the steady ground of a normal, stable life.

"Maggie said her parents were out of town. Her brother might be over there with some friends. She—she complained about them a couple days ago." Trish's mind seemed to waver.

Does she miss Maggie? Does she feel anything? Vicky thought.

"Anyway," Trish said, "Maggie said her parents would be gone for a week, due back in a couple days now."

"So, what? Are you just going to walk over there and get her?" Vicky kicked herself for asking at all. She never liked any of Trish's plans, and simply not knowing might've made things easier. But she couldn't help but ask. She was usually the planner. But who could plan to be…what she turned out to be?

"I don't know," Trish said. "We can't leave her here."

"Right. If she's here at all."

Trish shrugged. "Right. And there's only one way to find out." She turned her body in the driver's seat, facing Vicky.

"I mean, if she avoided everyone when she went in…maybe they don't know she's there? Have you ever been to her house before?" Vicky asked, spit balling.

Trish shook her head. Even though it was dark, Vicky felt as if she were seeing Trish for the first time. Her big dark eyes were focused, not worried. Her cheekbones pierced her tight cheeks, making her look like an emo model, passing for a frail twenty-something. She seemed like a wise old woman who was stuck in a young woman's body. But the more Vicky looked at her, the more touch-and-go Trish became. Immaturity clung to Trish in that sort of way. She planned, but she took risks that may have been unnecessary. *But are they really unnecessary?* Vicky's heart blurted a resounding, *No!*

But when Trish's eyes lingered a little too long on Vicky, her back straightened, and Vicky puffed her chest out. *There's no way in hell…* "No! Hell no, I'm not going over there—I'm not doing shit!"

"What?" Trish asked.

Vicky huffed, her insolence bleak.

"Hear me out—"

"No! I am not leaving this car. She is *your* problem."

"I—"

"No! And don't preach that bullshit to me about how you did me a favor by killing Steve. Maggie's people won't want me *anywhere* near their house. At least they know you! They don't know shit about me. How do you think that'll look? Some black girl, who looks homeless as hell by the way, walking around their house, which is *deep* in the cut. Jesus wouldn't be able to find that thing on the map. They will shoot me on sight! No! Clean up your child's mess."

Trish smiled. Then she giggled.

"What?"

"I wasn't going to ask you to do that. I was going to ask if you could watch Darwin while I'm gone."

If Vicky could feel heat, she was sure that her cheeks were on fire.

Trish looked at Darwin. He was looking at Vicky. He smiled at her and chuckled. He grabbed his foot and pulled his shoe off, tossed it onto the floor. "No," he said. That made Vicky smirk.

"I'll go in. But you have to watch Darwin. Deal?"

"Why'd you bring a baby to a kidnapping and/*or* murder?" Vicky was genuinely curious. Did Trish not have anyone else besides her husband? *Probably not*, Vicky thought. The woman had been alive for over one hundred years. Everyone she knew was dead. Vicky shuddered. That was going to be her one day. But she would not make the mistake of pushing a kid out of her monster twat. No one deserved to be that unlucky.

"You don't expect me to leave him with just *anyone* right now, do you?"

"I mean—" Darwin kicked his legs, having pulled the other shoe off. He spat and rubbed saliva on the window.

"I can't risk him biting someone and…" Trish looked in the direction of the house, "…someone finding out what he did."

Vicky knitted her brow. "You think it's safe? I mean, what if I'm stuck having to hide him and me if something happens to you?"

"Nothing's going to happen." Trish opened the baby bag and pulled out a pen. Then she reached inside the glove compartment. "Here's my number."

"I don't have a phone," Vicky lied. It was dead in her backpack, which was still lying on the floor of the back seat.

"I'm sure you can find one if the emergency is that serious."

"I—"

"Listen…" Trish put a finger up. Crickets chirped in the still November night. Loose leaves rolled across stiff grass. Laughter and music blasted from somewhere nearby, and waves crashed as they curled and kissed the shore.

"What?" Vicky said, now overloaded with sounds that she could not unhear.

"Do you hear anything?"

"Yes."

Trish smirked. "When I changed, the first thing I did was hide from everyone—I needed space to think. Was I dying? Was I bitten by something unworldly? What was that new taste that I was craving? Did you think the same thing?"

Vicky hesitated, wanting to say something, but she put her answer through a filter first. Then she said, "I hid with Steve. You see how that turned out."

"Welp, you might be on to something. I think Maggie's at home hiding. Somewhere beneath the noise, she is thinking in silence until she can figure it out." Trish looked at the woods. "I'm going to get her."

C H A P T E R   7

Property

It took Trish fifteen minutes to cut through the host of trees, some snagging at her skin. Low-hanging branches bare to the wooden bone made her wince as they clawed at her leather jacket and dark sweats. She quietly jogged on her toes, not breaking a sweat, but with hitched breath thanks to high knee raises.

Once the woods broke, she came upon a colonial, naked of drywall and windows. It stood as a house of lumber planks, an abandoned project or one that had just begun. Tall grass swayed in the evening wind, mildly disturbed by the moving atmosphere as it danced in the night. On the other side of that, Trish heard the small lake wipe the shore, moving in and out as the crescent moon allowed. The grass hid the shore and any small sandy beach that acted as a precursor.

On the other side of the empty house was what she expected to find: another man-made clearing that owned a piece of the private lake. The landscape was too perfect, accommodating the mini mansions that lined the sides of the lake, including the campground. The perfectly placed line of sheared fir bushes held onto their leaves as they would when the snow fell. The seclusion and inclusion of it all seemed wrong, but unsurprising.

Trish passed the line of waist-high, roundly trimmed firs and stopped when she stepped onto a massive, plushy green yard. The property was about ten acres, with the house sitting in the center.

The brick house rose two stories in the back, where a deck over-looked a lit pool. Fog drifted across the heated water—someone had been there recently, or was planning to be. As Trish crouched, using the bushes for cover, she thought, *No wonder Maggie's parents can't get rid of their kids.* The house was nice; immaculate, really. Something that she herself wouldn't mind having if she cared for such things. Tall windows offered a glimpse of the granite-coated kitchen with shiny appliances, and the TV in the living room was on with no one watching. It had to be 100 inches, taking up the entire wall. Trish scaled the wall of foliage, stopped when she made it to the front of the house. Yellow lights gleamed, shining on a row of four cars that were sitting in the driveway. Maggie's navy Prius, still an eyesore, was parked next to a red Mustang. The other two cars, a silver Mazda and a green pickup truck, blocked the red Mustang in, but Maggie's car was clear of all traffic.

Rowdy shouts and laughter erupted from underneath blaring music that seemed to get louder when the front door swung open, and a man wearing a black jacket and jeans strolled out. He hustled down the steps, went for the green pickup truck.

"Hey, Aaron!" A shout from the door. Trish could not see who the voice belonged to, but it was from a man with a raspy tenor. "Don't forget my beer this time!" A liquid arch came flying out the house, landing with a wet splat onto the paved walkway. "This shit tastes like cooter piss!"

Aaron chuckled, his hand on the door handle of the pickup truck. "Hey, fuck you, dude! How do you know what piss tastes like anyway?"

"Your mom," the man slurred. "Hurry up or we'll start the bong without you."

Aaron flipped off the man at the door, who slammed the door behind him. He got in the pickup truck and backed out, headed for the road which was about a quarter-mile away.

One less person to deal with, Trish thought. *But where is Maggie?*

Trish jogged across the yard, getting closer to the house. She crouched and peered at the garage, noticing a camera mounted to the edge of the roof. She clenched her teeth. *I guess everyone has cameras now. Luckily, I didn't come in that way.*

She dropped her shoulders, unsure of how to proceed. The house was big. There was an undetermined number of people inside. She didn't know the layout of the house, and she wasn't sure what Maggie's condition was. She bit her lower lip as she turned and headed back to the brush. But then she stopped, hearing something. The desperate sound passed so quickly that if anyone wasn't familiar with it, they would not have heard it. It was the pained yelp of someone taking their last breath. Seeing the last thing that they would ever see.

And it didn't come from inside the house.

She hopped over the wall of brush, safely hidden on the other side. She followed the sound, going toward the backyard. Aside from the glowing, foggy pool, it was dark—so dark that she couldn't see beyond it to the private shore along Bronze Lake.

Then she heard giggles.

She stepped out of hiding, heading into the backyard, looking, searching for the gateway to the lake. There was the dark silhouettes of the patio and patio furniture. The ruckus inside the house consisted of short bursts of laughter that died out gradually. The noise was pertinent in the air, but as she went deeper into the backyard, coming up on a narrow boardwalk flanked by tall grass, a new noise took hold.

Staggered squeaking. A grunting struggle.

***

The boardwalk sounded hollow underneath Trish's feet, forcing her to step lighter, walking on her toes. Beach grass clattered as the tall blades shoved at one another, making room for the freezing wind as it rushed by the shore. Clusters of pickerelweeds tangled with lake grass, only noticeable by the purple flowers that started to shed petals, preserving themselves for the coming months.

Crashing water spread over the sandy beach; it swayed, leaving a wet imprint on the packed sand. The moon glistened on the surface. The shadows of fall algal bloom swaying with its home on the watery surface. The boardwalk ended, giving way to wooden docks that extended out from the eight properties that surrounded the lake, one of them having to belong to the campground, which looked dark and abandoned. The docks that belonged to the half-lit homes were preoccupied by boats ranging from fishing boats to larger boats that could have been houseboats. For a fleeting second, Trish wondered if Maggie's parents considered such a solution to getting their full-grown kids out of the house. The boat on their dock was bigger than Trish and Randel's boat, *The Weston World,* which was a mini yacht in its own right.

But no matter how much she wanted to believe that things would be that easy—finding Maggie or whoever the squealer was on that boat—the grunts didn't come from there. She looked up the shore and laid eyes on what made things much more complicated.

It was the kicking feet that drew her attention. The bent knees of the owner of the combat boots ruffled the lakeside foliage, and as Trish slowly approached, crouched low, she caught glimpses of flailing fingers, swinging up and down. Whenever they landed on their shrilling target, they made a wet thudding sound. The lake swallowed the menial calls for help from the man, which came out as short-lived low groans and wet shrieks.

It would be easy to sneak up on Maggie, interrupt the assault by giving him a chance to live, run for help, and praise the stranger who pulled the dangerously manic girl off of him. Give him a chance to explain what the mystery woman looked like and tell them that she was the last one to see Maggie before she disappeared. Not him. He would be the survivor, telling his story to anyone who would listen.

She was crazy, he'd say.

Trish stopped, her vision lying as his fight wavered, the girl sitting across his lap, sure to hide the assault within the lakeside weeds. Maggie breathed heavily and cackled whenever her murderous frenzy allowed it, her fingers kicking up blood.

No. It would be easy to stop it all in that second. But Trish was enthralled with the discovery, studying the girl as she moved. *Was she going to feed?* She'd only turned an hour or so ago, thanks to Vicky not caring to watch Maggie or having Trish waste so much time trying to convince her to come along. Would Maggie want to feed this early? Trish thought about blood after smelling it in the woods all those years ago, but she only acted on it after nearly dying of loneliness, sunburns, and famine. It had even taken Vicky months to finally indulge in what she'd been missing. But Maggie? It seemed like she was playing with her food, not eating it.

Trish sniffed, only smelling the man's blood as it soaked the sand, set to water the roots of the beach grass for centuries to come, unless people decided that they wanted a shopping mall in that very spot, no longer upper middle-class hideaway homes. If Maggie had a smell, it was probably hiding underneath the man's bloody musk, or she simply didn't have one, like Vicky.

Like Darwin. Her son always smelled like milk and peaches and his father's aftershave. Trish's candied citrus perfume. She felt her breath catch in her throat. Her son's true nature had been under her nose…

No, not now, Trish thought.

Trish didn't expect Maggie to stop and turn, lay eyes on the woman—her boss—who had been watching, perplexed by the gory show. Trish couldn't smell Maggie and Maggie could not smell Trish.

Maggie ripped and tore at the boy's chest with sneers as hate pulsed through her petite frame. Small white feathers from his coat showered them. Her thick hair looked wild and unkept, soaking in new blood. Her fingers, not claws, dug into his face and chest, dark specks of blood rose and fell around him, and his screams were muted, caught in the convulsing shadow as the sand became a part of the mess beneath them. Maggie ripped chunks of flesh free, shedding tissue and sinew, distorting his features forever. She hungrily tore the boy apart but did not take a bite. Did not sink her teeth into his neck. Instead, she destroyed his jugular, washing herself in the shower of blood that his body released when the once-closed circuit adopted a gash, opening the system. In the dark, Trish could not see Maggie's eyes, but by the way she was grunting and sneering, her victim must have thought he was staring into the eyes of Satan himself. If his eyes were still open at all.

Trish imagined how Maggie must have appeared to the man in the house or wherever they met up before they ended up here. He trusted her enough to come outside with her. Maggie was wearing the same outfit, the same jeans and white blouse. The same puddle of blood on her neck and face. At least Trish thought so—it could have all been the man's blood now. Did he see Maggie in the house and thought she was sane enough to talk with outside? No one is that naive. Was Maggie able to turn off her feral urge long enough to get him alone? Maybe.

Does my child turn his meals feral if he doesn't drink them completely? His own stomach couldn't handle such a load. That's why he stopped feeding on Maggie and cried. *Tummy ache*, she thought. Cried for his mother to help him. Cried for his mother to explain what she had passed on to him.

Fix this, she demanded herself. She fixed Vicky's problem, and now it was time to fix Darwin's. *Take Maggie's head off and drown her in the lake*, she thought, eliminating the need to take Maggie away from the lake all together.

But the cameras? Hopefully none of those cars belonged to the dead man.

Of course one of those cars belongs to him, she thought.

The cameras would have spotted them leaving the house, but not what happened on the shore.

She looked at Maggie and spat between clenched teeth. *Fuck.*

CHAPTER 8

Party

The party raged, and Maggie did not stop tearing her friend's face with her fingertips. No claws. The more Maggie went at the body, because he was certainly dead, the more Trish could not leave it out in the open; she needed to hide it. She looked out at the churning waters. *If it ever dried up, the body would be found.* But throwing his body in the lake would require them to search for him. It would take them a while to find him in there, even if it was the first place they checked.

So much for leaving it up to the universe, Trish thought. Maggie liked using the universe as an excuse for her laziness, carelessness, and pointless failures.

Maggie, did you take your test the other day? Randel would ask once they'd gotten back home from a date night, which usually consisted of a movie and shopping for clothes for Darwin who was growing like weeds in the spring.

Oh, don't worry about it, Mr. Weston. I'll pass the class if it's in the cards.

Maggie, did you get your brakes fixed? Trish asked, caring only because Darwin and Randel liked Maggie, and she had come in a pinch for Trish a few times.

Oh, don't worry about that, Mrs. Weston. If the universe wants me to get into an accident, then it's going to happen anyway.

Maggie lacked every bit of common sense, but she was only gullible with parents who had too much money for her failures to be final. The girl lived life in a way that was easiest for her. But Trish knew Maggie didn't expect one of the kids that she babysat to turn her into a monster. This boyfriend or brother or whoever he was probably showed up at her house for one thing and got something entirely different.

If I hadn't shown up, there may have been a massacre!

Maggie stopped and threw her head back; her face glistened with sweat and blood, and her breath was foggy. Trish cocked her head. Her breath fogged when it came into contact with the chilly air whenever she did not have the ring on. But the sweat… That was different. If Maggie were anything like Trish, her body temperature would have fluctuated, making overheating impossible unless she was standing outside during a sunny day.

Trish may not be able to kill Maggie, but she could try to subdue her long enough to figure something out.

Trish put her hand over Maggie's mouth and twisted her head, breaking her neck. A thick *pop* shot out, her skin not thick enough to contain it. Her head lulled, but it didn't stop her from swinging her arms and pulling them both forward. Trish fell forward onto Maggie's back, her knees digging into the man's waist.

Struggling to keep hold of Maggie's mouth, her head heavier in Trish's hands without the support of her neck, she lost her grip on Maggie, who tried to run, gurgling blood. Maggie sounded strained and hoarse and wet as her broken throat had been made useless and her head lulled unnaturally, disobeying her advances for it to stand up straight. Trish pulled Maggie's pant leg, bringing her back down. Her head slammed into the sand, the earth's dust erupted around them, pricking Trish's skin and lodging into her eyes. She blinked as she sat on Maggie's back. Trish dug her knees into Maggie's back and pulled her shoulders up. Maggie's back snapped, leaving her at a right angle, her shoulders and twisted neck off the ground while her lower back, hips, and legs were pinned in the sand.

Maggie stopped moving her legs and arms. She stopped moving all together. Trish leaned forward. Maggie's eyes were closed save some intermittent twitching of her eyebrows and cheeks.

Is she dead? Is it actually possible?

Trish pressed Maggie's throat with two fingers, checking for a pulse. Her heartbeat sang, a little jumbled, but it was still there. But Trish could never be too sure. Nobody could. She looked at the man on the ground. His face was covered in bloody gashes and wasted blood. So were his neck and chest, his puffer coat doing nothing to protect him from his killer. Trish ripped Maggie's shirt off and shoved it down her throat. If Maggie was anything like Trish, she would heal, but not nearly fast enough. She'd be ripped to bits, burned, and buried before she had the chance. For a second, Trish wondered if that would work on Vicky. But for some reason, doubt and shame made her think differently about the girl.

Trish picked the bloody man up, making a note to burn her clothes when she burnt Maggie's remains, something that she couldn't venture to do to Vicky…her new companion.

CHAPTER 9

Homesick

Trish ignored her phone when it buzzed in her pocket. It had gone on to be the first of many times she got a call as she trekked through the familiar path that she'd taken earlier. But this time, she wasn't alone. Maggie was unconscious, her back still stiff and mangled, but it made it a little easier for Trish to carry her along, placing her shoulder in the new deep arch in Maggie's back. She hadn't stirred or made any noise. She only seemed to sleep as they cut through the never-ending woods. Maggie was leaving home for the last time, and for the first time in a long time, the abduction felt eerie.

The second time Trish's phone buzzed, she checked it, hoping it wasn't an unknown number with Vicky on the other end. A jolt shot through her. Darwin.

She pulled the phone out of her pocket, hefting Maggie over her shoulder as she started to slide off. Randel. *What does he want?* He was probably calling to complain about how he saw her pull off thanks to the unsanctioned cameras that he had installed at their home. He probably saw more than just that. *Dammit, did I turn the cameras off?* She couldn't remember if she was supposed to be playing dumb—*Oh, I forgot to turn them back on*—or if she had turned them back on and...

"Hello," she said.

"Hey, hon," he said, his voice not at all reaching the height of urgency that she had been anticipating. But there was a slight hitch to his breath, as if he were… *Exercising late?* Also strange. He usually worked out right after work or during his lunch break. It must have been a long day for him too. She wanted to laugh at the mere idea that his day had been anything like hers. He hadn't been murdering people, packing up and moving a storage unit, or walking in on a tragedy caused by their little son. Randel was at some office making some calls talking to some people about millions of dollars. At least he was paid for his time.

"Hey," Trish said, as she crossed the small crick that had been decreased to a muddy trail that let out into a dark clearing. It had to be the lake. She stepped onto the campground, hoping he'd get straight to the point. There had to be a reason for him to blow her phone up at…she looked at the screen…11:45 pm. It felt later than it was. Yeah, he'd call once, leave a text, and wait for her reply or returned call. But he never called four times. She held back her, *What the hell do you want?* and instead, very calmly, she asked, "Is everything all right? I didn't hear my phone because—"

"I'm coming back home early," he said. She could hear his breath beat against the receiver.

She broke through the clearing, Maggie still unmoving, still unconscious, and the car was where she'd left it. She could barely make out the outline of Vicky's head in the dark passenger cabin. Same for Darwin's car seat. "I thought you were not due back until Tuesday. Is everything all right?" Trish pulled her keys out of her pocket and popped the trunk, dumping Maggie. She fell inside without protest. The girl's limbs moved like Jello; she probably would have swung herself close enough to take a bite out of Trish if she were awake. Straight through her leather jacket that was much too small for the weather. But what did that matter? It wasn't like the girl could turn Trish into something that she already was. *Hm,* she thought, the phone still pressed to her face as Randel's breathing got louder. The trunk was bigger than Trish thought. She could've thrown Maggie's friend inside too. *Too late now.* She slammed it shut.

"Well," Randel finally said, "luckily, my client had something come up; we won't be meeting again until after the new year. So, I decided to move all of my meetings until then…I'm taking some personal time until January. That way, we can spend time on Darwin's behavior. His teacher gave me a few names of some psychologists. We can all go together and get him back in school by January. How does that sound?"

Alarm bells sounded in her head. *First the cameras, and now this? And a psychologist? I already said no!* Trish rushed to the driver's seat and put a finger up to Vicky, who was looking at her with a blank expression. She coughed, choking on spit as every emotion clogged her throat. She looked wide-eyed at Vicky, who lifted an open hand and hunched her shoulders as if to ask, *What?* Trish put up a finger against her lips, telling Vicky to shush. "That's great!" Trish blurted, opting out of the argument.

He went on. "Yeah, yeah. I'll be around for a while. We can get the house ready for the winter, invite my parents over for Thanksgiving and Christmas. We can even invite the neighbors over for Thursday night cocktails or something like that. It'll be a lot of fun hanging out with you and Darwin for a while."

"Sure, when will you be home?"

"Not until tomorrow around 5. I need to stop at the Grand Rapids office to drop some stuff off. I hope that's all right—and I'm sorry about how I blew up at you over the last few days. With Darwin's behavioral problems and the stuff that happened to the Jeep, I wasn't considerate of how things may be affecting you while you're dealing with all this on your own. I should be there. And I should have been there to make sure they installed the cameras correctly. I'm so sorry, Trish."

"It's fine. It's all fine. I-I can't wait to see you."

"Yeah, I mean, I think this is what we all need. Time together. We can work on Darwin's issues together, celebrate the holidays together. Find ourselves again. I just really feel like I need my family right now. I love you guys."

Vicky rolled her eyes, obviously having heard what Randel was saying.

Trish put her palm on her forehead. This was the last thing she needed. Or was it? A new plan formed, one having to depend on Vicky, a feat that she was slowly unlocking.

"I think that's a wonderful idea, Randel. Say, how about you and Darwin spend some time together? I think all I need is a break myself, you know? I've been under a lot of stress with all this stuff going on."

"Say less," he said. She could hear the smile forming around his words and imagined his tanned skin sleek with sweat. "I'll give you some money and you can start Christmas shopping. Take the day and go to the mall or the spa or even go visit Hilary in Indiana. Anything you want."

"Thanks."

"All right, I'm going to get some stuff done and get some sleep. I can't wait to see you tomorrow, Trish. I love you."

"I love you too."

After she hung up, she shoved the phone into the cupholder in the center console. She looked at her passengers. Vicky waited for Trish to say something, Darwin was fast asleep with drool leaking from his open mouth, and Maggie lay broken in the trunk. Panic rattled Trish's nerves. Vicky could not leave just yet. But she would have to soon.

PART 2

Murky Waters

CHAPTER 10

State

Vicky assumed Trish had been talking to her husband with all the *I love yous* and *I can't wait to see yous*. It made Vicky want to barf. Not physically, but emotionally. The fact that something like Trish could possess love never crossed Vicky's mind until then. Had Trish been pretending since she turned? If so, did any of her husbands have a clue about who she was? Vicky swallowed the lump forming in her throat. Trish had undoubtedly killed one or maybe two of her past loves—she'd be caught by now if she hadn't. Vicky couldn't imagine lying like that to anyone; she'd opt for loneliness. Steve's love was the mistake she needed to keep her off the idea of romance entirely. What did Trish need with a husband and a kid anyway? *I guess monsters can be selfish too.*

"Sorry it took so long," Trish said, starting the car and flipping it into drive. "Hopefully Darwin wasn't too much trouble. Did he sleep the whole time?"

Vicky's heart eased. Even though Trish may have loved her husband or was simply using him to look normal—the latter excuse made the most sense—she put her son above all. They were out there hunting down his first victim, after all. But Dawin didn't know any better. On the surface, Vicky saw him as any other kid. But instead of breaking a prized vase or spilling milk all over the kitchen floor, he drank people's blood. Vicky chuckled.

"What's so funny?" Trish asked, driving around the loop that led to the dirt road.

"Nothing. He babbled a little and reached for my hand. He really likes funny faces. And he kept calling me stinky. Like-like he… kept saying *ew* and *pee yew*. Did you teach him that?"

Trish's face crumbled. "I mean, I heard him say *ew* before—he says it to *everything*—but never *pee yew*." She gave Darwin a quick glance before looking at the road.

"Well, I asked him if he farted and he thought it was funny. He laughed himself tired," Vicky said. "He's a really nice kid. I bet he gets it from his dad." Vicky was sure he had, because Trish didn't have a reason to smile, not with all the chaos that she'd risen over the past century. There was a body in the trunk at that very moment. Vicky cringed.

Trish didn't respond to that. Instead, her face went serious, and she said, "There's been a change of plans."

"There was a plan?" Vicky asked.

Trish looked at Vicky. "Yeah, and I'll need you to get your hands dirty."

Vicky shook her head and faced the window. *This again.* She was already in enough shit with Steve's body still at the storage unit, if someone hadn't found him yet, and the FBI, police, whoever the hell, still out there looking for her. Then there was the added bonus of the babysitter in the trunk. Vicky's hands didn't need any more dirt.

"I'm serious," Trish said, her voice low. "Randel will be back tomorrow evening, and I need to get home and make sure everything is in its place. Meaning, no sign of you. No sign of Maggie. I really need your help now more than ever."

Vicky paused, Trish's words hitting her in the chest. A few hours ago, Trish went on about how Vicky should have been dead. Just a day ago, Trish trapped Vicky in a bear trap, and two months ago, Trish had killed Vicky, took her life, ending every dream that she manifested in her mind for years and years. Gone. And now, Trish needed Vicky more than ever. Vicky huffed, finding the oncoming shouting match and cascade of *gotchas* to be pointless. But she couldn't stop herself from starting. "So babysitting your son was…"

"Easy."

Vicky guffawed. She wasn't sure if she was mad at Trish for forcing her to help or infuriated with herself for thinking that babysitting was all she needed to do. Of course there was more. There was a body in the trunk, a baby who needed to be seen after, and an unsuspecting husband on his way home soon. When Vicky didn't reply, Trish said, "Look, I know I fucked you up, ruined your life, put you in a type of danger that no one could ever imagine. But you have to understand that I am holding up my side of the bargain, just like I promised. I'm teaching you to survive as you are, and one of the first things that you need to accept is that there will be times that you have to think on your feet and get your hands wet. Understand? The sooner you partake in those dirty exercises, the easier it'll get."

Vicky wanted to protest—no, open the door and jump out. Let the night and the rubble take her into its embrace and hide her in the woods. No one would find her and she'd be long gone before Trish had time to get someone to watch her son, backtrack, and search for Vicky. But then what?

Trish went on. "Now Randel is on his way home, and I can't simply burn Maggie in the firepit…"

Vicky frowned. "Really? That was your plan! Jesus, what… That's—"

"What did I *just* tell you?"

"How can you say something like that about someone who did so much for you? You're just going to toss her out like she was nothing? Like nobody loved her, like she didn't matter? You wanted to burn her? She trusted you. She thought she was safe at your house. But you… That's what you do. Like you did to me. You…" Vicky's breath hitched, her fists balled. The fervent need to strike Trish in the jaw was tempting. "I didn't know Maggie, but I know she didn't sign up to be killed. You *failed* her!" Vicky's irate declaration rung in her ears, lingering in the car.

Trish's nostrils flared as she pursed her lips. She flicked the rearview with her eyes, then laid them back on the road.

Vicky dropped her shoulders and sighed at Trish's silent answer to the tirade. "I'm sorry," Vicky said, shaking her head. "I know he didn't mean it…it's…" *Just like I didn't mean to drink Steve…* Vicky fought that same urge that pushed Darwin to drink Maggie. It pulled like a magnet to metal, her teeth sought but her mind resisted the taste, the need, the hunger… But then the opportunity presented itself when the need was at its greatest. And besides, if Trish had not been out with Vicky, then Maggie would not have been babysitting that night. Vicky waited for Trish to say just that, but her dark eyes stayed on the road.

Vicky's jaw dropped. Then she closed it. There was nothing she could say to Trish about letting Maggie go or finding another way to deal with the issue. But burning her to death? Vicky cocked her head. Trish carried Maggie to the trunk, and she looked dead, but Vicky wasn't sure how Trish had found Maggie, and based on how tight-lipped Trish had gone after Vicky's one-sided shouting match, there was no point in asking outright. Instead, Vicky asked *around* the question. "Would burning Maggie have even worked?"

Trish shook her head.

CHAPTER 11

Weston World

Vicky didn't need to ask where they were headed, because everyone knew that Lake Michigan was the farthest western point of Michigan. As they headed up the road, her mind rested with the girl in the trunk. There was no movement, no small bumps or growling. No begging to be let out.

"Are you going to be open and honest with me?" Vicky finally asked, breaking the silence that lasted for over a half-hour. But the state of Maggie egged on Vicky's curiosity.

Trish paused for a while, probably deciding on whether to lie or not—it seemed like a sport for her—then said, "Shoot."

"How did you find her? I mean, was she—is she like us?"

Trish said nothing.

"Look," Vicky said. "You are going to have to tell me—"

"I don't know."

Vicky narrowed her eyes. The answer felt wrong coming from Trish. She was well-versed in vampirism. She of all people would know if Maggie was turned or not. There was no time for bullshitting around because Trish was in her *feelings* about her family. It was only fair for her to be honest with Vicky, who was now the only person around who could help. "What do you mean you don't know?"

"I mean—" she said loudly, causing Darwin to stir. She lowered her voice and he settled down, his small grunts falling into sleepy breaths. "There is a body on Maggie's parents' private shore. I caught her killing someone, not drinking their blood."

Vicky drew her head back. "Excuse me? What? Who?"

"I don't know. That's for the police to find out and tell the entire county while they also talk about a missing person who was last seen in that house with *that* now very dead person. Any more questions that you or I don't have the answers to?" Trish quipped.

Vicky raised her brow. "Did Maggie have fangs?"

"No. No fangs. No claws. Only rage. She looked crazy as shit out there. Ripped the kid's face and chest off."

Vicky couldn't imagine the girl with the sweet voice, the girl with a cow mailbox, the girl who still lived with her parents, doing something so heinous. When she imagined a crazed young woman tearing someone's skin off their body on a dark, sandy shore, she only saw Trish. "And you left the body behind—"

"Doesn't matter. It's about what's about to happen now."

They fell into a silence full of unanswered questions. Within a matter of hours, Trish managed to leave another body lying around, and she waited to tell Vicky about it. *She is going to get us caught*, Vicky thought.

"It would be best if you and her stayed away from my neighborhood and out of sight entirely," Trish said. "I imagine you know how terrible the sun feels. I saw the burns on you the other night, and I'm sure you don't want to experience that again."

And there it was. Evidence that Maggie had indeed turned into a vampire. There was no way Trish would expect Vicky to sit around with a body. Maggie was like them and she, too, needed to stay out of the sun. Vicky dropped her brow, certain that Trish was trying to get her to beg for help or remind her that she didn't have a choice but to comply; Vicky had more at stake than Trish. Was she supposed to beg for solace and protection from the woman who changed her life for the worse?

Trish sighed, regretting or realizing that she was talking to someone that she royally screwed over. Vicky wasn't sure if Trish could feel guilt for anyone other than Darwin, and for his sake, Vicky considered him the safest kid on earth. But for Vicky's own sake, the story was different. Trust hadn't even been planted, let alone flourished, and Trish may have known that. "Since your boyfriend shot up the f— *the* storage unit, and Darwin bit the babysitter, and *Randel* is on his way home, I need time to clean the house and to get you and her"—she pointed her thumb to the space behind them—"somewhere to lay low through the day until I get back."

"Okay…" Vicky said, feeling another babysitting gig coming on, but not for Darwin.

"I have somewhere else to put you two for the day. But in order for you to stay there, you will need to help me. Deal?"

I guess the lessons are over, Vicky thought, as the request sounded more transactional than educational. Vicky considered her bag of tools, dead phone, and jewelry, and almost frowned. Her reinforced clothes were gone, destroyed by Steve and Trish, and tossed out. All she had on her back were the clothes that Trish had given her: a now bloody thin hoodie and yoga pants that were more for the spring. No way would they stand up to the sun.

She resented Trish for bestowing hopelessness, but Vicky's thoughts nagged at her, her accusations unfair; Trish kept Vicky safe even though it hadn't ended up well for the others involved. The monster had done a lot of damage, but she did keep her word. She'd even told Vicky about Mel, making her feel less bad about Steve. If only a little. Strange, because Trish didn't need to open up about her murdered old friend…but she did.

"The marina is not too far from here, so I need you to listen very carefully. I am going to drive up to the floating dock. My boat is on the farthest end to the right. It's called *Weston World.*"

Vicky scoffed, holding back a chuckle.

"Shut up. I didn't name it. It was my husband's boat before we got married."

"Sorry, husband, but I need to use your boat to dump a body. You don't mind, do you?" Vicky mocked a conversation that never happened, confident that Trish used the *Weston World* for just that. They pulled into the marina. A small building adorned with a motion sensor light sat in the darkness, a single pick-up truck in the parking lot. A slew of yachts, sailing and fishing boats lined up against the dark floating dock attached to the concrete platform. "No cameras or what?"

"That's why we park where we park, so that the camera doesn't see us carrying a body. I'm not a complete *idiot*."

"Yeah, okay."

"Anyway, I'm going to pop the trunk, and you are going to carry her—"

"By myself? No way! What if she's too heavy?"

"She's lighter than you think, and you are stronger than you think." Trish had her there. But if Maggie was light…

"*Is* she a vampire?" Vicky asked, snarky.

Trish looked at her. "I told you. I don't know."

"Oh yeah. Great."

"You have to be fast. Even though it's dark, there could still be people around. They gut and debone fish over there." Trish pointed to a building that sat up on the shore where a few fishing boats and a couple of mini yachts were parked off the dock. Vicky nodded. Of the forty or so spots on the floating dock, there were only about eight boats out. But some of those people probably went out on the water for one reason or another. Like they were.

Trish opened the glove compartment and handed Vicky the keys to the boat.

"Be careful and stay below deck. It gets really bright during the day. And be quiet. As you can see, there are many people who boat here. They can come and go as they please. Got it?"

"Do I have a choice?"

"No. There's a picnic blanket back there. Use it to cover her."

Vicky's heart slammed into her chest as she searched around. The boats bobbed carelessly, their owners probably at home, safe in bed. But Vicky wasn't safe. Safety lived only in her memories.

"The sooner you go, the sooner we can get this all over with," Trish said.

Vicky reached over to the floor and grabbed her bag. She got out and went around to the trunk. Trish popped it. Vicky shivered. Maggie's clothes and skin were covered in blood, so much so that Vicky could not tell if it belonged to her or the person that she had been attacking before Trish came along. Maggie wasn't moving, and a gag was lodged in her mouth. Her back was at a ninety-degree angle, her body unnaturally folded. Vicky picked her up. It'd be awkward to carry Maggie any other way but the obvious. Vicky put Maggie over her shoulder and covered her with the blanket with small boats on it. She wasn't very heavy, nothing more than a large load of laundry. Vicky used her free hand to slam the trunk shut. Before she hit the wooden path of the floating dock, Trish was already pulling out.

Vicky's knees threatened to buckle as she crossed the wavering platform. The wind blew, and the hint of fish guts rushed up her nose. Waves brushed the sturdy platform's concrete pillars. She went along to the far end, finding the words *Weston World* tattooed on the side of a monster of a boat. It bobbed nonchalantly on the water. It was much taller and wider than Vicky anticipated. Someone could live in it.

Vicky stepped onboard and her foot caught the lip on the side of the boat. She tripped and Maggie's weight dragged her forward and down.

"Shit!" she spat as she watched the sleek white floor come toward her face. Maggie fell against a small gate that separated the bow from a sitting area. The sitting area was beneath the glass covering, just behind the captain's chair and steering wheel. It was a boat for a small family and could have been considered a small yacht. The boat rocked beneath them, frazzled by the awkward disturbance.

Once the boat settled, Vicky pulled herself to her feet, kicking the pain out of her toe. She grabbed Maggie. With all the blood on her, there was no telling if she sustained any injuries from the fall. But it didn't matter, because she was still out and alive, somehow. Vicky felt her heartbeat—*Is it getting stronger?* —as she pressed her fingers to Maggie's neck.

No. No, right? she thought.

Escaping the sun, which would peek over the horizon in a few hours, was more important than figuring out Maggie's condition. Vicky headed to the short door that was to the left of the captain's chair, unlocked it. She pulled the handle and found steps. The space below was dark, and she hesitated to step forward. When she didn't hear anything, she proceeded.

There were only four steps that led down. She turned sideways and stuffed she and Maggie through the tight space, the broken arch in Maggie's back over Vicky's shoulder. At the bottom of the steps, she felt around on the wall for a switch. Finding one just next to the entrance, she flipped it. There was a table and another wraparound bench, much like the one above deck. It looked comfy, with plump pillows and a pillowy backing. Next to the steps was a small room with two cots inside. The mattresses looked thick, but they were small, fit for two younger children, each having a bed to themselves. Across from the table was a small kitchen with a sink, counter, microwave, and refrigerator that looked like it belonged in a dorm. The bathroom door was open and consisted of a shower, sink, and toilet.

The windows were covered in black paper. Vicky cocked her head, having imagined most people who had boats wanting as much sunlight as they could get. She imagined Trish told her husband a really good lie to get him to agree to black-out all the windows.

Vicky carried Maggie into the bathroom and placed her on her side, her body wedged between the sink pedestal and the wall. Vicky flinched and sprung back. Maggie's eyes cracked open, showing whites. The gag in her mouth was drenched in blood. Her head bobbed with the boat, swaying with currents. Her hair lay on her legs and her belly protruded out where her back had been snapped.

Vicky closed the bathroom door and blocked it with the microwave stacked on top of the refrigerator.

CHAPTER 12

Vincent and Elise

Trish pulled into her driveway and waited for the garage to rise at the demand of her controller. Darwin was still sleeping, snoring louder than she'd ever heard from him. There was no way she could take her son on the water with them. He didn't need to see what was about to happen to his only friend. His first bite. And he didn't need to learn that lesson at all if Trish could help it. Still, Maggie didn't deserve to turn into something worse than what Trish was. Killing with no purpose. Watching Maggie tear into her friend seemed unnatural; it didn't fit her. Not the girl who fawned over makeup, the internet, and ditzy TV shows. Not the girl who cared for Darwin.

Maggie didn't deserve what was going to happen next either.

But it needed to be done.

Once Trish pulled into the garage, she dreaded her very own immediate next steps. Randel would be home in less than 24 hours, and she still had a body to get rid of, a stowaway, a killing baby, the bullet hole in the front door, and no time to deal with any of it.

She closed her eyes.

Take it in pieces.

Lost in her to-do list, she reminded herself of the most immediate matter.

Darwin, she thought. Even though he was more like her than she wanted to see or confirm or know, he was still a baby. He couldn't be on his own.

Pita came to mind. *What if he bites Pita? What if he bites one of the kids like he bit that little girl in his class…* Panic rose in her chest. Warning signs. They had been everywhere and she ignored all of them. Now, she was contemplating putting her only friend in danger—thinking of her *child* as a danger.

But what other choice did she have? Trish trusted Pita and Darwin loved Pita and her family.

Darwin loved Maggie too.

She sighed. *Okay. Okay. But if Darwin is full, much like me and Vicky, he won't bite…* "Anytime soon…" She said that last part out loud, so loud that she heard him stir. She looked at him. He sheepishly opened his eyes, found her, and rested his tired gaze. Then his eyes fluttered, ready to doze back off, but he fought it as he always did, afraid he'd miss out on something. But there was nothing to miss. The level of damage that he could contribute had already been done. All he needed to do was rest and be a kid. Her heart throbbed, telling her that it wouldn't be that simple. That there was more to come to her doorstep. More to happen, more for her son to see. More people for her to dump. More deaths that she would have to help him hide.

Darwin frowned; her thoughts tainted the air in the car with a debilitating sadness. But this was their life together now.

A stray tear broke free, and she swiped it away. "Hey, baby," she said. "Are you okay? Are you tired?" He didn't break eye contact, but his frown slowly lifted. "You ready to go see Pita?"

To that, he smiled. Was he smiling because he wanted to hurt Pita? Or was he smiling because he really wanted to see her?

With no direction to go, she asked him, "Is Pita your friend?"

"Yes!" he shouted. It came out like *yesh*. His smile widened.

Her jaw dropped, and she covered her mouth. She giggled and her eyes watered over, tears spilling. "Oh, oh, you said yes. You said—" She wanted to record the moment and share it with Randel. She wanted to pull the boy out of the car and dance, swinging him around and kissing him on his cheek and forehead. *You're normal! You're still a normal kid!*

"Yesh, yesh, yesh!" He blew raspberries at the end of that.

She so desperately wanted to believe him. That his happiness and anticipation was real, and that there was no reason for him to feed again. For her, in the beginning, she had been warned to eat only once a season. *"A full-grown adult should be enough to get you through three months. Since you are so small, that is more than enough time to digest. Follow that schedule, and you'll have plenty of serum to get you through the next two centuries,"* Ally had told her with his strange Midwestern droll, his golden aura radiant in the wooden cabin deep in the Pennsylvanian wilderness. *"A full grown, stout, healthy adult would do."* And she was told that she would feel full and live to continue to blend and experience. Living forever was rare, and she promised to take full advantage. That's all he wanted. But after her first kill, her feeding schedule changed for the worse.

Glutton became a crux.

***

After leaving Ally's, Trish trudged through the wilderness, stumbling upon Weatherton, Pennsylvania. The mountain town was full of mountain people doing mountain things: drinking, climbing, digging, and farming. It wasn't hard to fit in. All she had to do was be her old West Virginia self: a young girl a long ways from home wearing a patchy burgundy dress, leather boots, and a wool coat that Ally had given her. She found her way into a pub in what she assumed to be the town square, easily finding herself laughing. Men with alcohol on their breath grabbed her hand and swung her about as they danced to the local banjo band.

After sleeping in the basement of an abandoned cottage on the outskirts of town for a few nights, she got a job working at that very pub. The owner, a man named Vincent, with his wife, Elise, were of the church and strongly believed that a young woman should never be without a home.

Elise greeted Trish with a smile, her round face reminiscent of a porcelain doll, down to her even, papery skin and long dark hair. She smelled sweet like honey tea. "You remind me so much of my little Ellen, God rest her soul. She could have grown up to be as pretty as you. The way you smile at the people in the bar… You're so polite and helpful. Well-mannered and an all-around wonderful child. We are honored to have you stay with us. I—Since we lost Ellen to the flu, I never thought I'd get another chance to be a mother." Elise searched Trish's face with hopeful eyes, believing Trish was fifteen years old, and not nineteen. "Sweetheart, you're a gift from God."

"Thank you, Mrs. Elise, but I'd have to say that you and Mr. Vincent were sent from heaven," Trish replied, better at hiding her Southern accent than she anticipated.

Elise pursed her pink lips. "I know I didn't ask you this before—Vincent said that it isn't any of our business and that we are helping you because we need to. We *have* to. No way can we leave a child on her own. But please, child. Tell me. Where are your parents? Did you run away? Did they send you away?" Her round eyes went droopy, pleading.

Trish repeated her story as she had rehearsed during that lonely night in her abandoned cottage: "My parents died in an avalanche in late winter. I escaped, but after their bodies were pulled out, I ran. I couldn't stay there. I—" She mustered up real tears, thinking of Momma and the hell she must have gone through as she searched for her child. Though it was only 25% true, she cried when she told the story, because she knew she'd never see Momma again.

Trish watched Elise's heart break in real time. She hugged her. "You never have to worry about being alone ever again. I promise. God's got you. *We've* got you."

Their belief came with a side of job security. And they fed her for free, or so they thought. She stored the food and left it in the woods for the animals.

All she had to do was be respectful and attend mass twice a week. Easy enough, until the hunger pains engulfed her gut, forcing her to strike Elise's jugular. One dead woman later, Trish found herself and her full belly on the road again.

Every day she thought about going back to West Virginia. Whenever she got the urge to head in that direction, she thought about what Ally had warned: "You are not like them. Going back home is a death sentence, especially because they are plenty aware of your kind. A monster—a demon. A witch. You'll burn for it."

Still, it haunted her dreams. Her heart thudded in her chest as glimpses of the thing that bit her came back to haunt her. Its mangled body hung from a burning tree limb, its eyes bulged and one swollen shut as Cutler and the boys beat on it.

Trish moved forward, staying in one town or another. Picking up a job here and there. Killing a loner, a drunkard, or an unsuspecting elder when her stomach growled or when the people in town smelled better than good. It had gotten so easy that once a season turned into once a month; that is, until she got to New York. Droves of people on the streets and in the boarding house meant more authoritative supervision. With the risk of capture great on her shoulders, she abided by the once a season rule for a long while. Or at least until Darwin was born.

Wake

It was daytime. The black paper covering the sun-bleached windows turned brown as it absorbed the sun's rays, saving Vicky from the scorching burns. She was in the master bedroom, the large bed taking up most of the space, leaving enough room for that and a white metal cabinet. She opened the cabinet and found towels, a phone charger, a brush, a black scrunchy, and fresh clothes: Trish's signature yoga pants and a striped, long-sleeved shirt. Vicky changed, brushed her hair back into a puff ball, and placed her backpack on the bed.

Vicky put her phone on the charger, and took stock of her small inventory. She pulled the notebook out and slouched, not having a pen to write with. She looked around, then thought, *Who would waste time writing anything when they were on a beautiful excursion… or dumping a body?* She rolled her eyes. She thought she'd have a boat like that one day. She'd lounge on the long beak, the railed-off bow securing her from the rambunctious lake water. She'd wear an expensive bikini and sip rosé as her skin absorbed the sun's rays. Steve was in the captain's chair. The dark red hole in his head leaked onto his pale face, his red hair darkening into a glossy crimson.

She shivered, shaken from her stupor, then flipped the notebook open, hands itching to find what she needed: Dr. P's address and his offer.

Please meet me at this address. I have a set-up in my house that will keep you comfortable and safe. There are so many treatments that we can try. All natural, all humane. I went over everything with your parents, and they are on board. I promise to keep you away from the Feds, and I will not stop until you are cured.

Dr. P, 1960 Willow Lane, Grand Rapids, MI 49506

Vicky wondered if the offer still stood. She didn't want to stay as she was. She didn't want to learn how to stalk people, kill them, and then dispose of their bodies. No. Trish could keep her training. She could keep her advice and have fun keeping up with her and her child's killings. Vicky read Dr. P's letter over and over, once for every day she wasted with Steve, once for every day she drifted further away from the woman she once was. Once for every ounce of disgust she drowned in.

She thought through the night as she lay in bed, beckoning rest that never came, her mind begging for preservation and to be rid of the nightmare before it got worse. But Vicky could not leave just yet. Her clothes were too thin, fit for the summer. Instead, she hand-washed her bloody hoodie and pants in the kitchenette sink and hung them over the edge of the table. The red stain on the gray hoodie remained, but no one would see it if she wore it underneath the thin striped shirt. Same for the hot pink bottoms: she'd double up. Vicky made a ski mask and neck scarf out of the pillow casings on the couch. She tried them on for size, the fabric scratching her face, but thick enough for the sun, she hoped. She found a first aid kit on the counter and checked the rips in her calf and the holes that had been in her waist and collarbone. They healed up beautifully, leaving scabs.

A big *thwack* made Vicky shoot to her feet.

The eerie sound of familiar music humming from a new medium filled the cabin. Vicky stepped slowly, approaching the sound that didn't belong. She stopped in front of the bathroom door and waited. Listening.

The humming stopped. "Are you going to let me out?" The voice sounded much louder than Vicky remembered yesterday afternoon. In fact, as Vicky lay in the trunk at Trish's house, she remembered Maggie sounding squeaky and pleasant. Not this voice. It was droll but sweet. A lower tone.

Maggie giggled. "I know you hear me, baby girl."

Vicky pressed her tongue to the side of her mouth. How was Maggie speaking, or moving at all, with her body bent and broken as it was? She looked down at her barrier. Maggie wasn't getting out unless she crushed the mini fridge and microwave. She was trapped.

"Hello? Can you hear me? I know you're standing out there, looking around. Listening to my voice." She chuckled. "Just let me out and we can do anything you waaaannnnnt," she sang, holding the note, making it vibrate in her throat.

Vicky had questions. Lots of them. She and Maggie could talk all day. But just as Mom had told her to never antagonize a stranger's dog…

"Oh, come on. I know you want to let me out…right? Aren't you hungry? Don't you want some of my blood? I have a lot of it."

When Vicky didn't answer, the doorknob turned, jostling, but the door did not budge.

"Stop messing with the door," Vicky demanded.

Maggie hummed a tune that sounded familiar, but Vicky could not place it. It could have easily been some pop song. Either way, it was eerie and off-putting, making her insides crawl.

"I said—"

"You should let me out." Maggie's voice was clear but raspy.

"No."

"Oh, come on. You know that she doesn't care about either one of us. But he does. He always has."

"Who?"

"Him. Darwin."

"I—"

"He set me free. Allowed me to see the world and the people in it as they really are. Monsters. Things that need to die. Go away. Let the ancient beings reclaim the land—people are poison." An evil chuckle. "Huh, wish I could have played a little longer."

"Who did you kill?"

"Huh?" She sounded exhausted. Her sigh wavered in her throat. "Oh, Oliver."

"You killed a man? Why?"

"He wasn't a *man*. He was a disease," she said matter-of-factly. "Always wanting to stick his meat in something that never wanted him. I always wanted him to go away. And it isn't just me, no… It's all the other girls who gag when they see him. He thinks he's special. A gift. But it turns out that he was made of meat and bled and died just like anyone else. And I loved it. I liked pulling back the layers of his being. Offering a glimpse at the man that started off as a small meaningless sperm in his daddy's ball sack. I saw his life as he grew and burst out his momma's hole. I saw him take his first steps into mediocrity and drive into the same job, the same town, the same house, the same dream as his *daddy*. I watched him fawn over me, that young girl with the pretty hair and thick lips. I watched his dick stiffen in those tight-ass pants. Then I watched him let me in. My bloody face. Wounded neck. It didn't matter. He wanted me no matter what. And I let him think he could have it. I wanted to watch his entrails glisten in the white sheen of the moon."

"Why?" Vicky said, keeping Maggie talking as she panicked, looking around and finding nothing. Maggie was alive and mouthy. And moving.

"Because Darwin loves everything. He is everyone. He… I had to protect him."

Vicky stopped looking for a weapon and glared at the door. "Did Oliver want to hurt Darwin?"

"I don't know. But Oliver didn't understand—okay—he didn't get why Darwin made me bleed. Why Darwin wanted my essence. He didn't know—he didn't listen. So—I had to look inside him. I needed to know why…"

Vicky froze. Oliver must have seen Maggie covered in blood and made the mistake of asking what happened to her. "Darwin's just a baby."

Maggie slammed on the door. "You don't get it then. I thought you would because…because you smell like you would. But I was wrong."

Vicky could not smell Maggie. This took her by surprise. "What do I smell like?"

"Like Patricia. Like his *momma*." She chuckled. "Yup. She got that wrong too. I smelled her coming, I knew she was standing there. But I couldn't stop."

Maggie slammed her hand into the door and it bulged, absorbing her strength. Vicky watched the mini appliances, her false awareness of them holding quickly deteriorated. The hard plastic cracked and bent, and every time Maggie rammed her body into the door, the temporary divot got wider and wider. Vicky wasn't sure if it was the result of Maggie's head damage wearing off, or if she had fully healed. When Vicky dumped Maggie in the bathroom not even six hours ago, the girl's back was bent backward at an unnatural angle. Now, based on the way she rammed her body into the door, she was standing up straight, and her back was no longer broken.

"Stop it! Or I'm putting you outside!" Vicky said as she searched around. She ran over to the room and looked through her things. If Maggie was anything like Vicky or Trish, or hell, probably even Darwin as a full-grown adult, a mallet to the head wouldn't do much.

"You're stronger than you think," Trish had said. And she wasn't wrong. Vicky could have killed Steve a long time ago if she had known her own strength.

"Let me out!" Maggie shrieked.

Vicky didn't answer; she knew what Maggie wanted. *I wanted to watch his entrails glisten in the sheen of the white moon.* Those words. Vicky hated that they painted her memory in such gore, such elaborate lust, such… *Focus! Focus.*

"I need him now!" Maggie said, less angry and more desperate. "Don't you get it? I'm starving for his warm blood, his split body to cover me, shield me from the cold, bring me back from death."

Maggie banged on the door, almost breaking it. She slammed an open hand into it.

"Stop it, or you're going outside!" Vicky warned.

"Fuck you, liar!"

"I'm not—"

"You're not putting me outside!" Maggie stopped banging and breathed hard. "You wanna know how I know that? Huh?! Because she told you. She's like you. If you open that fucking door, then you get burned. I'm not stupid. I heard everything she told you in the car," she said.

"Okay. Then if I let you out, where are you going to go?" Vicky asked.

Maggie stayed quiet. As the silence spread between them, Vicky dropped her hands to her sides.

Then one loud thud and the door flew open, crushing the microwave and splitting the refrigerator. Maggie stepped out, her eyes wild and dark, her head and face coated in dried blood. Her shirt was ripped, showing a flat belly with dried brown and dark red blemishes.

"You," she growled.

Maggie rushed for Vicky, forcing her back, her tailbone hitting the table's edge. Hand outstretched, Vicky shoved Maggie in the chest. As Maggie stumbled back, she swung, her nails slicing Vicky's right cheek.

Vicky grabbed Maggie's arm, snatched her hand, and flung her around, throwing her into the counter. The boat rocked beneath their feet, making Vicky's knees waver. Maggie growled and ran for Vicky again. Vicky swung a fist at Maggie's face and missed as Maggie ducked, wrapping her arms around Vicky's waist. She lifted Vicky and slammed her down on the table. The table's leg collapsed, sending her and the tabletop to the floor. Maggie climbed onto Vicky's lap and clawed at her face with fast swinging hands, and nails. Vicky grabbed Maggie's wrists, but the girl writhed and gnashed her teeth, ready to use them as she leaned forward. But they were not fangs. And her fingertips were not claws. Her wild movements made her unwieldy, but she was not heavy and she was not stronger.

When Maggie leaned in closer, Vicky headbutted her in the nose. Maggie blinked, face frozen at the shocking blow. Vicky shoved her off, sending Maggie flying into the second bedroom. Vicky climbed to her feet, her face leaking, and stinging pangs rode her cheeks. As she stood straight, Maggie was already charging, hands first, intending to grab Vicky. Vicky grabbed Maggie's wrists and pinned her to the wall near the door.

"Maggie! Stop—"

Maggie sank her teeth into Vicky's wrist, and Vicky shrieked. Blood poured from her arm as Vicky slammed Maggie's head into the wall, jamming her wounded wrist deeper into the girl's mouth.

"Let go!" Vicky shouted.

Maggie snarled and bit down like a wild dog. Vicky lifted her arm and smashed Maggie's head into the wall, one, two, three times. Still, she didn't let up. Vicky grabbed Maggie's hair and pulled her into the bathroom, her legs barely keeping up as she grunted through the barrage of head injuries and a mouth full of Vicky's flesh and blood. Seeing red, Vicky headed for the shower, where a hard white tile patterned the walls. She swatted the wall with Maggie's head until she heard a crack.

Maggie's jaws unclenched, unveiling ragged skin from a ferocious bite. Unresponsive, Maggie fell onto the shower floor.

CHAPTER 14

Sullen

The night was uneventful, with Darwin falling back to sleep in Trish's bed beside her, and her watching him, crying to herself. When he woke up at his normal time—around six—he refused the bottle, and he didn't touch his Honey O's. He didn't even bother to crush them up and throw them on the floor. He only looked at the white of the highchair table.

Nothing she did made him smile. Not talking to him. Not playing with his toy trucks or magnet blocks. She put them together for him to just stare at them before looking at her. He was obedient, and she welcomed a tantrum in place of his obscene silence. She touched his hand, and he looked at her fingers as if they didn't belong there. She continued to move and play, but he didn't return baby babble or interest. Only preoccupied silence.

Giving up, she sat Darwin down in front of the TV and got to work. She pulled out a couple duffle bags and packed a black hoodie and a pair of black sweatpants that she wore throughout the third trimester of her pregnancy. She looked around the closet and in her drawers. It'd been a long time since she'd been caught in the sun without the ring; outside of the incident with Mel, her best friend at one point in time, there were no other times.

Trish stopped, realizing that it was November. Mel used to make a big deal about the month, forcing Trish and whoever they were travelling with to celebrate her month-long birthday. If she were alive now, she'd be seventy-one. But instead, she was frozen at the age of twenty-two, stuffed in a barrel in the middle of nowhere California. Mel only had herself to blame, and because of her, Trish vowed to never get close to another human again. Yeah, Trish got married, and she did feel for her husbands; she wasn't a complete cynic. But husbands were different than friends. There was no need for reading emotions or considering feelings. Sex or mending personal space. Friends didn't react to her every move or need to know where she was at all times. Friends took the load off her shoulders, reminding her that it was okay to be human.

Trish went to the garage and pulled a big tote box from underneath the bench that held shelves of storage boxes. Inside were winter clothes, something she needed to sort through anyway because the weather was changing. She stopped, wondering if Darwin would need a new coat; he'd grown a lot since the last time they had snow seven months ago.

Does climate affect him? Because it didn't affect her or Vicky.

Of course it does—it does!

She dug through her memory, trying to find him sweating at all. Trying to remember if he woke up with a wet neck or damp hair.

Darwin didn't like sleeping with his blanket, so she'd never know. She grabbed a ski mask, and tinted ski goggles that Randel's mother had bought for her. She hated the set because it reminded her of Mrs. Weston's main gripe about Trish not getting out of the house. She shoved the gloves and scarf that came with it into the duffle bag. Then she headed to the bathroom and looked at the iron pills. She opened a bottle and grabbed ten.

***

When Pita showed up at 9:30 am, Trish carried Darwin in his car seat out to the car and peered inside. Pita's kids, Katie and Brady, were in the back seat. They looked just like their mom, with tanned skin and silky dark brown hair.

Brady waved, and Katie said, "Hi, Darwin's mommy."

"Hello," Trish said with a smile. Though the kids seemed chipper, Pita's mood was sullen. They'd briefly discussed the incident on campus earlier. Trish took on the role of listening as Pita spilled whatever tea she had: "Gabby said she saw Dr. Webb at some shit bar near campus with a pale boney woman with long black hair. She swears she thinks that woman had something to do with what happened to him because she'd never seen her on campus before. She said the woman had a chilly glare, like a vengeful ghost or an ice demon. I don't know where she got those weird descriptions, probably from all that damn anime that she watches, but it wasn't very helpful to the police. How many pale, skinny women with black hair do you see walking around anywhere? Uh, a lot. Just go to the nearest emo club." They agreed not to discuss the massacre in front of the kids, but Pita promised to tell Trish more when she found out more information.

Trish put Darwin in the car, placing his car seat into the empty space behind Pita. Then she handed Pita two hundred dollars.

"I don't need that," Pita exclaimed. Her almond eyes ignited with surprise.

"No, please. Take the kids and do something fun. I really appreciate your help."

"Well, okay. Of course. When do you want him back?" Pita took one hundred and put the other one back in Trish's hand.

"A few hours. I just really need to get my mind together and get the house cleaned. I have to admit, I'm still a little shaken up about what happened to the Jeep and with the cameras and… I hate my new car." She flicked a finger at the closed garage door. "It's way too small compared to my Jeep." Even though the trunk was big enough to fit Maggie inside, it felt tight.

"I am so sorry that that happened," Pita said. "Take all the time you need. I'll take them to the aquarium and the mall. Then we'll go to the park and out to eat. I'll wear the little guy out for you. That way, you can have some peace once he gets back home. What time do you want me to drop him off?"

"Can you drop him off at 4? Randel will be back at 5 and I'm sure he'll want to see us." *And I need to make sure Darwin's bloody mess is spotless.* The living room could do with another once over.

"That's perfect. I don't have anything planned later, so if you want me to keep him a little longer, I can. You and Randel could have some alone time." She smiled and tilted her chin up. She winked. "Know what I'm sayin.' Should I bring him around 7?"

Trish didn't plan on leaving him with Pita that long, and she didn't want Darwin to end up at Pita's house. At least he would be distracted by the public and the activities; no way would he be interested in biting anyone.

He's not going to bite anyone because he is full.

Stop it!

"No. No, that's fine. But I really appreciate it. He should be here to welcome his dad home," Trish said.

"All right then. See you later, girl."

Trish waved to the kids in the back and blew a kiss at Darwin, who returned a bored eye.

CHAPTER 15

Below Deck

Trish pulled into the marina, half-expecting the entire state to be standing around, staring at the commotion. But there was none. The boats were unmoved and there was no activity, just the smell of freezing fresh water and phantom boat exhaust. Still, she expected Vicky to struggle with Maggie, who was still alive and did not go down easily to begin with. Trish had to break her back to get her settled down; it was surprising she stayed out as long as she did. Maggie was violent, her hands lusty for blood, but she wasn't heavier than she should have been. For Trish and Vicky, their bone densities made them half as heavy as they looked. But Maggie lacked that attribute. Maggie didn't eat; she attacked. Maggie didn't have claws or fangs. She…she wasn't a vampire.

Then what the hell did my kid turn her into? Trish wondered. She jotted down whatever she could before she left the house, making it the last thing on her list of urgent shit to tend to or figure out.

Trish grabbed two duffle bags from the trunk and made her way up the dock. One bag had items consisting of ski accessories and an over-sized sweat suit, and the other one, the heavier of the two, consisted of a cinder block, duct tape, and a roll of plastic.

When Trish walked up to *Weston World*, there was no movement, no sounds other than the water pushing up against the bobbing boat. The dock was as peaceful as it always had been on a chilly

November morning. Trish climbed aboard, noting the blood on the floor which was wet with condensation.

What the hell? But no sign of Vicky or Maggie. Why would there be? The sun was blazing on that chilly autumn morning.

Trish knocked on the door after finding it locked. It made sense that it was locked, because having it open and casting the hot sun on them would make noise. A screechy, painful noise.

"Yeah," Vicky said. Trish could hear tiredness through the door. But Vicky was fine. The windows were blacked out. They were like that in the summer because of Trish's headaches, but they'd left the windows covered year-round anyway because Randel wanted to protect the interior. *Whatever the hell that means...* She asked him about putting the boat in one of those storage places, and he said no and complained about how expensive it was. They went on to compromise, starting the tradition of putting the boat away in early December before the lake froze over. She was happy about the end decision because she never knew when she'd have to, well, do what she was there doing in that very moment.

The latch unlocked.

"Let me know—" Trish started.

"Come in," Vicky said, sounding farther away than she was before.

Trish let herself inside and caught whiplash. The floor was sleek with streaks of blood. The table had a bent leg; the surface flattened to the floor. The pillows were bare, devoid of the wraps that she and Randel had carefully picked out. The bathroom door was busted, and the minifridge and microwave were cracked on all sides, crushed and sprawled across the floor.

Trish closed the door behind her and found Vicky cradling her arm. New scrapes and big scratches etched her face, and her clothes were different. She was wearing Trish's extra outfit that she'd left in the bedroom. The clothes that she had given to Vicky the day before were haphazardly shoved underneath the broken table. Trish turned her head to find Maggie slumped over; a dark red circle was impaled on the shower wall and leaked down to where she was lying. Her hair covered her face as her blood leaked down the shower drain.

"Uh."

"I—" Vicky tried.

"No. No. Let me say it. She got up, caught you off guard. Attacked you, which is why you have those deep scratches on your face. Then you bashed her head into the wall until she stopped moving. Like *stop*, stopped."

"She… I had her trapped in the bathroom."

Trish raised a brow. "Oh?" She crossed her arms and shifted her hips. "Then how did this happen?"

"She…she broke out this morning and attacked me."

Trish wanted to scream, having cleaned so much in such a short period. Granted, she left Toby's house and the storage unit a fucking mess. But this?

Of the two bags that Trish had hauled over her shoulder, she tossed one to Vicky.

"What's this?" Vicky asked.

"Clothes. Put them on so we can get started. The sooner, the better. Hand me the keys so we can clean this shit up and be done with whatever *she* is."

"She bit me."

To that, Trish stopped. "She did?"

Vicky put her arm out, showing Trish the damage. The teeth marks were long, flat imprints. The wound was bare, the skin gone, the remaining tissue mangled and chewed. Destroyed. "They weren't…"

"No. No fangs." Vicky said. They both looked at Maggie.

"Is she dead?" Trish asked.

Vicky scrunched her face. "I don't know. I didn't check. I'm not going anywhere near her. I—"

"Fine." Trish went over and pressed her fingers against the underside of Maggie's right jaw. Her chilling skin did nothing in response. "Damn. Looks like you killed her."

"I—"

"Unless her heart rate is so slow that I can't feel it. It looks like you killed her. This will make things a pinch easier. Now, take those iron pills, get dressed, and come up when you're done. I'm going to start the boat and get us out to sea. Stay down here until I shout for you."

"Okay," Vicky said, her voice lower than a whisper.

Trish climbed back topside and threw her head back, allowing the sun to wash her face, and her sunglasses to absorb the UV rays. She looked around. There was no one in sight. Even the boat house looked dead. The forecast said there was a high of 32°F, meaning that most of the boat people were indoors or somewhere else.

Trish set the bag of supplies that she had been carrying onto the floor next to the captain's chair.

A blow to the head was all it took, eh? Trish thought.

Either that, or Maggie wasn't a vampire at all. But she was something. No longer normal in any sense of the word. The Maggie that Trish knew didn't attack people. And for Vicky to do what she did, and that bite mark...

Trish shrugged and sat in the captain's chair; the blue expanse opened to her travels on the minor shores of White Lake only to be spilled out onto the massive body of water that lay ahead by two miles. Lake Michigan could carry her to Wisconsin if she headed west, Chicago if she went south, or the U.P. if she went north. But dead center was where they needed to be, and dead center was where they were going to go.

CHAPTER 16

Lake Chippewa

The bow of the *Weston World* tore through the lake's surface, slicing and distorting it to make way for the speeding lump of hard plastic, glass, and metal. The boat moved waves and travelled the distance that the lake owned, disturbing the peace that the lake kept. The wind shouted in Trish's ears, scowling at her for yet another desecration of the water, a home that didn't belong to her. But she needed the space, and she needed to bury her first family secret. The frothing water leapt out of the way, not daring to slow her down.

Maggie could never be found. Not as she was. Not as she had come to be. Even as she sat slumped over on the shower floor, Trish still saw the pricks in her neck, dark underneath the curtain of blood that turned the old Maggie into a tortured shadow of herself.

But her heart had stopped. She was dead in a way that Trish never thought possible. People would comb the streets, every town, every city along the west coast of the state. They'd probably go to Detroit and Chicago looking for Maggie. She was loved. Looked after. Cared for. Randel even cared about her.

Trish had let Maggie down, just like Vicky said.

"Sorry," she said. But she couldn't take it back. She couldn't even help her own child. And for that, Maggie had to disappear. They would never find her. As would be the case for all of Darwin's meals. They would be swept under the rug like unwanted dust, left for nature to help them decay in silence.

The only upside was that Darwin's victims were killable.

So fucking be it, Trish thought as she headed into the openness of the two shades of blue: one of the sky and one of the water. With the throttle in high gear, they were cruising at 35 knots, expecting to reach their destination within the hour. If Maggie were anything like Trish and Vicky, a simple bashing of the head would not have ended her so easily. Trish commended Vicky for finding that out for the both of them. Trish may have owed her more than that. She'd been through enough and overpaid any debt that she could have owed Trish. Watched her kid, helped her deal with Steve.

Told me about the Fed across the street.

Maybe that special brand of loyalty that she reserved for her son for eternity and her husbands for the short times that she knew them needed to expand a bit.

Using the forty-acre bog as her vantage point, she veered southwest for ten miles. When she finally stopped, she dropped the anchor.

"All right," she said once she turned the boat off and shoved the keys in her pocket. She headed below deck and found Vicky covered in the layer of clothing Trish had given her.

Trish put her hair up in a ponytail. "I need you to help me. There's a bag next to the captain's chair. Get the roll of plastic out of it and cover the bench above deck. Make sure the plastic covers it completely. Like enough to tuck it underneath the bench and enough to ride the length of the window. But before you go, make sure that you have everything that she showed up with."

Vicky stared from behind the ski mask, the tinted goggles big on her face and her dark clothes loose on her body. She looked like a sloppy, introverted ski instructor.

Trish clarified, "Like earrings, money, shoes—"

"She's wearing shoes." Again with the low voice, as if she were hesitating to speak.

"Are you all right?"

"Yeah, I'll—" Vicky turned and headed upstairs.

After waiting a few minutes, listening to the sounds of plastic ripping and smoothing, Trish picked Maggie up and carried her to the deck. She placed her on the plastic, happy that she didn't need to repeat herself. Vicky seemed to always understand the assignment, which made things a little easier.

"Do you do this often?" Vicky asked.

Trish didn't answer.

"I didn't know there was an island out here," Vicky said, her voice shaking a little at the end of her words.

"Oh, yeah. That's the forty-acre bog."

"A what?"

"Yeah. It's a floating island that they use to cover up Lake Chippewa."

"Oh," Vicky said. "I remember learning about that: the deepest part of Lake Michigan. Why do they cover it up? Wouldn't we want to put Maggie there?"

"No. We wouldn't." Trish placed the cinder block next to Maggie's body and stuffed the gag that she had been wearing in her pocket. She rolled Maggie up tight. "We don't want to put her there because people are drawn to that area every year. And when I say every year, I mean it. There is a community of boaters from Wisconsin that get together and use their big ol' boats to move the bog back to that very spot, 'cause, you know, floaters gotta float."

"Interesting," Vicky said, not sounding very interested.

"You should get to know your dumping grounds."

"Ah, so you *do* do this often," she said, answering her own question.

Trish smiled.

"Did she have a phone on her?" Vicky asked.

Trish's heart dropped. When she abducted Maggie, she didn't think to check her pockets, but she would have felt it or noticed it when she carried her off, right?

Trish shrugged. "Well." She picked Maggie up and dropped her overboard. The frazzled lake pulled the plastic bundle into its depths.

Vicky looked over the side and watched Maggie sink. For a second, it looked like her body had jerked.

"What—Are you all right?" Trish asked again. "Are you cry—"

"Are you serious? Doesn't this *bother* you? No, this..." Vicky flicked her hand at the lake's surface that sucked Maggie in... "Not the sneaking around and killing? Missing persons posters or the people that will disappear because of you? Because of your son?"

"Because of you?" Trish asked.

"None of that bothers you?" Vicky skimmed over Trish's question that time.

"No," Trish said. "Look, if it makes you feel any better, maybe you can think of it as us getting rid of a psycho who I caught ripping an innocent man apart in her very own backyard. She wasn't going to stop. Look at what she did you. How is your arm, by the way? I'm sure your last meal and those iron pills will help you. You're welcome!"

Vicky coughed, her body buckling in grief. "This is so fucked!"

"What the…what the hell is wrong with you? Did you two become friends while I was out? Listen, Vicky, you better change what you target with your emotions, right now. Instead of worrying about Maggie, worrying about her being dead, you better hope her phone was left at her parents' house. That should be your number one concern."

With that, Trish went back to the captain's chair, crafting a lie to tell her husband about how she wanted to go shopping alone, but instead, spending time cleaning the lower deck of their boat where her stowaway and feral babysitter had a bloody fight.

CHAPTER 17

Dash

The boat rocked beneath Vicky's feet, bumping up against the currents, splitting the lake's ceiling with its abhorrent speed. The engine cut through the atmosphere, drowning in the rolling tide and shouting into the moist air. Vicky's insides shifted, crashing into her stature, forcing her to hold onto the rail with one hand and hang onto her stomach with the other arm, the arm where the pangs of a bite crashed into her, making it throb. Making it hot. It was strange feeling heat engulf her face, a sensation that she hadn't felt in months. And it wasn't from the sun that usually stung her skin before tearing it apart, digging its UV rays into her flesh and leaving blisters and slits in its wake.

But that wasn't what she felt as the heat swallowed her neck and cheeks. Her mouth moistened, and her knees clacked together. Her joints screamed, assaulted by the too-quick movement, the fast-coming shore, the stern waters that they'd left behind. It was also the fake calmness of the surface once it recovered after they left it. But the lake wasn't calm. It was accommodating.

Maggie was in there. A normal girl who'd turned into a monster less than 24 hours ago was now sinking to the bottom of her watery grave. And no one would find her unless they were looking. Vicky's lungs felt like they were inflated. Her belly twisted and turned. Her heart was loud in her ears. Vomit surged up her throat at the unwanted nausea. She doubled over the railing, pulled the mask up to her nose, and threw up. It looked like clear water, fitting in with the blue mass that carried them back toward land. Her lips and jaw prickled at the onslaught of sun rays burrowing into her skin. She pulled the mask down, eyes trained on the watery landscape. The dark blue water tore her vomit up as if angry that she dumped it there. She silently apologized to the fish that had to smell it or whoever accidentally ate it in passing. She apologized for the dark secret that was dumped there. A secret that the underwater world would pass by, accepting it as part of the party.

"Ugh," she exclaimed as she pushed herself back and sat on the hot bench. It reminded her of Teresa's seats in her Mustang in the late summer. They'd get in with shorts or club dresses that stopped at the top of their thighs. She frowned and looked at it. She forgot what that felt like. Then she wondered why the weather invaded her skin now. After all that time…two months. She overheated, wet all over. She felt her forehead, imagining it moistened. Anticipating feeling it wet with sweat. She was sweaty. So sweaty that she was tempted to tear her clothes off. But the thought of burning alive with a nauseated stomach was more unappealing.

She looked at Trish and found her steering and watching the lake as they approached the shore.

"Are you all right?" Trish shouted, not moving her vision from what lay ahead.

"I've never had sea sickness," Vicky barely said. Her throat tightened as she shouted over the cacophony of noises erupting around them. Her stomach rolled, threatening to toss more of what looked like pure water out of her body. She cocked her head, realizing that the vomit wasn't red like blood. It looked clear and thick, slimy like mucus. Was motion sickness another symptom? She had felt sick below deck as she sat there staring at Maggie's bloodied head and broken skull. Vicky was nursing her throbbing arm where the bite mark turned into a gnarly scab. It looked like it dried quickly, tattooing her arm with a scar that she'd carry forever, unlike the other damage that she'd sustained in the last couple months. The iron pills seemed to work…again.

"You sure?" Trish asked. "Have you ever been on a boat?"

"Wh—" Vicky cut through the forming cloudiness around her head to put the privileged monster back in her place. Trish wasn't the only one who had access to boats and large bodies of water. But as she continued her impromptu rant, it fell by the wayside, sank into the lethargy that had stolen the vigor of cussing someone out to the point that they submitted. "I've been on a boat before… What the fuck do you mean?" The words came out sheepishly and made her body feel viler. She wanted to explain that her parents took her and Moody out on Lake Huron every summer. That she and her family went out on the Atlantic Ocean every year with her grandparents who moved to North Carolina right after Vicky was born. Papa Moses had a boat that was too big for him to keep up, so they went out to help him get it ready for the summer. She wanted to explain that she also knew how to deep-sea fish, thanks to Papa Moses, who refused to believe that such an activity was heavy on his back. Moody always jumped in to help him reel in his mahi-mahi or wahoo. But she could not tell Trish any of those things about her past, her lore, her upbringing, because every time she attempted, her stomach churned, her bones shuddered, and her arm screamed for her to take a knife and gouge the bite mark out of her flesh. So, she opted to keep her answer short.

"I'm just saying… Did you get sick on the way out here?"

Trish's authoritative tone was back, sounding nothing like the woman who begged Vicky to watch her son last night. It pressed on Vicky's nerves. Trish showed so much care for Darwin, but carelessly abducted and tossed Maggie away as if her life had no meaning. As if no one wanted her to remain a part of their lives. Vicky seethed underneath her ski mask. What were Trish's plans for Vicky? If she knew how Vicky was really feeling, would she toss her overboard too? Her rattling heart screamed with worry. *She would. She's done with you, and her husband is coming home.* There was no way Vicky was making it any easier for Trish than it already seemed to be. She needed her own plan.

"No," she said.

Trish stopped a few miles away from the shore and sprayed the deck with a hose. "Make sure you keep your throw up off the deck. And after you *do* get some on the side of the boat or on the deck, spray it off," Trish said. "You might not have DNA that they can find, but Steve sure does."

Vicky didn't answer. Steve. He was still in her gut, unless she tossed whatever was left of him overboard. And no DNA. She reminded herself to add it to the list of symptoms once she found a pen.

After cleaning the deck, Trish said, "You can hang out here on the boat. I have to find another storage unit for you to stay at. That shouldn't be too long. Give me about a week or so. All right?" She didn't wait for an answer. Instead, she plopped back down in the driver's seat.

They continued their unstable ride until they reached the dock. There wasn't a lot of traffic, but there were more people around. Which was fitting for Vicky. She ran down the steps, not giving herself time to process how sick she really was. She grabbed her bag and rushed out.

Trish was pulling the boat it, tying it to the dock. Vicky didn't bother asking if she needed help. Vicky hurried over to the dock on wobbly legs and hopped over the side of the boat. She landed on the wooden planks, her bruised tennis shoes thudding. She bent her knees, absorbing the jarring pain that shot from her ankles through her knees, up her middle…

"Where are you going?" Trish asked. Vicky knew what she'd been expecting: Vicky was supposed to stay below deck and be dealt with. Just like she dealt with Maggie. But Vicky wasn't giving Trish the pleasure.

She walked up the dock, new fear weighing on the pain.

"Hey!" Trish called out, clever enough not to yell Vicky's name. Covering her own ass if anyone was listening. Vicky would have done the same thing. Not for her own purposes, but to shield the other person from harm. But Trish wasn't Vicky. She was selfish and cruel. A destroyer of lives.

"Where are you going?" Trish shouted.

Vicky didn't answer. She fell into a sprint, her backpack tapping against her lower back.

Trish didn't chase after her.

PART 3

Sought

Disgruntled

Trish had a few hours to check the state of her house, a once over to make sure there was nothing of Maggie's lying around in wait. She also had to sort through the shit from the storage unit and put everything that was useful in the trunk of her too-small car. Randel didn't need to find anything when he decided to fall into a cleaning frenzy, and Darwin didn't need to adopt a new toy, be it a brush or rogue lip gloss. Or a phone. *Where is the girl's phone?* It was bad enough that Randel had hidden cameras in the living room. She looked around to see if there were more. She found none.

Trish went over to the couch and shoved her hand between the cushions, finding a penny and a nickel, a long lost scrunchy, and a Cheerio.

When did Darwin eat Cheerios in the living room? she thought as she dropped to her knees and gave a sweeping glance underneath the couch.

Maggie probably allowed him to eat on the furniture, a secret those two shared. They probably bonded over it as they sat watching one of his annoyingly bright, severely loud sing-alongs.

But as Trish looked over everything, from the office to the kitchen to the living room, all places where Maggie could have been, there was nothing of the girl. Did she even take her purse when she left? She was able to drive a car, so that said as much about her state.

She drove home. She let herself inside. She attacked a man and didn't take his blood…but Maggie bit Vicky the first chance she got, then she died from a bashed and broken skull. She went down so easily and quick, thanks to Vicky, that the disposal took far less time than Trish anticipated. Too bad their time on the water didn't carry over to the shore. Trish frowned. Then she tensed, flustered. Vicky seemed to crumble, sick with guilt. Trish rolled her eyes as she went for the kitchen, grabbing the measuring tape from the junk drawer by the sink.

One day, Vicky would learn to deal with what she was, a cannibal. One day, she'd choose survival over missing persons posters and family press conferences. *She will.* And once she did, things would get a little easier. Vicky probably saw the missing persons videos and press conference about herself, and still, she stayed in the shadows.

She'll figure it out, Trish thought. Trish headed for the front door, the black tape over the bullet hole screaming at her, *Don't forget about me!* She hadn't. She'd looked online and the home improvement store up the street had a few to choose from. She'd hang the new door and move onto the next thing, putting it behind her.

Vicky would make memories for herself just as Trish had. And there was nothing Trish could do to train her any better than the mistakes could. Vicky would stub her toes and snag her teeth. Come close to what felt like death and walk away with blood on her hands. But, just as Trish had, Vicky would have to come to terms with what she had become before she could learn anything.

Darwin would too.

A lump formed in her throat.

But how? she thought, uncomfortable with the idea, unsettled by the reality. She went into the office and grabbed her car keys, then caught a glimpse of something outside her window. The person that marched along, with purpose, seemed out of place. It was the neighbor. Pete. He was dressed formally, his bald head covered with a fedora. His brown face freshly shaven. He was wearing a long peacoat and slacks with shiny shoes. But it wasn't what he was wearing that made Trish uneasy. It wasn't the manila folders that he was holding. It was where he was headed.

He knocked on her front door.

***

Trish stared at the doorknob as Pete knocked.

"I know you're there," he said.

She clenched her teeth.

"Or I can speak to your *husband* instead."

Fuck. Of course he didn't need to talk to Randel. He was there for her, so she'd deal with him only. *Whether he leaves here alive or dead…* She opened the door, hoping he picked up her dismay.

"Good afternoon Mrs. Weston. Do you have time to talk?" He grinned, his scent strong with mint. Her heart throbbed, stealing the words that she wanted to say. She never dealt with the police, though she prepared for it just the same. But he stood before her, looking her in the eye, waiting for her move, for her lie, for her distraction that she could not deliver.

She contemplated a simple *Get off my property*. But her tongue formed different words. "What is this about?" she asked.

"Your Jeep," he said.

"Oh?" She crossed her arms and leaned against the doorframe. "What about it?" She squinted, getting another look at him. "Did you see anything?"

His smile grew somehow. "Hm. Where are my manners? Let's start over. I am—"

"Peter Morgan, also known as Pete from across the street. I know who you are—we met the other day." Trish allowed a faux smile. "How is you wife, Cecelia, doing, by the way?"

His face dropped into a scowl as he collected her threat. Disappearing an FBI agent's wife was a high risk, but Trish would do it.

The pregnant pause deflated when he said, "I'm Agent Peter Morgan of the FBI."

She lifted her head, pretending to be surprised. "Did the police turn the Jeep over to you? I'm—"

"Cut the shit," he spat, baring his perfectly white teeth. "If you want to play this game, I'll make this a whole thing. I'll get news crews out here, make sure your clients know what you are. Make sure your neighbors know what you are. I'm sure you know what people will do to something like you."

Trish inhaled a heavy breath.

"Are you going to let me in to talk or are you going to explain my presence to a lawyer?"

She bit her lower lip. No lawyer could defend her from a man with crime scene photos, which were undoubtedly in the folders he was holding. There was no telling how many years he'd investigated her. How long he'd been waiting to have that very conversation.

His grin returned. "So?"

"What is there to talk about?"

"I have something to show you."

"So, I'm not under arrest?"

"No. Not today."

"Then—"

"Patricia, you *want* to know what I have. You want to talk to me. But I don't want to talk about it out here. And I'm sure you don't want to either." He eyed Mrs. Pepper's house. It was quiet and her car wasn't in the driveway, but somehow the woman still knew who walked their dog and what yard it shit in at any and all times of the day. Pete, or Agent Morgan, had a point.

"Are you alone?" she asked, plotting.

"Always," he said.

Good, she thought. It would make it easier to strangle him and shove him into the trunk.

She moved aside, allowing him in. He looked around the house like a museum patron.

"Doing some cleaning?" he asked. She cringed. The bleachy smell was strong and plentiful on the many splotches of blood that the couch and floor had seen recently.

"My son is messy," she said. "We'll sit in the kitchen." She shuffled him into the kitchen and pointed at the table.

Once he sat down, he wasted no time. He opened his folder and placed pictures of the crime scene at Toby's house on the table. Then he crossed his arms and looked at Trish. He raised a brow. "Well…"

She looked at him. "Well, what?"

"The people at the bar ID'd you. Do you remember going to Young's Bar and Grill?"

She swallowed the lump in her throat. "No," she said.

"People said they saw you at the bar with Toby Webb on the last night he was seen alive. They said you looked a lot like the girl in the sketch. Well…they said you looked like her mother or aunt…But I know it was you."

He put the sketch on the table. Her round eyes and thick lips were familiar. So were her cheeks and dark eye shadow. "I wasn't there," she said.

"His friends told us that Toby was taking you home… Is that a lie too?"

"Yes," she said.

"You made quite a mess that night," Morgan said. He pulled out a picture of the bathtub and then the photo of Toby's wrapped-up body. The sheet was snug like a cocoon.

"I bet he was the target, wasn't he? You knew he would be at home alone, but you kept getting interrupted by the phone calls and then, eventually, by unwanted guests." He put down a photo of the blood in the living room. Blood drops tracked from the couch to the bathroom.

She looked away.

"You must have been hungry that night, huh? Was it greed or desperation? How did Toby get so lucky to cross paths with you?"

Toby wasn't a saint, she thought. *He was a male whore dressed in robes. He wasn't a victim. He was a fraud.*

Agent Morgan pulled out another picture of Tay. His back was caved in and blood fell out of his mouth and onto the tiled basement floor.

"Oh, that one was nasty. It sucks when an innocent person dies a brutal death. You didn't even take any blood from *him*," he teased.

Then there was Barbie's mugshot and her ripped-up face. Her blonde hair matted with fleshy chunks as her skull was reduced to bloody gashes.

"Rarely see claws get pulled out on victims. You messed her up bad. Was it because she had a big mouth?"

Trish's insides went cold. *Rarely?* she thought. How many did he know about? How many did *they* know about?

Agent Morgan threw down a familiar picture of a trailer, and Trish fought her reaction. The rusty trailer looked abandoned, the door hung on with rusty hinges. The grass around it bleached in the Kentucky sun. "We found drops of Johnny's blood, but none of yours. Those people down there still think that you're dead." A wedding photo next to the trailer. She wore Johnny's mother's wedding dress, and he wore a tux that he borrowed from a neighbor. "The people that are still alive swear that you and he were so happy. A little chaotic at times, but perfect. But his death and your disappearance is the biggest mystery that they'd ever seen. They say you were a good woman. A kind soul. And they think Johnny went and got you and him killed."

She glared at him, pressing to ask the question, but knowing the answer. He slid another picture of what was left of Johnny on the table. "The public doesn't know that we found him," he said. "And it looks like you didn't know either." He was reduced to bones coated in slime and moss.

Then there were the photos that caught her breath. Mel. Her plentiful glossy orange hair and forever gray eyes. That mischievous grin that trapped so many secrets. "Found her in 2007. Didn't know who she was until we got a DNA match to some blood that was retained from a brutal crime scene out in Santa Barbara. Same MO. And what I mean is…" He dropped a photo of them together at a concert. Trish couldn't remember which one; they'd been to so many as they travelled the country. As they robbed and pillaged, they looked out for one another. "She was bloodless and beaten. Left at a construction site. She was so horrendously beaten that it took decades to identify her." He shook his head. "You leave a lot of death…"

You should see what happened to Tucker, Trish thought. He and Mel spiked Trish's water with PCP, then tortured her for days in that garage. But when Mel took the ring off Trish's finger, intending to sell it so she and Tucker could elope, Trish changed. Tucker was ripped apart, limb by limb, and burned in the firepit. Having loved Mel, Trish stopped short of tearing her to pieces. Instead, she drank the backstabber dry, figuring Mel could sustain Trish as she fled the area, never to return to California again. Mel had only herself to thank for what happened that day. *The things jealous people do for money.* Still, the thought of one of her only friends formed a pit in her gut. "What are you going to do?" Trish asked before she could stop herself.

He sighed. "Where is Victoria Scott?"

"I—"

"Don't say that you don't know because I clocked her coming to your front porch a few nights ago. She was here. She did that shit to your Jeep. And she was here last night. So tell me, where is she?"

"I don't know."

He narrowed his eyes, frustrated or intrigued; she couldn't tell. *Both?*

"If she killed someone, I didn't have anything to do with it," she said through a trembling throat.

"I never said that."

He pulled out a folder, opened it, and laid it on the table. In the photo, blood darkened the walls and floor of what looked like an old, dank basement with cinder block walls. The sprawled bodies were unrecognizable. Pale faces twisted in horror, throats sliced deep, flesh and inky blood embraced the lifeless room like a black sheet. Eyes wide and still across the mass grave, bodies so mangled it was hard to tell where one started and the next began. Senseless and unfamiliar. "I—That wasn't me... V-Vicky did that?"

He chuckled. "Vicky? Huh. I've only heard her friends and family call her that. You sure you don't know where she is?"

"I-I don't understand..." When would Vicky have had the time to tear through someone's home, leaving... Trish scanned the picture, counting the bodies. *Five or six?*

"Patricia?"

"I told you, I don't know where she is," Trish said.

He leaned in. "Look closer. Describe the picture to me."

She frantically searched, wanting the man out of her house. Wanting this all to be a dream. Wanted… "The clothes are from… the 1930s? Uh, did Vicky go to a costume party or a cult meeting? What—"

"Describe the picture."

"It's hazy. Tinge. Aged around the edges… It's—" She frowned. "It's from another time." *It's not mine!* she screamed in her head. Her hunts were never that sloppy, that lazy, that *arrogant.*

"That's right. It was taken in 1931 in Baton Rouge."

She looked at him, shook her head. "Someone else did this."

"Where is your son?" he asked.

"What?" Trish was taken aback.

"Where is your son? A straightforward question."

"Sleeping," she lied. "Why?"

He sat back; a quizzical gaze took his features. "Are you willing to strike a deal?"

She cocked her head. "Who did this?" she asked, pointing at the picture. "Because it wasn't me," she said.

"Hm," Agent Morgan said. He pulled out another photo, set it on the table.

Trish's eyes widened.

The hole in Steve's head was still wet and round, and the slits across his neck covered Vicky's bite marks. "She didn't do that," Morgan said. "Now, she may have drank him; I mean, he was empty like most of your victims. But I don't think Vicky killed him. She loved him and, according to the footage we pulled from his property, he kept her hidden for two months. But somehow, he ended up dead in your storage unit…Him and Earl. Well…Earl was in the trunk of Steve's sedan. A bullet in his head."

Trish bit the back of her lip. *Earl.* He never asked questions. Never pried. Only took her monthly payments and watched his TV. The man who was nothing more than a glimpse of stability in her otherwise chaotic world was now one of Steve's many victims. *I'm sorry, Earl.*

"You didn't think Earl had electronic backups of who owned what units? You should know better." He snickered. "And this kid." He pointed at Steve's corpse. "You shouldn't have picked that one to vanish. His uncle has the whole town looking for whoever did it. Doesn't surprise me that some of his more fucked up friends knew about a vampire, and that the medical examiner left town not too long ago. They are corrupt as *hell* over there, but you'd be surprised at how quickly they cooperate when you have piles of evidence to throw in their faces. I mean, drug trafficking, torture, mutilation… The prosecution writes itself. Imagine how upset my colleagues were when they were called off of Steve and the sheriff. I mean, I would be too. Years and years of surveillance all down the drain. And for what? I had to strike a few deals to get to you uninterrupted."

He pulled out another photo, and Trish hoped it was his last. He held it in his hands, its back to her. "If you cut a deal with us, it would make both of our lives so much easier."

Trish imagined her next moves: Packing up Darwin and driving straight to Maine until she figured out how to get out of the country. Randel could meet them there. Randel would have to trust her. Trust that she knew what she was doing. Trust that she knew what was best for them. Deal or no deal, Morgan wasn't going away. "Wh-what do you want?"

He placed the portrait on the table.

The wind left her lungs and tears filled her vision.

"I need you to help me stop Randel."

Watcher

Trish jumped to her feet, her heart pounding. "No…" She stifled a whisper.

"We've been tracking him for a long time," Agent Morgan said, the deliberate cadence of his voice echoing in the quiet room.

She gasped. "No…"

"His bite marks are all over American history," the agent said.

"I can't…" she squeaked. This cop, this agent, this government official, Morgan, was lying. He had to be. Even though everything he said about Trish and Vicky…was true. *Fuck!*

"Patricia?"

She shook her head, tears flowing. "How?" she rasped.

"Do you want to make a deal?" he asked, insistent.

"That's not…" She wanted to snatch the photo, throw it on the floor. Stomp on it. Set it on fire. But she was lost in Randel's familiar eyes as they watched her back. His smile was the same, his hair long and thick…silky. His skin, smooth and golden. *Randel…Randel…*

Agent Morgan opened his folder again. "You know…" He placed another crime scene photo of a woman splayed out in an alley. Her once pale throat was ripped and shredded, her orange leather tank top and feathered mohawk stained red. "We lost count after one hundred sixty…" Another photo of a man in a bed, naked and bound. His head covered with a bloody pillow. "…because we couldn't tell…" Another one with three people dead on a bedroom floor, faces twisted in agony. "…where his—Randel, as you call him—atrocities ended, and where yours began." Another photo, another body, another wet, gory, untimely death. "We saved saliva and hair, but that didn't seem to matter." Agent Morgan walked around the table, headed toward her. "We realized back in the early 2000s that blood typing and DNA wasn't going to catch it. Then and only then did we realize that we didn't need trace evidence. We only needed our eyes. Our imagination. The will to study the stories that deteriorated into myths. Some bodies had bite marks and were low on blood. All the bleeding out…the wounds should have been nastier. Should have been *wetter*." He sighed, narrowed his eyes. "Nah. Those victims had their blood stolen by something that severed the jugular, and in some cases, the femoral. Then, and only then, did we take a different approach."

"This doesn't make sense," Trish said, hiding her face in her palms. "No, it…" Her tongue absorbed what remained of her thought. It was all *impossible*, permanently out of favor, not registering in the universe's cards. *Implausible*. "This shit's fake." A nerve-infused chuckle. "AI-generated shit!" She peered at him. "Is that what you're doing? Lying on Randel to get to me?" Another chuckle. "Never thought *this* would… Not at all. Nowhere on my Bingo card."

He raised a brow.

"You're using my husband to get me to talk. You have *nothing*." She felt her chest lighten; the idea of rotting within a jail cell or some government facility diminished to a near miss. The agent had nothing.

His shit-eating grin appeared on his cleanly shaved face again. "You really think you're smart, huh? You can't fathom the idea of someone getting past you? He hid in plain sight, and you didn't catch him."

She cringed.

"But guess what? I'm sure you've been married many times over the course of your disgusting life. All those men were real humans who probably tried procreating with you because, let's be honest, you are an attractive woman."

"You flirting with me now?" She grabbed onto the edge of the table, ready to flip it on him.

"Trust me, sweetheart, you aren't my type. I prefer my women to have a taste for farm animals, fish, and plants. Not my blood."

"Hm."

"You probably convinced those men that you were infertile. Not able to carry a kid for whatever reason. Why do you think it happened this time?"

She didn't answer, safe with the belief that Randel had a genetic defect that carried over to her womb. Nothing more.

That is the defect; Randel is just like you, she thought. Her face flushed.

"I'll make this a little easier for you." More pictures. How did the man have more pictures in that folder? How could she not have anticipated more evidence? "Look at the photos, Patricia."

There was Randel with mutton chops. Randel with bell-bottoms. Randel in a black and white photo helping a woman out of a horse carriage.

"We have been after him for a long time…"

She glared at the photo again. There was her husband. Her seemingly human, innocent, caring, loving husband. *Don't lie to yourself*, she thought. Not loving, not innocent…not human. "Since when?" she asked, bristling.

He slouched. "We don't know." His stern glare seemed to pierce her thoughts, digging for an answer that wasn't there.

"I-I don't know what to say. What am I supposed to say? Why…"

"You don't have a choice but to help us."

"What about my son? If I—"

"Not our problem."

Our, she thought.

"Finding a babysitter should be the least of your worries. If you don't help us, you won't have to worry about seeing after anyone ever again."

She pursed her lips, searching for an out and finding none. She doubted that Agent Morgan had been spying on her alone with his comfortable use of the words of *us* and *we*.

"You know the difference between you and him?" Agent Morgan pointed at the bite marks on the photos so carefully laid out on the table. Randel's victims—if they *were* his victims, or victims at all—shared the tell-tale signs of an attack. "You care enough to cover your tracks…faking suicides and ligature marks with broken necks and slit throats. Even with Victoria, you were careful enough to pull your fangs across her neck, which was sloppy; the parallel cuts gave it away. But I get it…you were in a hurry. You got sloppy, and you tripped up. But him…Randel…he never gave a damn…"

"I can't…"

"Don't think he won't try to get rid of you too, Patricia…"

She scoffed. "Now I know you're full of shit because—"

"Yes, he can…because he has." He pulled out another photo. "You aren't his first wife. He's been married to women just like you. Vampiric and all."

She blinked, shuddered. "What?"

"Yes. Of course. We found the last one in the Louisiana swamp. Locked up tight in a barrel. Dead. I thought it was strange that they lived in the hot humidity of a Deep South swamp, but they did. Until she was killed and he was never seen again."

"Stop." She felt dizzy.

"There could be other instances throughout the years, but…"

"Please stop."

"Looks like you don't have many options. You can either help us or—"

"Get out."

"Patricia."

"I said get out!"

He gathered the pictures, slid them into the folder. Then he reached into his coat and set a card on the table in front of her. "Just a reminder that if you don't help me, then I'll be coming for you before he gets the chance to kill you himself. You have 48 hours."

48 hours. Randel would be home in four.

The Bares

As the countryside route cut through Deedum, the land shifted from forest to farmland. Randel's temporary home away from his temporary home, the shitty RV on his parents' property, sat quietly on their one hundred and twenty acres of land. They lived in a small, single-floored brick house, its rusting gutters barely hanging onto the chipping roofline. The white front door's paint job had deteriorated with time, and the concrete porch was littered with small potholes. They had all the time and money in the world to fix their house and land, and if it were up to him, it'd be sold by now. But Randel couldn't give a damn about the house or the land or the people who owned it. That wasn't his problem, and they weren't his parents.

As usual and on time, Randel showed up unannounced, parking his SUV in the graveled driveway, its clean glossy midnight-blue finish misplaced on that shit-heap property. As he headed toward the RV, he felt their eyes on him. Their hushed whispers flooded the space, full of hope that he'd just swing by to pay rent and be on his way. He smiled, stuffing his hands in the pockets of his padded denim jacket.

"Sorry, Mom and Dad, you'll have to deal with me for another four years or so," he sang. The tall grass surrounding the house was gray and brown, appearing frost-bitten before frost became a thing that season.

"Hello Betsy!" he announced as he approached his old home. The weathered steel looked more brown than white as dirt and aged moss clung to the roof and sides. The words *Race Around* scrolled over the bent vent and dusty hooded headlights. Black paper shielded the windows, impenetrable by the sun. The passenger side tire sank into the ground, flattened, while the others were bald.

"Gotta get those changed," Randel muttered to himself before stopping in his tracks. His shoulders dropped, his face went hot as rage morphed his intentions, shredded his plans. The door was ajar; the rusty hinges creaked in the calm winds.

"What the fuck?!" he shouted as he jogged for the opening. He searched the door, looking for a reason. Searching for cause. The lock had been obliterated, busted by some kind of tool. He yanked the door open; it smacked the metal wall outside the vehicle. Once he reached the top of the short staircase, his face fell.

These fucking people, he thought. Inside, papers were tossed on the driver and passenger seats and thrown all over the narrow floor. Pots, pans, and glass labware had been pulled from the cabinets and shelves around the kitchen sink and placed on the counters. His portable fume hood, which he'd installed where a bed would have been many years ago, was gutted; copper tubing was bent, broken, and scattered across the floor.

"What the fuck?" he spat as he picked up the useless pieces. "Thousands of dollars, gone!" he shouted. *Why were they…* His eyes landed on the mini refrigerator, an old small thing that came with the RV that was stationed in a cabinet below the sink. He dropped the copper tubing and rushed for the cabinet. He opened it. It was empty. A red sheet coated his vision as his antsy palms moistened. He closed the door, inhaled a deep shaky breath, and opened it again. No jar, no contents, no nothing. The same empty cool space taunted him. *No*, he thought. *They…*

He inhaled deep, nostrils flaring as the night ahead, the visit ahead, shifted in front of him. He closed the door again. "This can't be…" He opened it again. Nothing. "…fucking happening!" He growled. He kicked the refrigerator, denting the door. Starting over…the whole idea of starting over made him want to run his own head over with a bulldozer.

"It isn't time!" he shouted as he kicked the door again, again. The door fell to the floor, exposing the refrigerator's emptiness to the world. "Dammit!" he roared, spittle flying from his mouth.

There were more things to get, more things to do, more things… more things… He needed an RV, he needed a new fume hood, he needed…he needed. He needed new parents.

***

The couple that he'd met at Moose's Bar in town all those years ago sat on their worn-down flannel couch in their shitty house that matched the farmland: dreary and unkempt. The place reeked of cigarettes. The couple, a burn out and a sweaty pervert, approached Randel, a seemingly young townie, and asked him if he wanted to swing. He declined, thoroughly grossed out by their collective stench and the fact that they had a full set of teeth between them. Instead, he hired them for a long-term acting gig after he paid for their dental work and wardrobe. It wasn't long before he moved from the campground and onto their land. They never asked why, never snooped. They only took three thousand dollars of rent and whatever clothes or story he fed them. They'd been perfect contenders over the last seven years, until now.

"Welcome home, son," Shannon Bare said, using a flimsy wooded end table as a foot stool as she polished her toes red. Her skin was as rich and brown as rust as she sat with her legs up, her short gown leaving nothing to the imagination. Her silky black hair was tied up into a bun.

"You got rent?" Paul Bare asked, tapping a cigarette in the ash-tray that rested on his round belly as he reclined in one of the only new things in the house, a leather La-Z-Boy. His sleeveless white t-shirt stained deep yellow as if he routinely pissed on it.

"What were you doing in my RV?" Randel said, rage eating his words. He shifted, planting himself next to a table with a lamp on it that worked overtime, revealing the mess of clothes, paper, mail, and cigarette butts on the dark carpet and on the glass coffee table. Cups of spent brown chew sat on the end tables and entertainment center, which was adorned with a 64-inch flat screen. Next to that, a gun safe stood up against the wall. It reminded Randel of an old wooden casket that the pilgrims used.

Shannon's face crumpled as she stuck the polishing brush into the bottle. "Why would anybody go in that piece of shit? Ain't got shit in there." Her tongue was so clean and proper in front of Trish that the trash mouth that sat before him seemed fake.

"Well, the door was open, for starters…" Randel hoped they'd be honest. Now, he would have to go review the footage for a month's worth of time. He couldn't find the patience for such a tedious task.

"You got more money?" Paul asked.

"Answer my question first," Randel said.

Paul patted the cherry of his cancer stick on the ashtray and set it on the arm of the sofa. Then he leaned forward, struggling to keep his breath straight. "Look, it smelled funny out there the last time you left…"

"Okay… And?" Randel quipped.

"Well, I don't want no meth lab on my land…so I checked it out."

"Hm…and what did you find?"

"Some shit in the refrigerator—"

"Where is it? What did you do with it?" Randel's body pulsed as heat rose in his chest.

"Poured it down the toilet," Shannon said.

"Why?" Randel shouted, the word searing the air, forcing them to flinch. So many years. So…many…years…down the drain.

"Look, we don't know what the hell you got going on out there," Shannon said as she stood. Her husband stood next to her. "But it's weird and it needs to—"

"It looked like blood," Paul spoke up. "So, it's either you pay more, or you leave."

"You want me to leave?" Randel said. He chuckled. "You went through *my* stuff! Not the other way around. If I leave, who is going to pay you to sit on your asses all day? Huh?"

"What the hell does it matter, Randel? We didn't tell nobody; we just don't want to be involved in whatever you got going on out there. It smells like gas and brimstone, and you had blood out there *in a jar*. Now, I don't care if it's from an animal or…whatever. But it's freaky, and I don't want it here."

Randel narrowed his eyes. "Unless I pay you more. Right?"

Paul seemed to stand straighter when he looked at his wife. "Well, yeah."

"Do you understand what you destroyed? What you snuck into my RV and dumped into the garbage?" His voice tore through the air, savage and raw. "It took years—years—to make that, and you just pissed it all away!" He lunged at the coffee table and kicked it so hard it shattered; shards flew, and wood splinters ricocheted off the walls. Shannon squealed. Paul flinched. "You have no idea what you've done!"

"Anything on this property is my property," Paul protested.

"The hell it is!"

"Just leave!" Shannon yelled. "Leave or we're calling the sheriff and your wife. We'll tell them everything!"

"Go ahead, bitch. I dare you!"

She bent to reach for her phone on the couch. Randel rushed for her, grabbed her neck, and squeezed. She croaked and swung her thin arms, her blows landing like falling confetti on his face and chest. "It wasn't…us…i-it…" she squeaked.

"Let her go!" Paul shouted. The bastard moved faster than Randel had ever seen, his gelatinous gut and neck led the way to the other side of the living room. The yellow light disappeared and Paul slammed the butt of the table lamp over Randel's head. Randel didn't flinch. He squeezed Shannon's neck, her slaps and scratches frantic against his wrist. Her heart was erratic, beating against her neck in his palm. Her blood struggled, leaving her face. Veins in her forehead popped and her eyes went bloodshot and wet.

"I-it..I…" Shannon whispered.

The click of a handgun loaded and ready to shoot. "I said put her down!"

Randel looked at Paul, whose pistol was set on him. He sighed. "Okay." He turned, Shannon's back facing her husband, and squeezed. Her neck snapped, bones breaking like twigs. Then he jutted her forward, throwing her at Paul.

"You son of a bitch!" Paul yelled as he pulled the trigger. Bullets tore into Shannon, who landed on Paul. The couple tumbled to the floor.

Randel went over to Paul, who squirmed beneath his wife, awash in her blood, his gun hand pinned underneath her body.

"All you had to do was stay out of my shit," Randel said. He stood on Shannon's back. Then he jumped.

"Ahhh!" Paul screamed, the pool of blood growing larger. "Stop! S-stop! We didn't do it. W—"

"But since the contract was infringed upon…" Randel jumped again. Shannon's bones popped and snapped.

"Ahhh!" Paul screamed as he worked his arm, trying to break free of all the weight.

"I guess the contract has reached its end." Randel jumped to the side, his boots landing on Paul's face.

CHAPTER 21

Bigman's Oil Refinery

The oil refinery was on the trajectory to buy up all the warehouses and any business that existed on Industry Row in Lakeshore. But it would take time. When Vicky planned the protest, she rode around the area, having to bribe Teresa, her roommate, with a gas card so that Vicky could have her Mustang for a few hours off campus alone. The area housed loads of boarded-up, abandoned warehouses. The buildings were comfortably hidden within the bustling area that was once clogged with the smell of production, manufacturing, and hardworking people who came and went. The refinery would change that. It would taint the air, kill the environment, and destroy lives. The objective of the protest was simple: be loud, and don't stop until the police got physical. But as Vicky passed through town on foot, heading to one of those very abandoned buildings, she found it odd that anyone could live so close to such a disruption. People and life were everywhere within the vicinity. Though there were no smells associated with the goings on of the refinery yet—they were set to open just after Christmas—there would be. But if the town had a say on whether the refinery was allowed to share their lakeshore, she'd bet they'd allow it—refineries brought good-paying jobs to the lucky few, but they also heightened the chance for shit like lung cancer and asthma. People didn't know what was best for them until it was too late.

How do you push off an invisible threat? she thought as a migraine rolled through her head. The sickness entrenched her veins and mixed in with her blood. Her stomach cramped as nausea tore away at her insides.

The sun ducked behind the clouds, soaking the town in a late autumn gloom that dulled the afternoon with a dark gray that used to make Vicky sleep all day. It felt like she'd caught the flu as she sweated profusely, only feeling wet as she felt heavy. She wanted to tear the ski mask off her face but knew better. It was still day out, and the sun would tear her to pieces. She trudged along, looked around for a place to lay low, but not to sleep because it wasn't a thing anymore. Even with the pain coursing through her body, tiredness was lacking, but exhaustion bloomed, ripening in her limbs as she watched the refinery grow in the distance as it sat on the outskirts of the industrial park, about a quarter-mile away from where she headed.

The once booming warehouses hid in the shadow of the refinery. A large chunk of them were marked to be sold with real estate signs in their yards. Some of them were marked sold. She paused when she came to the building that sat in her memories from her lonely drives around the industrial park. Oddly, there were no signs, and nobody home. Vicky walked around the off-white building with a sluggish gait. The horizontal metal siding rode the length of the L-shaped building, reaching the flat roof. The body-high windows were centralized in the very front right-hand corner of the building. There was a dumpster next to the bottom point of the capital L, and an abandoned parking lot. There were two garage doors on the bottom portion of the L, big enough for semitrucks to back into and unload. Vicky counted a total of four boarded up doors along the sides of the warehouse portion of the building, and one glass door that was obstructed but locked when she tugged on the handle.

She peered inside. All the lights were out, and there was a lone reception desk with a closed door next to it. She went around to the first garage door and slid her fingers underneath, minding her own strength. She pulled, her back straining as cramps gripped her muscles. Tears and sweat mixed, plastering her ski mask to her face. She grunted as her knees shook, holding her body upright as the pain threatened to consume her, end her in that parking lot. Her arms throbbed, her right wrist locked, refusing to move. Something broke and metal hit the hard floor on the other side. She waited. No alarms went off. No one came running to see who was breaking in. The place was truly abandoned. So much so that they got the power cut off along with the security system. Maybe the refinery was in talks of buying the building? Surely the bank laid claim? There were no signs in the yard; she had no idea who kept watch.

Inside, the many smells of the different people and stored products clung to the air. The gray walls were bare and so were the pillars that held the place up. There was nothing but dust. Vicky's right hand pulsed, hot with aches as her arm went limp. She huffed as her nose and eyes leaked, the flu encompassing her body, her right arm dying at her side. She went toward a pair of metal double doors. She pushed through them and found the receptionist's area, the glass door facing the cloudy late afternoon. To her right was an office area: a desk, no chair, no computer, nothing else that made it an office at one point. Brown stains adorned the lime carpet, and cables were strewn across the floor, connecting to nothing. A lone black ink pen lay tangled in the mess.

The warehouse's metal walls felt like a modern fortress, and Vicky made the empty office her own. She pulled the drenched mask off her face and hung it off the edge of the desk. Then she sat on the floor and opened her bag. She took the cash that Maggie had in her jeans pocket, happy that she had stashed it after the fight. Trish must've paid Maggie up front; two hundred dollars was a lot for a baby-sitting gig, if that was where the money had come from. Based on where her house was, Vicky imagined that Maggie had money stashed every and anywhere.

How long before her parents come looking for her? Vicky thought. Her gut turned and pain tore through her arm. She pulled her sleeve up and looked at the bite. Maggie's teeth prints had turned into crusty scabs, and pangs radiated from the source. Vicky winced and sucked her lower lip. The iron pill's effects seemed to wear off or stopped working entirely; it healed the outer damage but did nothing for her other symptoms.

Her stomach buckled, so she stood up. She paced, her knees cramping as she leaned forward, sweat dripping down her nose. She watched it fall to the floor.

She breathed heavy, her heart speeding as she went for the window, watching her reflection back in the dark. Her sunken eyes and cheeks belonged to a corpse. The honey of her eyes drained for two black balls of despair. Her sleek face was beige, faded of all color. Her plump lips cracked, dry angry slits of blood crept through. Her troubled features were unrecognizable…as was the person jogging all alone on the road. His steady run was well-paced as he went by wearing a shock of light blue and orange.

You'll never fully heal until you eat, Trish had told her that faithful night when she left the building feeling better, and Steve never left alive again. "No," Vicky cried, her feet refusing to leave the window, the vengeful pain kicking her in the ribs and arms.

She grabbed her stomach when a cramp crackled like lightning. She sucked air between her clenched teeth when her right arm answered with an inflamed throb.

"No…" she cried. "I…" Her mouth watered, the sweet nectar soaking her teeth, pushing the pain away long enough for her body to communicate another feeling.

"Do it, Vicky," a familiar but distant tenor of the only man who knew what she needed before she did. His breath brushed against her ear as he kissed it. She looked down. Pale arms wrapped her waist, squeezing her tight, holding her captive in his embrace. "Eat, Vicky," Steve said.

***

The street in front of the warehouse adopted a yellow sheen from the night lights that flipped on as the sun set in the west behind the tall wiry towers and jumbo vats that made up the eyesore of a refinery. Vicky listened to the jogger's tennis shoes tap against the concrete that could have been a dirt road but wasn't. The semi-trucks weighed heavily on it, adding deep potholes and dragging pebbles and rocks across the tormented road.

The man's run had slowed to a modest night jog. He was short, and from the waist down, he looked thin, maybe having spent a lot of time, every day even, walking or running around his neighborhood and that very industrial park. His white hair lay flat against his glistening ivory face as he moved to a catchable cadence. He kept his eyes forward, not minding the industrial buildings on either side of the road. Not fearing the block of empty warehouses that were soon to be sucked in by the oil refinery a quarter mile away. Not considering the stranger who had just made it to the slew of thick brush that was unkempt, unclipped, and left to grow wild when the owner of the abandoned warehouse sold out.

The breeze carried the sound blasting from the light blue headphones that he had plugged into his left ear—at least that's what Vicky saw—as he whizzed by her shadowy spot. His puffer jacket snuggly fit his torso, but the hood jutted out enough for her to reach out and yank it. He was lean, and he was alone.

But does he deserve to die? she thought. His shoes looked expensive, Air Maxes to be exact. His running clothes were bright, light blue, orange, white, the type of stuff celebrities wore during their yoga YouTube streams. He was important to someone, rich or no. But she knew for sure that someone would be looking for him. Someone was probably at home, cooking dinner, timing it just perfectly to come out of the oven when he was done with his run.

She doubled over as her belly curdled. The yellow light took on different colors as her vision played with her mind. Pink, lime, red. Red. Red. Her fingertips sizzled and bled as her fingernails widened and elongated, tips pointy and hardened. Tingles ripped through her gums as her fangs extended. She dropped her jaw to give them room.

She groaned as pain shot through her body, her transformation so complete, so full, so…

She wanted to tell him to run. Tell him that he was stupid for being out alone. Warn him to beware of the monster who had broken out of her hiding spot. Pick up something and throw it at him to get his attention as she ran after him. Scream at him as she reached out and snatched his hood.

He yelped as the collar dug into his neck, and his legs flew up as he landed.

"What the—"

His words died on his tongue when she put her hand over his mouth and dragged him by his head into the brush and back to the warehouse where he kicked and threw his head every which way. But her grip was still too strong, even with the illness chipping away at her bones and eating away at her guts. His muffled cries almost made her let him go.

But once she dragged him away from the opened pull-up door and deeper into the shadows of a business that was once teeming with people, stored products, ringing phones, and honking truck horns, his fate was sealed. He wailed against her hand. It sounded like he was begging her… *Please.*

She quaked and allowed the tears to roll. She looked down at his ashen face that was pink through her eyes. She dug her claws into his jaw and tightened her grip on the back of his neck.

"No, no, no," it sounded like he was saying. She didn't know if he was shouting at the form that was upon him, or if he was screaming at what she was about to do. How he was about to die. Could have been both reasons.

Her lips quavered as she moved them to speak. "I'm sorry," she whispered.

His eyes widened. "N—"

A chalky, thick crack whacked the walls, filling the space with the last sound he'd ever hear. Up close, the small wrinkles around his horror-stricken eyes made him look forty-something, a little younger than she thought he had been as she watched him from afar.

His phone. His phone, her mind screamed. But it didn't sound like her. The voice belonged to Trish.

Where is his phone? Vicky thought as she stabbed him in the jugular with her thick, pointed teeth.

What kind of watch is he wearing? she wondered as her mouth formed a suction, pulling his clean savory blood into her mouth. The waterfall of free food filling her belly. Her eyes fluttered at the delightful taste of the savory goodness.

Where are his keys? House keys, car keys, whatever keys?!

The questions played on her mind for several minutes, until there was no more. She wiped her mouth with the back of her hand and pulled his wallet from his pocket.

She ignored his license. She didn't want to know his name. She opened the middle of his wallet and pulled out five hundred and seventy-two dollars. Together with Maggie's, Vicky had seven hundred dollars now. Then she pulled the phone out of his pocket. It said he had no service.

Good, she thought. She dug in his pockets, finding a keycard. His face smiled back, his suit well-tailored and his dimples deep. Kimmel Wroth. Senior Production Manager, Bigman's Oil Refinery.

CHAPTER 22

Soup

Randel loosened his tie with a huff as he buttoned up his sport coat. He wished he could keep on his sweatpants and padded flannel shirt. It suited the man he evolved into, one so bland that he blended well with the pathetic humans he walked alongside. But the suits were a tired costume that he wore for *work*. Trish believed that lie, so long as she got her own space to commit her own atrocities. He'd have to bear the burden of playing dress-up for a little while longer. He grabbed his empty leather laptop bag and hopped out of the SUV, deciding on a lie, because he knew Trish would present one of her own.

He hadn't planned on rushing back home but, surprise, surprise, Trish found the camera that had been snugged in the fake plant on the living room end table. Shannon Bare had given him that vase and that out-of-the-way plant. Or at least that's what Trish believed. And he had no reason to stay in Deedum after what the Bares had done. *Fucking idiots.* He gritted the backs of his teeth when he opened the app on his phone and watched Trish's discovery. She knocked the damn thing off the end table and then crushed it once she realized what it was. She wouldn't say anything about it, pretend that she hadn't seen it. *Or would she?*

Yeah, Randel was upset that she found it, and yeah, he was mad that it was gone. But he was more curious than angry. Curious that it was broken on Friday, after Trish carried someone who was bigger than the baby through the house. The carrier's gait matched Trish's, no doubt. But the victim was a black girl that he hadn't seen before… *No clue…*

Not only had the eyes in the back of his head been compromised, but there had been a stranger within their midst.

He entered the garage but stopped to give Trish's new compact car the side eye. He hated it. There was no way she could get rid of bodies with that thing. The Jeep was far more superior in many ways with that being the biggest. There wasn't even enough room for her to clean it out, let alone making a mess in the first place.

It didn't matter. At the rate she was going, she'd be done soon.

He let himself inside and sniffed. Trish had sweet cherry blossom candles raging. The perfumy smell coated his throat, making his mouth taste soapy. He'd bought her candles years ago, just as he bought her apple pie, gingerbread, and lavender scents, anything to watch her turn her nose up. Anything to see her façade fade away.

Just like the others.

His slow steps were buried underneath the raging stove fan, his eyes finding a piece of black tape plastered on the back of the front door. He ran a finger over it then shrugged.

Bullet hole, bite mark, scratch, who knows what the fucking woman's been up to.

As he went deeper into the house, the candles fell behind the abrasive sulfuric scent of garlic and onion. He smirked when he found her in the kitchen, her back to him as she cooked. He stopped at the door and watched her thin frame. Strange, because, unlike him, she couldn't tolerate the sulfur-based foods. He wasn't sure if it was her age or her sheer unwillingness to adapt to the blood bags, but it was amusing when her eyes watered or when her stomach made gurgling noises, especially when Randel ditched her to watch Darwin, forcing her to miss her monthly feedings. She was just like the others, so resistant to change and misconstruing tolerability for adapting.

"Hey, babe," he said, setting his bag on the chair at the kitchen table.

"Hey," she said over her shoulder, her smile too big to be normal. He thought maybe she felt bad about what she'd put him through.

Dragging all that negative attention to their home. *Seriously, how stupid and careless could you be?*

"Whatcha cooking?" he asked as he went over to her. He wrapped his arms around her waist and kissed her on the neck. She hesitated to drop her smile or return love. It was always fake, he could tell. She used men as a cloaking device just like the women before her.

"Roasted garlic soup," she said sweetly.

"I didn't know you liked that stuff? I could have made it for you. My mom has a great recipe." The lie tasted good on his lips. His mother was long-dead, somewhere in upstate New York in an unmarked grave in an unmarked location. But the mother he was referring to was also dead and dumped in a well on unkempt land in middle Michigan, not from Seattle like Trish was told.

"I bet she does," Trish said. It was facetious of course. "And it's fine," she went on. "I was in the mood to cook something different."

"Yeah. What happened to the door?"

She tensed in his arms. He knew the answer would be a lie. He felt the outline of a bullet hole underneath her half assed attempt to cover it up. She shot the door with one of the many guns she hidden around the house. This was his favorite part about returning home. *Ask for a lie. Such a one-sided game.*

"I shot it."

"Why?" he asked, curious that she told the truth.

"I thought someone was breaking in. I didn't tell you because I didn't want you to worry. I'm really sorry. It's just…what happened to the Jeep has me on edge."

"Hm," he said. He let her go, stepped back. "Have you had a chance to talk to Detective Woodward yet?" He pulled his coat off and hung it on the back of the chair. A pregnant pause. She was getting ready to lie about something. Just about *everything* that came out of her mouth was a lie. He paused and sniffed, surprisingly finding something underneath the abusing garlic and onion. *Is that mint?*

"Yeah. They finished taking samples and I have to come get it and take it to the car wash."

"Okay, when?"

"Tomorrow sometime." She said that really fast. Too fast. Even her lies were getting sloppy.

"That's great news. I'll go pick it up," he said. He'd liked trolling her more than fantasizing about her death.

"Thanks," she said. "Soup's ready!"

"Where's Darwin?" he asked, so taken by her unusual activities that he veered away from his routine. *Always ask about the kid, just as any caring father would.*

"Oh, he's taking a nap. You know how tired he gets around this time. So, I lit candles and made dinner for us because I feel really bad about what happened this week. And I want to make it up to you. So relax. And welcome home."

"I'm happy you finally got around to using them," he said as she placed the plate with a full bowl and spoon on top of it. "Was wondering if you liked candles at all."

He watched her sip her spoon, and she didn't contort. Were they eating the same thing? She hated sulfur. Just the other day, she covered her nose to hide from scrambled eggs. But now?

He watched her sip again, and this time, a small grimace played on her lips. He smiled and followed suit. "Wow. If I knew that you made soup like this, I would petition for you to cook more."

She shrugged. "I can if you want."

Her thick lips made him want to suck on them, then chew them off. Her lies turned him on, but perhaps he'd hold her to that one. And the one about the Jeep. "I'd like that."

CHAPTER 23

Refresh

Vicky woke up in the office, her head finally landing on straight. Nightmares riddled the lingering remains of her psychosis as she drifted back into reality. Back to the warehouse that she'd found. Her belly was full and her head spun like it had when she woke up the morning after smoking pot all night; she had to convince herself that everything was real. Drinking the jogger was different than drinking Steve. When she drank Steve, she saw beautiful colors, felt her pupils shrink to pinpoints and her insides fill up, pulsing with joy as she'd finally given her body what it wanted. But the jogger, Mr. Wroth, made her see colorful lights that didn't exist. She almost forgot the glimpses from the night before. They fell prey to the teeth that felt good in her mouth. Her tongue sucked on the red stream like two lovers swapping spit.

And now, it was time to go.

Vicky sat up. Her stomach was unnoticeable, and her body was stable, no longer shaky. She looked at her arm. The bite marks were gone. She cocked her head. It was the bite that brought on the debilitating flu and body aches. Not seasickness. Not Steve. It was Maggie. But why? What was it about Darwin that made him so different from his mother? Different from Vicky?

"He's not like you and his mother," Steve's strong tender erupted, echoing around the space. Vicky looked around, panicked. The room was empty and there were no footsteps from beyond the office. She rolled her eyes and sighed. Maybe she was still high after all—from Maggie's bite or Mr. Wroth's blood, she wasn't sure.

She dusted her pants off as she stood, knocking off the powder from the dry wall and long-forgotten dust. She listened to her temporary space. Its inhabitants, some rats or whatever animals from outside, skittered around on the concrete floor that had been used to load and unload merchandise. Then there were the chants. The sounds that she had been hoping to hear. The sounds of the voices that refused to stay quiet while rich corporations remained hellbent on destroying the planet—their only planet—for millions if not billions of dollars that they did not need. The voices of the students.

She looked around, finding her bag underneath the desk, and her ski mask hanging off the edge of it. She pressed her fingers against the dry fabric, then slid it on. Everything was accounted for, including her partially charged phone and dead people's money.

***

It was dark for 7 am, but Vicky kept her ski goggles on, hoping to blend with the frosty morning. As she approached the cluster of students, she felt proud. There were about fifty of them, holding up signs that said, *Save the Planet*, and, *Keep the air clean*, and there were pictures of oil refinery tanks full of blood.

As she drew closer, she saw faces that she recognized. Teresa wasn't among the group, which she expected. Teresa didn't care about clean drinking water and breathable air. She was in school practicing education, wanting to teach the kids that would drink dirty water and breathe tainted air. Though their debates were idiotic, Vicky missed Teresa. The way she used to snore every night, forcing Vicky to keep her headphones in as she slept. The way she used to get them into elite parties and hole in the wall dive bars just because of her elegant wardrobe. They wore the same size, so it always worked. She missed how Teresa was overprotective of her, and how she wished she could tell her that she was right about Steve. That he was *worse* than either of them imagined.

Vicky fell in with the crowd, all too enthralled with their shouting at the gates of the refinery. She smiled as the group moved on to chanting *"Stay out of myyyy air!"* There were two men in hard hats looking back at the group, but they remained undeterred. So much so that they didn't notice the monster amongst them. Notice that there were things more important than what they were doing just then. Notice that they were full of blood. Her heart leapt up to her throat as their smells, all smells, crept into her sinuses, living there. It had purged her hunger and taken away the nastiness that she'd felt after Maggie bit her. She felt her teeth in Steve's neck and his wet blood on her lips and throat…in her mouth, in her stomach. She was full on him.

As the group moved on to another chant, Vicky stepped away, jogging, jogging, heading away. She wasn't one of them anymore. She teared up. They didn't share the same goals. They didn't want the same things. Their fight for equality and redistribution of resources for everyone to live side-by-side on a clean planet had died in her lonely world. Vicky rejected the great fight for a new one. Dizziness encompassed her view, and her middle weakened as her body refused to push forward. She tripped over her toes and stumbled forward, slamming a foot into the ground to stop her fall.

I can't do this, she thought. She'd killed a man. *Mr. Kimmel Wroth*. She knew where Maggie's grave was. She stole Steve's blood. Vicky shook her head. They were all dead. And there would be many more if Vicky didn't change…if *Trish* wasn't stopped.

But how? she asked herself as she finally cleared the enormous property, leaving her stance and ultimate purpose behind. Her face crumbled as a new agenda came to mind: there was only one way to undo the coming damage, and she had to get there before anyone else died.

House Call

After meandering along the sidewalks of the small downtown square, fully covered in Trish's old ski attire and oversized jogging suit, Vicky ventured into a small library that could have been a cream-colored Victorian style mansion that was donated by some lonely rich donor. No library card required, she bypassed the rows of shelving units and the librarian, who was nose-deep in whatever book he had been reading. She sighed, relieved to get out of the sun and away from the many smells of food and people. Although she was full and the shakes had disappeared, the sun that hid behind the thick clouds had a way of playing with her head, beating down on the cloth that barely shielded her from its hate.

She sat at a computer at the end of the long table that acted as a desk, with stacks of random books and seven computers stationed along its length. She surfed Craigslist incognito, finding many prospects for cheap temporary wheels that could make the forty-five-minute drive to her last hope. It didn't take too long to find a person on the outskirts of town with an old car for sale, a Buick Century was uploaded eight months ago. Vicky ran there, and no one batted an eye at the woman dressed in all black, running top speed, ready to go skiing. She imagined that she looked like an experienced jogger, like Mr. Wroth from the night before. She slowed at the memory. His terror-stricken eyes begged for the reason that he had to die. Petrified that his death was a possibility at all. If only he skipped his jog that night…

No, she thought. *Don't go there.* The brick buildings, apartments, and luxury townhouses were reduced to farmland and dirt roads as she came up on the house on the main stretch. Only then did she notice that she was tired, more tired than she'd ever been when she was out running at night. *Add it to the list*, she thought. She snapped her fingers at the many other things that belonged on that very list. About what happened on the boat. About the bite.

The Buick Century was parked on the curb at the head of a massive yard. It was burgundy with minor rust spots, and dark tinted windows in the rear, matching the photo in the post exactly. She walked around it, and a man in his sixties came out of the farmhouse. He looked as if he spent most of his time outside, working on the mass of land that had grown some type of crops and the barn that sat even farther from the road.

"It's still for sale," he shouted, the gravel in his throat confirming his age.

"Does it run?" she asked. She peered through the driver's side window. The burgundy cloth seats were covered in old stains. The dash looked outdated with a radio that operated with oversized silver knobs.

"Yeah." He shook his head eagerly. "Yeah, I take it up the road every morning just to make sure. My grandson rebuilt it…"

"So why isn't he driving it?" she asked.

He chuckled. "Can't drive a car when you're spending life in prison," he said frankly.

"I have four hundred," she said, stepping back.

He stopped and blinked his hooded eyes. "The post says seven hundred."

"I know what the post says. But this car doesn't have a title. And it's been sitting here for eight months. Nobody wants a car that don't have a title. Do they?"

He ran a hand over his thinning silver hair. He shook his head.

"I'll take it off your hands for five hundred. That's my final offer."

***

The traditional style house stood three floors high in the East Grand Rapids luxury neighborhood of Cedar Peaks. The neighbors' houses were a mixture of contemporary and Victorian colonials. Vicky bet that there were no less than four bedrooms on each lot. But the house of interest, the one with the poorly decorated pumpkins on the porch steps and the tall windows that could see for days, had an empty driveway. This much, Vicky had assumed. It was 11:30 am after all; Dr. P would be at the hospital.

She grunted. *Later*, she thought. *He'll be back later.* With that she took off. The old farmer was right about the Buick—the engine was strong, and the gas was cheap. But as she drove through Cedar Peaks, the thunderous muffler crackled, deafening her to the radio. As if the sounds were not loud enough, and a cop car that passed by gave her pause, fully equipped to read the stolen plates from the much newer Buick from the gas station thirty minutes west.

Vicky pulled into a pharmacy parking lot. She watched the people go in and out of the CVS, all wearing coats and jeans. Sweatpants and hoodies. Vicky didn't miss being cold. She could leave late fall and the entire winter behind for good. But she would miss the summer. The feel of the sun on her skin. The hot days on the porch with Momma or riding down to the River Walk with Brit and Moody and whoever else wanted to go along. That was the first time she smoked weed, sitting in the back seat of Brit's car. They got out and walked the length of the Detroit River until they reached Belle Isle. In the late evening, everything breathed and everything soared. Everything was important and everything was beautiful.

Vicky would feel that again, as soon as Dr. P got home.

***

Under the cover of night, Dr. P's awning cast a deep shadow over his porch. Vicky stood on the sidewalk out front, waiting for a light to shine through a window or listening for faint music or chatter.

It all felt like a fantasy: Vicky approaching her future home after a long day at the law firm. Her thinking about what to cook for dinner. Her wondering why her husband's car was still not in the driveway. She spent nine hours in the Buick, waiting and writing, watching and preparing. 9 pm came and went, and Dr. P's driveway was still empty.

As Vicky drew closer, she frowned.

The smell of rotten meat entangled the air, forcing her to hold her breath, leaving it out of her nostrils. It was strange really. She turned to look at the curb. The dumpster was there. Then she looked up the street. Everyone else's was not.

Were the dumpsters on the curb this morning? she thought.

She walked past it and sniffed, smelling nothing. She looked at the house, and headed for the porch steps, the air growing more pungent as she got closer. She threw her hand over her nose, and looked around the house, up the driveway. There was a two-car garage past the open gate in the backyard, but no cars in sight.

She hopped off the porch and headed up the driveway for the garage. Standing on her toes, she looked inside the small windows on the aluminum garage door.

There were two cars inside. Vicky's heart dropped into her stomach. She looked at the house again. All the windows were dark. She shook her head. The sun had settled into the horizon, giving way to an early evening around 6 pm. She knew. She'd written it down for her own sake.

"So why…?"

She looked at the ground. "Maybe he's sick or in bed early?" she whispered to herself. She ran up to the back door, the nearest entrance to where she had been standing. She pressed the doorbell. There was no movement, no call outs. She pressed her ear against the door and held her breath. No sound. She knocked and knocked.

Nothing. She didn't want to be a creep, just going inside without an invitation.

You do have an invitation, she reminded herself. *Just tell him you got lost or something.* Even though it was a couple months too late. *Better late than never,* she reasoned. She was sure he wanted to see her. He probably had more information, a cure.

Oh God please, she thought. Even though she blamed Trish for all the terrible things that happened over the past couple months, Vicky would cure Trish and Darwin too.

She knocked again.

Nothing.

Vicky sighed and turned the knob. It was unlocked.

CHAPTER 25

Wolf

Trish spent the better part of the last two days studying Randel. The way his throat moved up and down when he swallowed food. The way his straight teeth looked pearly and white when he smiled. The way he watched Darwin play and how he'd get on the floor and play with him. The way he went through and cleaned the entire house. The way he laughed, the way he moaned. The way he ate.

She hoped Agent Morgan was messing with her. If he were, she could ignore it. Write it off as a close call, an agent who had nothing. She could deny everything because there was no physical evidence to tie her to anything.

But if he was telling the truth about Randel…

I hate you, Randel. The only words she could grab from her tormented mind as she lay next to him. She trembled at vile thoughts. She could choke him out, slit his throat. Torture him for months before leaving him to cook in the sun. And still, he might not die. He didn't flinch when he ate the soup stuffed with garlic and onion. Italian herbs. Nothing. He sucked it down like he kissed her deeply.

What do you want? she thought. What, was he going to kill Trish and Darwin and then go on with his day? Find another woman, have another baby? *Wash, rinse, repeat.* Her face flushed. *How could he?* Her thoughts felt wet with tears.

She got out of bed, her bare body exposed before she threw her silk robe on. She left Randel lightly snoring and naked in their bedroom. She grabbed her keys and headed for the garage. Popped the trunk and pulled the garbage bags out, searching for the one that held her notebooks. It was at the bottom of the pile. She grabbed a stack of journals, notes from her lifetime. She flipped pages in bundles: September 10, 1905, April 6, 1909. Next book: February 26, 1972, May 17, 1973…

Randel ate regular food without getting sick. Randel loved the sun. Randel felt warm. Randel could have kids. Randel smelled like…Randel smelled like…

She froze. Her shoulders dropped. She smelled blood on him before, but not enough to know if it belonged to him. For the most part, he smelled like the house they made: aftershave, baby formula, body wash, cologne… Her hands shook as her vision smeared the inner workings of her garage. *Their* garage. "He has the serum," she whispered.

And he knew she had it too. *The camera in the vase. The cameras outside. Are there any more?* He had been watching her in plain sight. Her eyes darted from the car to the garage door, to the door that led back into the house.

"I gotta go…" she declared. "I gotta…"

Heart pounding, she rushed inside the house and up the steps. Thinking, thinking. *Grab anything. Grab nothing. Get Darwin, get…*

She rushed to Darwin's room, finding him fast asleep. She grabbed him and carried him downstairs, heading for the kitchen. *Uh, bottles, uh…d-diapers, uh…* She laid Darwin in his playpen in the office and rushed for the kitchen, mind jumbling, thoughts scattered. *Get the baby's stuff, grab clothes, change later…*

She headed for the refrigerator, searching for bottles. *Where are they?* She slammed the fridge closed and looked around the kitchen. It spun, misplacing objects, lives, and worlds. *Get Darwin's shit!* her mind screamed.

She froze.

"What are you looking for?" Randel asked, no longer naked, but wearing flannel pajama bottoms, his hands in his pockets.

"A bottle. For Darwin…"

He scoffed. "He's sleeping."

"I know. I—" She rushed past him, heading for the office. Heading for her child.

"Are you in a hurry? The garage door is open."

She kept for the office, eyes wild. *Where are my keys?*

"Trish!" he spat.

But she kept going, heading for Darwin, going to grab him. Going to leave.

Cold pain slammed into the side of her head, beating her temple. The force sent her sideways; her computer monitor hit the wall as her body collided into the desk. She rolled on her back, seeing double. Two men standing over her. One was the man that she had grown to know and love. The one that gave her a child, and in return, she protected their lives. And the other. The liar. The killer. The cheat. The monster who dwelled within her and Darwin's sanctum.

She watched Randel's brass knuckles come down again, breaking her nose, splitting her lips. She lifted her hands, fending off the blows, but his hands were too strong. A sharp pain bashed into her cranium.

"Ahh!" Darwin's high-pitched shrill. "No!"

Randel grabbed her hair as she kicked and screamed, her body dragged from the office, down the short staircase, and into the garage. Her ears rang as she slammed into the counter beneath the shelving unit in the storage room. Sounds drifted in and out. Above her: Christmas decorations, tote boxes, and all the stuff that they deemed unworthy of a permanent spot in the house.

He crouched in front of her, reminding her of what led to the undoubtably nasty crack on the side of her face. Blood spritzed his bare chest. He was wearing a piece of her, and it felt wrong.

He stood. "This isn't how I wanted this to go," he said as he slammed the door closed, shutting Darwin's cries out. Trish's body flailed as her knees collapsed, fumbling her to the floor. Her head banged intensely.

"You have fucked up royally, you know that?" He kicked her in the face, and her mouth responded with loosened teeth. She spit one out. She turned on her side, shielding her face from another blow.

"Answer me!" His monstrous demand made her shudder. The fury in his throat was brazen and the anger in his eyes was foreign but unmistaken.

"Please don't hurt Darwin." But the kick to the mouth made her tongue feel inflated, and the words didn't come out right. She mumbled.

He turned and went for the tool set that he rarely used and pulled out a mallet and a long, pointy stake they used to pin the gazebo down in the backyard.

Trish slid back, fighting to get on her feet, but her body didn't comply, still lost in the assault from moments before. Dizziness banged around her head, confusing her arms for her legs and her mouth for her ears. The world fell together and separated, allowing Randel to advance. He set the mallet and the stake on the counter and crouched.

"You can only blame yourself for this. You know. None of them in the past have fucked up as much as you have. And now..." He sighed. "You've made things just a *pinch* harder for me." His demonic chuckle sent chills through her. "I don't do well with being inconvenienced. But don't feel bad. The Bares *really* messed shit up, way worse than you ever could."

The Bares?

Randel grabbed her hands and yanked her up, forcing her on her knees. He planted them onto the counter. He held her wrists together with one hand. She pulled and pulled. Managed to say, "No! Randel. Stop!"

He grinned. "You ever notice how much stronger you are when it comes to *them*? How you always seem to overpower them with little to no strength cost of your own?"

She threw herself back and grunted. "Let me go! Let me go, you fuck!"

"Feel free to scream all you want! Ahhhhh!" he shouted and laughed. "Scream at the top of your lungs!" He shouted again. His yelling made the hanging tools clank, and the concrete floor vibrate. "No one will hear you! You want to know why? Huh? You want to know why, *Trish*?"

She screamed so loud that her ears rang and her lungs tightened. So loud that she didn't care who came running—not for her own sake, but for Darwin's.

"Ask me why!" Randel said as he squeezed her wrists. First there was a pop that made her scream freeze in her throat. And then the collapsing of bones as the space between her wrists depleted. She let out a pained yelp.

"Ask me why!" he demanded.

"Why?!" she shouted as pain shot up her arms, and the sensation in her fingers disappeared. She tried to move them, tried to tussle and break his grip, but her body refused.

"Because this room is soundproof."

He stacked her wrists on one another and used his fingers to place the stake into the back of her exposed hand. He raised the mallet and slammed it onto the stake, nailing her hands in place on the shelf.

Her throat felt raw as she screamed.

"Oh, it's about time you woke up! I thought you *never* slept. I mean, I do; you don't know how."

He rammed the stake again. She wailed and kicked, pinned in place.

"Shit, you couldn't relax if I drugged you. You know how many times I wanted time alone in my own *house?*"

He rammed it again.

"Stop," she begged.

"You never fucking leave! So I have to wait for you to go to *Indiana.*"

Again.

"No," she squealed.

"To go see your dear old friend."

Again.

"How is she anyway? Huh? Did they find Josef Bradford?"

In the corn mill off Route 30. "Randel!"

Again.

"Mike Tate?"

In Lake Michigan, near Chicago. "Randel, please!" she blubbered.

"How about Hughie Nathan? Did you hang out with him too?"

Buried in the woods behind the Seaside Motel. "Stop!" She pulled, but her flesh tore with the effort.

"Be careful! You don't want to tear your hands in half. You might need them if you ever want to carry your son again."

"Stay-stay away—"

He crouched and shushed her. "You want me to stay away from your son?"

She nodded, glaring at him through a blanket of blood. Tears and leaking wounds felt exposed in the face of the inciter.

Randel leaned in and whispered in her ear, "He's my son too." He slammed her head into the counter, and everything went black.

PART 4

Pry

Chat

The man in Trish's yard, who Vicky ventured to be the elusive Randel, was adjusting the cameras that spawned shortly after Vicky's initial arrival. He looked a lot like he did in the many family photos in their living room. His tanned skin looked even in the late morning sun, and his face was well-sculpted—an attractive middle-aged man who ate good and worked out often. One of those guys who grew into being handsome.

But after he finished messing around with the cameras, he looked throughout the yard, and for a second, Vicky wondered if he felt someone watching him. But he wouldn't see her unless he looked six houses down, near the corner, not in front of anyone's house but a small grassy lot that was well kept, a perfect place for a dog park. Vicky sat in the back seat, behind the passenger seat, surrounded by tinted windows.

Throughout the morning, Randel spent a lot of time raking leaves and glaring at the houses across the street. He fiddled with the cameras and went in and out of the garage.

Is he nervous?

She'd never met him up close, so she didn't understand his mannerisms. And she didn't know if he could hear Darwin as clearly as she could. The boy had been crying on and off, his loud screams growing hoarse but the urgency remaining unchanged.

Trish had yet to make an appearance. After finding Dr. P, Vicky needed to speak with Trish more than ever. But that was impossible with Randel out in the yard. Vicky wished she had put Trish's number in her bag. But she didn't; she let the paper fall between the passenger seat and the door of Trish's Honda.

"Oh, to hope," she said aloud.

"You were always so hopeful," a voice said.

Vicky gawked at the driver's seat and found Steve looking over his shoulder at her. His gray eyes smiled and the gory hole in his pale face was prominent. His neck leaked where Trish had slashed his throat…

"… *and* where you bit me," he said.

Vicky's eyes widened, nostrils flared as her heart threatened to jump up her throat.

"Oh, don't look so surprised."

"How… You're dead."

"Am I?" he asked, blood spilling from his head and neck as he cocked his head. "I look as fine as I did when we met. Remember that? At the 7-Eleven with Teresa? You were so smart and gorgeous. And your body… You also smoked, just like me. I never thought you would—"

"Stop it," Vicky snapped as she blinked hard, fighting tears.

He chuckled. "Huh, I guess you want to believe that I hurt you?"

"You did. You—"

"Kept you safe? Kept everyone else safe from you?"

She closed her eyes, swallowed hard. *I'm losing it…* She gasped, searching for breath.

"Look at me, V," he said, his voice soft and somber. Forgiving and welcoming.

She shook her head. *Hallucinations*, she thought. *Another symptom. Another…* The face of the dying Mr. Wroth hid behind her eyes. She opened them, and there was Steve, wearing the same jeans and leather jacket he'd been wearing that night, the last night she'd seen him. The first time she truly tasted him.

"I miss you," he said, his blue lips barely moving.

She rubbed her eyes with the back of her hand. But he was still there.

"Did you hear me? I miss you, V."

"You—No." She looked at her lap. "I'm losing my fucking mind," she said, her throat shaking.

He snickered. "No, you're not." He leaned over the center console. She didn't feel any air coming from him, but she heard him sniff. He didn't have a smell. No weed, no strong cologne. No blood.

"You can try to ignore me," he whispered. "I know you better than you know yourself. I accepted you well before you did…better than the doctor."

"No…no."

"Dr. P waited all that time, just for someone to get into his house and put a bullet in his chest." He made a pistol with his hand and pointed to his own chest. "Bang," he whispered. "Left him there with a mangled heart, dead at the foot of his spiral staircase in his all-white, all-fur, all-porcelain and crystal tower. Been there so long that his tanned skin went pale." He chuckled. "Vicky, he didn't know you. He didn't care about you like I did, because if he did, he would have come looking for you. He didn't care about where you went. I wonder if Nurse Cammy suffered the same fate. You know how the government is about their secrets."

"Shut up," she cried. "Dr. P—"

"—was executed because of you. But it's okay, V. We all make mistakes. You made the right decision. You came to me, and I told you to eat to make you feel better. And you listened. You…you did it…twice. Kind of funny that I did that for you. Now tell me, how do you feel, V?"

She sniffed, peering past Steve and at Randel. *Trish, where the fuck are you?*

"That's not how that works," Steve assured out loud. "Trish will not help you either."

"You're wrong!"

"Okay," he sang. "Your friend over there looks *really* nervous, don't you think?"

Randel moved fast, fiddled with security, leaving Darwin in the house to cry. Trish fawned over her son, who shared their secret. He was new to this life, just as Vicky, but at least she was older, was capable of looking out for herself. Trish would have tended to him, calmed him down, and for some reason, she wasn't doing that. Why?

A cynical chuckle. "He's moving like he's hiding something. Like he lost *control* of something."

Vicky inhaled, wanting a closer look. Wanting to…

"Now, don't be stupid. You can't just walk in there and think they'll welcome you. Remember what happened last time?"

The bear trap left a scar. Even though the physical pain subsided and the wounds were superficial at best—

"Thanks to *my* blood," Steve said.

—the mental scar made her stomach turn. "I have to talk to her," Vicky said. "She's the only one who can help me. Who can…"

He scoffed. "She turned you into a killer… But I…I was helping you. I made sure no one—"

"This is different," she said. "You tried to keep me as your pet. But she wants to teach me to survive."

"…so that she can relieve herself of the burden of someone who…"

"It doesn't matter. You don't matter. Everything you said before was gas. You didn't care about me. You just wanted me to help you get rid of bodies, Steve. I was wrong for thinking otherwise. But if you don't have fangs, and you haven't been held by the government, and you haven't gotten away with it for one hundred or so years, then kindly shut the fuck up. All right?"

Steve didn't respond. He was gone.

CHAPTER 27

Cameras, Calls, and Cars

Trish went down easier than Randel expected. He bet Trish never imagined herself in that very room one day, the same room she used to prepare a woman for disposal a few years back. He watched her do it on one of the many cameras he had around the house. In that room, there was one attached to the box labeled *Christmas*, a small hole engraved in the bulky letters. Holidays were one of the many things he forced her to ingrain within her miserable existence, but when Randel was alone, he didn't bother with festivities. Instead, he used that special time of year to pick people up at crowded stores or parades. The unsupervised teenagers were the easiest to snatch up—he only needed to give them a look and a smile. It was so easy to pull them in, so easy to get what he wanted from them. But he stopped with the younger ones. *Not worth the risks,* he thought. But maybe they needed to be, because soon enough, thanks to the Bares, he'd be out of serum, and soon enough, he'd be tied to the night. What's worse, Trish dragged unwanted eyes to their house. The police would be around again.

Oh yes, he thought as he went through the bags that Trish had thrown around the garage. They were full of papers, journals, and clothes. Stuff she'd hidden somewhere else. Things that she used for her hunts. Things he could use to frame her for his coming onslaught of victims. He'd spent the bulk of their marriage doing just that: digging through her things, weaponizing her secrets.

Randel sat at the kitchen table, eyes planted to the laptop screen. Running the camera back, he skimmed over the storage room. He watched himself kicking Trish, dragging her inside from the garage. Then there was darkness, the room quiet. Then… He paused the recording. *There's that girl again.* The black girl was frail, her bloody clothes nearly hanging off her body. Trish treated the stranger's busted leg, talked to her like a police officer, questioning her about someone. "Did he do this to you?" Trish had asked.

Who is he?

Randel rubbed his forehead, wishing he'd checked the indoor cameras sooner. He rarely did because Trish wasn't stupid enough to bring anyone into their home, not since the woman in the storage unit *years* ago. But there she was, bringing a stranger who Randel had seen Trish carrying through the living room before the camera broke. There she was.

Where is she now? he thought.

He switched to the Security Plus app for the outside cameras, but the account had been locked. The passwords—Mannygray@78 and DarDar@West24—did not work.

"Fuck," he shouted, slamming his hands against the keyboard. Trish changed the password and locked him out. Tied up with draining the Bares and putting *them* in jars, he hadn't checked the outdoor cameras since the day they were set up.

He dreaded calling the company and hated the idea of asking Trish; she wouldn't answer the question straight out, she'd lie through her busted mouth. In her current state, he'd be lucky if she told him anything at all.

She wasn't always like that. In fact, she had showed some sort of respect for her cloaking device, her fuck bag, the father of her child. That's all he was to her, and he was fine with it because she, *too,* was giving him something precious.

No harm, no foul.

Randel searched his memory, seeking out who or what a young black woman would be doing with his wife. The camera caught her inside the storage unit suffering from some bloody wounds and Trish had given her iron pills, nursing her. No doubt the girl was a vampire because why wouldn't she be?

How the hell did that happen? Trish knew better than to turn anyone, especially since she had a child at home. *How stupid and dangerous*, he thought. Then he cocked his head, hope blooming in his chest. *Unless…*

"Nah, that can't be—" Randel huffed and headed out to the garage. He grabbed the rake that hung against the wall between two exposed wooden studs and opened the garage door, the slow rise wearing on his thinning patience. The satisfying crunching of distorting leaves as the rake combed the freezing grass was welcoming to his ears. The motion slowed his heart and mind, conjuring up a plan in plain sight as the breaking leaves and grass allowed thoughts to circulate, come clearer.

The Bares were dead, and Randel had a new lab space and enough blood to last him for a little while once the serum ran out. *Yes.*

Which would be in two more removals. Dammit.

He was going to kill Trish and dispose of her body…somehow. *Her fault, entirely.*

And Randel would be a single dad. *Just for a few years.*

His phone vibrated in his pocket, pulling him from his thoughts. He pulled it up and glared at the screen. The name clicked instantly: Maggie's emergency contact, Bianca Poloski, her mother.

"Hello, Mrs. Poloski." He sounded cheerful, saving face.

"Hi, Randel." She didn't waste time getting to the point. "I was wondering if you've seen Maggie?"

He raised a brow. "Uh, no. I haven't seen her in a week or so. I just got back in town."

The woman sniffed. "Okay. I-I was just asking because her brother hadn't seen her in three days since she came home after watching Darwin. He said she didn't say anything to him—they're *always* bickering, driving me nuts. Anyway, he said she rushed by when she came home the other night, didn't even talk, looking like she *hurt* herself. She locked herself in her room before he could see anything.

Me and Mark just came back from vacation yesterday morning, and she still isn't here."

"That's strange," Randel said. Maggie was usually very social.

"Anyway, uh, I'm—" She started sobbing.

"I'm sure she'll turn up soon. She's a young adult, they venture off and come right back, right?"

"Well, that's the thing. Her car is here, and her phone is in her room. I was hoping that you guys picked her up and had her watching Darwin or something."

"Did her brother see her leave the house that night?" Randel peered in the garage at the back of the closed storage room door, then he looked at Trish's car. Then he looked at the door again.

She couldn't be that stupid, he thought.

"Well, no," Bianca said. "She had company, and that kid…he's missing too. I— Oh my god. Mark is talking about calling the police and getting divers out here."

Maybe Trish is that stupid, he thought. He stomped inside the garage, and into the house.

"Maybe he should," Randel said, knowing that Mark would do it anyway.

Mark was protective over Maggie; well, according to Maggie. "But he won't do anything about Mav and his friends drinking and carrying on in the house whenever *he* visits," Maggie had said that day Randel met her at a Starbucks to help her with her homework.

Inside the kitchen, Randel snatched up Trish's keys off the counter.

"Yeah," Bianca said, sobbing while trying to speak.

"What makes him think that they're in the lake? I mean— Maggie can swim, right?" Randel unlocked the older car by putting the key in the passenger side door. He looked inside. He sniffed and smelled Darwin's apple juice and milk. There were also small hints of a pissy diaper, which was normal for him.

Randel slammed the door and rounded the back of the car. He stopped at the trunk; the faint smell of cheap body spray lingered in the air. His chest caved when he popped the trunk, the sweet smell of isopropanol and chemical strawberries hit him in the face.

Small specks of blood spritzed the light gray carpeting. He tsked then mouthed, "Dammit."

"Yeah. I mean, she's not here. Her phone was in her room, and her and her friend's cars are *still* here," she said again as if rehashing clues. But Randel was a few steps ahead. "They left somehow. Mark wants to have the police jailbreak her phone and see who called her last. I-I just don't understand. And…and there's blood. I… She never does this, and we are really scared."

Ah, so you hope that she's here, one of the worst places she could be, he thought. "I'm sure she's fine," he lied, knowing that she was more than likely anything but fine. She was probably dead somewhere. And Trish had her in the trunk and dragged her off. That much was a fact. *But why?* Yeah, the soft of Maggie's neck was tempting, and Randel planned on using her in case of emergency—a lot like the one he was in now—but what the hell did Trish want with the babysitter? "Do you want me to come help you look for her?"

"We can use your and Trish's help… Can you ask her if she'd seen Maggie? I called her and got her voicemail."

"Well, Trish is going to stay here with Darwin. But I can ask her, and I'll be over in an hour or so. Is that all right?"

"I really appreciate it."

"All right, bye. I'm on my way." He hung up and clenched his jaw.

CHAPTER 28

Monitor

After what felt like a few hours of the serum mending the cracked bones in her wrists, Trish pulled her hands away and up the stake, tearing her flesh as she slowly widened the new holes stamped through the middle of her palms. She was sure there was a camera somewhere that she couldn't see, so she slowed her advances.

When she wasn't trying to break her very involved restraints, she listened for whatever Randel was doing. He spent a little under an hour banging on the other side of the door while it stood ajar, installing a barrel bolt on the outside of it. Or he spent time reminding her of how stupid she was for not recognizing him as a threat.

"Remember when we first met," Randel had said as he opened the tool bench and tossed tools into a tote box that they once used for Darwin's old clothes.

"I had been watching you for so long. I was actually at the hotel bar with Victor, listening to him talk about his wife and how he was going to stop cheating, because it lost its appeal. It was no longer *fun*." He chuckled. "I was like, *Sure, buddy*. Then, just in time, and just as you had every week for the last two months, you strolled into the bar. You looked beautiful with those plentiful lips in that sexy black cocktail dress as you shopped around for food. You never looked at me. Never noticed that I was the most handsome person in that place. Or, better yet, you could not *smell* me." Trish cocked her head, having known that Victor and Randel were acquaintances, but her eyes were on Victor, not his drinking buddy.

Randel dropped a hammer into the box. It clanged against the other tools. "I told Victor to take his little pudgy ass over there and talk to you, because just like I saw you walk in, he damn near drooled at the sight of you. I told him that his wife wasn't going anywhere. He's the bread winner. And he believed me. He took his ass over there. I thought you were going to kill him. Call it bait. Call it another one of your *missing persons* flyers to add to the stash. Call it what you want. But when he answered my email about a fake project proposal, I was surprised that he was still alive." Randel sounded elated. Trish rolled her eyes. She had left Victor alive because the hunt wasn't bearing fruit. A suck boy, a repeating blood bag who could keep a secret, was warranted, until it wasn't.

"And then when I met up with him, his watch was on his left arm, not the right arm, where it had always been when I met up with him. Now, I know that's weird, but he kept looking at his right arm, found it bare, and then quickly looked at his left arm to see the time. His balding head and clean-shaven face looked paler than I remembered. And I found it especially odd that the watch had blemishes of off-white make up on its golden finish; it barely concealed the bruising bite mark. Anyway, I asked him about what happened with the chick from the bar and he told me everything, about the little game you guys played. He thought it was exciting. Made me swear to secrecy. And I did. I laughed every time he emailed me with blood drop emojis." He dropped a handful of bolts into the box.

Trish pulled her hands away from the stake, a jarring pain shot through her fingers. She stopped when he looked at her.

"But I guess you didn't want to play anymore, because he went on to slit his watch wrist in a hotel room off I-96, 13 miles away from home, 30 miles away from Lakeshore. I was kind of surprised that you bothered to show up to the funeral. Dressed in black. Face covered with a gothic shawl, still hiding from the sun even though you had the serum coursing through those pretty little veins. But then I remembered: you had to make sure that he was embalmed. Make sure he was fully dead. I made my move after his wife chewed you out, not fully understanding what she was doing. You were just some whore that drove him to commit infidelity. Who drove him to kill himself when you wanted to break it off. But we both knew the widow had it all wrong, and you let her stay wrong when you rushed out—no doubt blushing underneath that sun drape that hung over your face." He glared at the wall, lost in a memory. "There was so much grief and love in that chapel."

Trish shook her head, having killed Victor because *he* wanted to cut it off. *"My blood is low, and my wife is pressuring me to go to the doctor. I think she knows something is going on. I can't afford another divorce. We have to stop,"* he had said as he sat on the hard mattress, the rings around his eyes pregnant with tiredness.

"I chased you out the chapel and apologized for the widow. I *soothed* you."

Trish looked away. Her heart felt heavy when an unassuming stranger hugged her and said, *"Please excuse her. She's just upset that she couldn't keep him happy. She's taking his death off on anyone who isn't her."* Randel's soft voice and warm embrace was the pillow that her soul needed.

"Did you ever wonder why it was so easy to fall for me once I had your undivided attention?" Randel asked as he lifted the tote box, stealing any weapons she could use to kill him once she broke free. "Did you think it was my charm? Nah. Well, maybe a little." He chuckled.

"Would you like to walk with me? Victor was my best friend and I—I'm going to miss him." His smile welcomed her in, making him a different contender. Trish had been single since Johnny, and living without the convenience of her traditional cloaking device, a husband, was becoming dangerous.

"Us being together had nothing to do with your strategy or whatever plans you concocted in that pretty head of yours. It was the force between us, our atoms drawn to each other. But let's be honest, you could never love anyone more than something that fell out of your womb and I made sure to give it to you."

He kissed the air. "I love you, Trish."

Then he left her alone.

***

Randel came back into the room wielding a black folding chair, a baby monitor, and a piece of bread that soaked the room in a horrid stench. Greenery and foliage clung to his skin as he ate what smelled like a garlic butter biscuit. Her stomach turned and he grinned. He set up the chair in front of her and sat. He licked his fingers and slung crumbs at her. Annoyance dragged his brow as he scowled at her.

"I'm taking your car," he said. "You don't mind, do you?"

As if it matters. She sneered.

"You know, I've been with some really scrappy women. It's fun to catch them when they are on a hunt or in the middle of their serial killing period."

"*You're* a serial killer," she said carefully, hoping he heard every bit of disdain in her voice.

"Yeah, but no. See, I mean a serial killer because, just like humans, you have to take the time to sneak around and cover your steps—you want to avoid the Feds and the police and the law and politics and the conspiracy theorists—all those who are incredibly inferior. They don't mean shit to me," he hissed before taking another bite of his food. She willed him to choke on it, but he didn't. "And I mean *serial killing period* because it comes every three months, then there's a baby, then they come every month. You can ignore the new need to feed more often…but you gotta do something about those *pangs*…"

She swallowed hard, feeling her mouth water around the edges of vomit threatening to surge. The fact that he knew a schedule that she carefully hid from him was sickening on top of his incessant chewing on something that he should not have been able to tolerate. But she skimmed over that. "So you don't care? Even though they own the planet? They make the laws. They have the numbers. They are the main being."

He tsked. "Ah, see, that's where you're wrong, my love. It shouldn't be you who is afraid of them; they don't have your DNA, fingerprints, leads, imagination, nothing! Nothing at all! There are virtually no rules! None! It's all a mirage, walls that you built around yourself that make you afraid."

She frowned. Hands hurting as blood leaked, pooling on the floor. The stake pulled at her, forcing her to dig her knees into the concrete floor.

"You aren't following me, are you?" Randel asked.

She knew what he meant. She knew this wouldn't end well. Not only was he preaching the opposite of what she had taught herself, he'd been at it just as long as she had if Agent Morgan's pictures held any weight…and they did.

"It's cute how you all think the same. You think you're the lone wolf on the planet. No one else is *like you*. No one else is as unique or superior *as you*. You're the only monster that *lives here*, unstoppable in your own right. And then I show up, knowing *everything* about you. Knowing where you're from. Who you are. What you've done. And I'm thinking: Wow! I am about to give her the best gift she could ever ask for: a child. A loving husband who only pretends to be *kind of* interested. I'm going to give her space to feed and make missing people. Imagine the look on her face when she finds out that I am no *savior. No normie."* He chewed on the stinky bread. "Did Ally tell you why his family lived in the wilderness?"

Trish's throat tightened. *Ally.* She knew she'd never see him again, never planned on it. But the fact that Randel knew him was… dangerous. "How do you know him?"

Randel sighed. His smile rose as excitement lit up his dark, unassuming eyes. He crossed his ankles. "I was walking around the forest, drowning in the sounds and smells of a settlement near my haunting ground. See, America didn't always belong to the people who settled here, unprovoked. I had been plotting on infiltrating them, but I had to be smart because…guns, you know. Anyway, there was a woman, gray-haired and shriveled, out there all alone picking berries and digging holes, storing dirt in a bag. I grabbed her, then stopped because she stank of sulfur. The smell was so horrid that my gut told me to leave her alone. But I was *hungry*, and it had been months since I'd seen a human out in the wilderness all alone. She knew what I was, called me a vampire right off the jump. *You blood suckers love the dark canopies.* Her voice was so low that it felt far away. *Love wet caves. Love…You're not extinct. I knew it. I seen. I…The Ancient One lives.*" He paused, shifted. "And right then, I did not drink her, but I knew I had to kill her. Couldn't have humans walking around smelling like brimstone, with skin that looked golden in the moonlight. They'd stink up the whole forest…couldn't have that. As I squeezed her neck, she said in a small voice, a timbre as small as she was, 'I can help you with the sun.' And that's when she told me about a serum that she'd been working on, among other things."

He looked off, entranced.

"I didn't believe her, but I also didn't understand why she was out at night all alone. I also didn't understand that invisible glow shining from her aura. I didn't understand how she knew about my opposition to the all-seeing star. But she did. She took me back to her cabin. Inside, there were more people: kids, men, and women, who looked just like her. Who smelled just like her. She handed me the serum—it was in a golden charm bracelet—and told me to wear it. I did, and I felt better. She told me that it would run out, but it should last for a while. She was smart enough not to tell me how long because, back then, it only lasted for three weeks, so I visited often. It all came with a caveat though: I had to help protect them from the settlers who lived in a new town. Turned out, people didn't like witches or alchemists. I don't believe in monsters, but I do believe in science, and she impressed me with hers. I protected their settlement…there were only twelve people there at the time…and I got to keep the serum, and I got to feast on the blood of the people in town who, eventually, blamed the family of witches in the woods for their disappearing kids and women and men. That was in 1807. Ally wasn't born until 1828. By the time he was born, there was a little less *conquering* of Appalachia and more *building up*, as they say. Running low on food, I ventured out and came back to find the old hag dead, and that Ally's father was running things. But he didn't have any serum…he had a theory on how to make a longer-lasting formula that he needed a special ingredient for. And that's when he gave me a name…a very *special* name."

Words didn't come to Trish as her thoughts stumbled on questions as the black box known as Ally's life was starting to fill in.

"You look perplexed. Did he tell you something different about the serum?"

She frowned. Ally told her nothing. He only promised her life.

Randel chuckled. "Well, Ally died the way he lived: a lying asshole. See, his father, and eventually Ally himself, spoon-fed me those unique names, keeping leverage like his grandmother had for all those years. Instead of protecting their land, I was providing this important ingredient that reinforced the serum. If I used it as instructed, I would have had it for about one hundred and fifty years." He chuckled. "But, you know, shit happens. My bracelet was confiscated in D.C. in 1888, so I had to go get more serum. Then after that I was lucky to get fifty years out of a serving; it's always important to keep a back-up batch because I love to eat." He popped the rest of the bread in his mouth, dusted the crumbs off his jeans.

"Why would they do that?" she asked, the question raspy in her throat.

"What? Make more serum that lasted longer? I don't know what the hell they needed it for, and for a second, I wondered if they got joy in deploying monsters out into the world to destroy the people who 'settled' on their land." He shook his head. "It happened to the best of us. But the moral of the story is that I don't work for anyone. Eventually, I figured things out. I looked at the equipment and minerals, picked up on all the smells. Knew the main ingredient."

He leaned in. "I just needed the names."

She sobbed, knowing that her name was on that list.

"Don't cry for Ally. If anything, you should hate him, because if not for him, I wouldn't have known how to find you!" He smiled.

She tussled with her restraints, pulling her hands, opting to tear them open just to get away. Just to tear his face from his skull.

"You won't break free."

"Where's Darwin?" she growled.

"He's fine. You didn't hear him? He's been cranky all day and finally went to sleep."

Alarm shot through her. Sleep could mean a short slumber or a really long one. She did not know who Randel was anymore; he could have meant one or the other.

As if reading her face, he said, "An *actual* nap."

He set a baby monitor that she didn't recognize on the counter. "Watch him until I get back, will you?"

Darwin was sleeping. He tussled, his face scrunched deep within the clutches of a nightmare.

"I don't know how long I'll be gone. Maggie is missing and Bianca and Mark asked for my help. I told them you had to sit with Darwin, so…" He paused, his eyes narrowing, expecting.

Her heart kicked at her chest.

Dropping By

Vicky watched Randel pull off in Trish's car after pulling his SUV into the garage.

"Now why is he taking her car?" Steve asked from the driver's seat.

She ignored him. He'd only just come back, proving that Maggie had done more damage than Vicky thought. Ignoring his voice seemed to work, pulled her back to reality.

She adjusted her shoulders, keeping an eye on the car as it headed up the street. Darwin had quieted down, so that was a plus.

"Doesn't mean that Trish wants you there," Steve said.

She felt her heart lurch, not because the sun had found skin or because she was hungry. It wasn't because of the uncertainty that plagued her for the last several months. No. Trish hadn't made an appearance in the last several hours. Something was *wrong*.

"Why is Randel taking Trish's car?" she asked. Vicky watched Randel all day—covered up nicely, making the sun less of a threat—searching for a break as she stooped low underneath the cover of the tinted windows of the first thing she'd owned in a while. Nothing was stopping her from getting into that house, Randel included. Still, she failed to make sense of his explosive movements and odd behavior.

"Because she belongs to him, just like you belong to me."

"I don't belong to anyone. And especially not you!"

"*There* she is. There's my girl. I knew you wouldn't ignore me forever. Must be really lonely sitting here, thinking about us. Thinking about what you did to me…to Mr. Wroth. Now, you want to grovel at the feet of—"

"Fuck off! You are dead. Okay."

"You are to."

"I know that!" she shouted, her pained voice boomed in her ears. "I know what I am. Alright? And I did that to you. You're dead because of me. Don't you see that I get that? I can't bring you back. I can't fix anything. I can't—and I'm sorry. I am *so sorry*. You were a terrible person and…" She closed her eyes and sighed. "You were there for me when I had no one. The doctors, the government, my family and friends were gone. You kept my secret. You kept me hidden and safe and I should have left. I should have left a week into my stay at your house. Right after you healed my burns—made me feel like I wasn't crazy, like nothing was my fault. I didn't go because I loved you. I loved you so much. I love your smile, your laugh, how you listen and you were so fucking smart. But you tortured me—just like a lot of other people probably *would*. Probably *will*. You cut me open so many times." She put a hand on her belly, over the phantom incision. "You hurt me so bad." Tears fell down her face. Steve's blade slicing through her fresh sutures made her jerk in the present. "And you kept going. You kept…trying to get me to eat. But I didn't. I wouldn't." She wiped the tears away. "I need Trish because she gets it. You don't. You can't. You didn't! And you're dead now and you're n-never coming back. And I—I'm *never* coming back!"

A knock on the driver's side window snatched her focus.

Steve had gone.

"Miss Scott," Agent Peter Morgan said, his voice muffled by the windowed barrier. He was wearing a jumpsuit, fresh off of a neighborhood walk. His dark eyes studied her, and his sly grin held many meanings, untrustworthy being the most apparent.

Vicky glared at him and then put her hand over her nose; a pungent sulfuric scent was tangled in the air. She could have vomited on the back seat.

The agent smiled. "Something wrong?"

There was a small hint of mint hidden somewhere deep within his musk. He could have been her uncle, walking to the car just to check on her. But he was everything but… The man from the hospital, the man who lived in the house across the street was everything but a welcomed guest. He was familiar in all the wrong ways, and Trish's secret agent neighbor was no longer shy. "I'm sorry," she said, finally aware of how rude she may have seemed. But then the conversation between him and Dr. P resurfaced. Then Dr. P's bloodied chest plagued her thoughts. No, Agent Morgan wasn't a good man.

"I know who you are," she said through her cupped hand.

"And I know who you are, Victoria Scott." Her name knocked the wind out of her chest. Her stomach turned as if someone with morning breath was blowing in her face.

"You were at the hospital that day, weren't you?" she asked. She needed to get him talking about what he wanted, not only her, but her *kind*. She narrowed her eyes at him. She was in his house. There were no pictures of him, and she didn't see his face. But she knew that voice, and she knew that name. Agent Morgan. Agent *Peter* Morgan. She looked at Trish's house, and then back at him, thinking of how this chance meeting could benefit her. It was quiet over there; Darwin must have cried himself to sleep. She didn't need the agent standing outside her car window, calling attention. "Are you—"

"Come inside and I'll tell you. I think we're after the same thing."

"Like what?" she humored him. But she was only torturing herself. The longer he talked, the more she had to smell garlic. She couldn't imagine what his house smelled like now.

"Like, why do you think I ate two cloves of garlic before I came out here?" He looked at Trish's house. "As I said, we are after the same thing."

"I don't trust you," Vicky quipped.

"I can assure you that you are not the one I want."

"You sure wanted me at the hospital. You wanted to take me away from Dr. P and family and friends and lie about what had happened to me. Remember?"

"I knew you were awake." He smiled, assured of himself.

"I guess we're both lucky that I left."

"Yeah. We are. But Steve wasn't."

Words caught in her throat. They *found* Steve. But she didn't ask. Was it a trick? Was Steve just…

"He found my body," Steve said. Vicky neglected the driver's seat where he liked to sit. "Oh, V, baby, they are after you. They know what you did. Don't go with him."

"Look, we can make a deal that ends with you going free," Agent Morgan said.

"He's lying," Steve said.

"But we need to go inside and talk."

"Why can't we talk here? Why can't you just get in the car?" Vicky asked.

"Because the occupant in that house," he pointed to Trish's tri-level, "knows who I am. And it would be best if they did not see us talking."

She couldn't argue with that.

"And if you don't come with me, I'll make a call, and have you dragged away right now. It isn't hard to track stolen plates, Miss Scott."

CHAPTER 30

Missing Persons

Randel pulled in front of the Poloskis' house after driving up the long narrow driveway that could pass for an abandoned dirt road. Nerves prickled his neck; police scoured the area. The more viable paved driveway that led up to the two-car garage was full of cars; the navy Prius belonged to Maggie. He wasn't sure which one belonged to her elusive friend. Two uniformed officers crouched next to the opened door, looking for something. The front door of the large house was open, allowing the outside inside, showing off a living room that was worth more than Randel's entire house.

Randel did not go inside. Instead, he went around the perimeter, looking, but not touching the grass or brush that outlined the property.

How did they get the police here so quickly? What did they find?

As he neared the backyard, he peered at the property next door, a skeleton of a house. It was bare of walls; wooden studs outlined the structure that could have been. Police officers searched inside the frame.

The backyard was also a heavy sight. Three cops wearing gloves walked slowly, searching the large wooden patio and long pool area which fogged at the surface. Heated.

Bianca stood at the mouth of a wooden walkway that cut through a thick bed of lake grass and tangled pickerelweeds. The lake's sandy shore littered the end of the narrow boardwalk. She was speaking with a man who donned an overcoat and a silver badge hanging around his neck.

"And you didn't hear her leave the house?" the man, who Randel assumed to be a detective, asked Bianca.

"N-no," she said. "I was on vacation." The woman's face was ashen and bloated; sacs ballooned underneath her tired emerald eyes. Her blonde hair was tossed back into a loose ponytail, and her silk pajama smelled like they could use a wash. The wino stench wafted from her panicked nerves.

The smell of blood dragged Randel's attention away from the conversation and onto the people wearing CSI jackets who were crouched along the edges of a disturbance in the vast water plants' bed. They took pictures and collected swabs, their tips sandy and crimson. The scene along the shore was barred by yellow tape.

Randel would have gone over, but the last thing he needed was to be yelled at or have the attention of the detective. And then he wondered… Should he be there at all? The police department that was responsible for Maggie's neighborhood shared resources with the same department who had Trish's Jeep. He cringed.

No, no, no. You need to know what they know. You need to know if Maggie is…

"Oh my God, they found something?" Mark shouted from the shore. His baseball cap, jeans, and long-sleeved black button-up looked damp, as if he were acting as a one-man diving team before the police showed up. He, too, was several feet outside of the crime scene tape. Bianca rushed over to her husband. The detective called into the walkie-talkie that he pulled from his oversized pocket.

"Woodward here. What is it?"

Of course. Randel stopped himself from rolling his eyes. *The same dickhead who took Trish's Jeep.*

Out in the center of the manmade lake was a boat. In it sat one occupant who was staring at what could have been a monitor.

"He found a body," someone said. "He's pulling it up now."

"Is it her?" Bianca shouted as she rushed back to Detective Woodward.

"We don't know yet," Detective Woodward said.

"Is it her?!" Bianca yelled, her watery eyes landing on Randel.

"I don't—" Randel started.

"Please tell me it's not her! Please! I don't…I don't want it to be her!" Bianca's words fell into blubbering chaos as she cried.

Randel looked to Mark, who had pulled his cap off and nervously cradled it in his hands.

The diver resurfaced, and the pully attached to the boat pulled the body out of the water. The corpse wore a plaid shirt, khaki pants, and black and white tennis shoes. Scraps of what could have been a puffer coat barely hung onto his shoulders. Which was strange. The last time the kid was seen, it was about thirty degrees outside. Humans loved to cover up from the cold. The men on the boat laid the body inside and pulled the anchor up.

"It looks like a young adult white male," the voice on the walkie said.

"Roger that."

The boat bobbed lazily on the aggravated currents before rushing in.

Relieved, Randel smirked. His hunch was correct: Maggie had been in Trish's trunk. But why?

Where did you put her, Trish?

Bianca and Mark ran onto the dock, meeting the boat there. Randel followed close behind, curious about the corpse's condition. Did the boy actually drown? Was this boy related to the Poloskis' household in any way? The sooner he knew, the better.

"Oh my God!" Bianca shrieked. She fell into Mark's arms. "Oliver!" she wailed.

The body looked pale, but fresh from where Randel was standing. The slits and welts across his chest and face had been washed out, cleaned of blood, but they left his features distorted.

He was attacked to death or caught in a boat propeller, Randel thought. *Nah. Too much of a coincidence.* He fought a smile, having seen such an attack before. But he still wasn't sure.

"Maggie, where are you?" Mark asked, his question hidden beneath his wife's shrill screams.

"Sir." A tap on Randel's shoulder. He spun around to find Detective Woodward standing toe-to-toe. "We need you to clear the area."

Randel nodded and went to head back up the dock.

"Randel," Mark said. "Thank you s-so much for coming. Can you—"

"Randel," Detective Woodward said, a spark of recognition in his eye. He pulled a notebook from his pocket and flipped back a few pages. He stopped. "Magdalena Poloski babysits for you?" he asked.

"Yes. She—"

"She babysits for them," Bianca proclaimed between sobs.

"Hm. Patricia Weston is your wife?" Detective Woodward said.

"Yes. That's why I'm here. I want to help find Maggie," Randel said. "This is all really devastating."

"Yeah, it is. Can you stick around for a while? I need to ask you a few questions. Bianca told me Maggie worked for your wife the night she was last seen. Is that true?"

"Yes, of course," Randel said, even though Trish hadn't told him as much. He hadn't seen Maggie enter or leave that night because Trish fucked up the cameras, locked him out. Randel hadn't even seen Maggie on the living room camera, which was also compromised by his dear wife. But in the efforts to seem like a cohesive unit, he agreed. There was no telling what happened inside the house that night or how Maggie ended up in Trish's trunk.

"Detective!" the boat driver called out.

"Stay close," he said before answering the man's call.

"Sure," Randel said.

"Justin and a couple of volunteers are searching the woods. Can you help them?" Mark asked as he swiped away tears. "W-we need to call Oliver's parents."

He nodded. "Sure, anything you need, I'm here," he said.

"Thank you." Mark huddled with his wife, who had pulled her phone out and put it on speaker.

Randel turned and strolled up the dock and to the boardwalk, his brisk pace ignored by the many volunteers and investigators. He passed through the backyard, and by the house. He zeroed in on the Honda as the heat of the policing presence burned his back. He hopped in, fumbled with the keys, and drove off, leaving the chaos behind. The police had nothing; Maggie's car and phone were at her own home. Woodward would waste time questioning Randel. Besides, Randel was doing the assignment—just not in the woods where Maggie would never be found.

Where did you put her? he thought, thinking about what he would have done. Maggie was long gone, especially if Trish had anything to do with it. *Where else would...* It was smart to put Oliver in the lake close to the house. He'd be found one day; it wasn't like Trish could go into the house and get both sets of keys and make them look like runaways. That was improbable. *And with this small-ass car, there is no room for two bodies,* he reasoned. *Perhaps she brought her guest along? And Darwin?*

Trish didn't give a damn about them finding the boy because he was still human when he died. *But Maggie?* If she turned, a man-made lake wouldn't be a fitting hiding spot. She could get out if she wasn't permanently immobilized.

"A hit to the head," he said aloud.

Still, Maggie would need to *never* be found. Her corpse would raise questions, and nowadays her blood would be studied. *Trish wouldn't risk that. I wouldn't risk—*

There was one other place that came to mind. At the stop sign a mile or so away, he leaned over and opened the glove compartment, finding the boat keys in the same place he'd stored his copy in his SUV.

Why would she need these stored in her temporary car? he thought.

CHAPTER 31

Coffee and Cloves

Vicky stood in Agent Morgan's office, a familiar space. The white-board was still full of Trish's crime scene pictures with her at the epi-center. The walls and the suede blue love seat were covered in photos and documents. Stacks of file folders were piled on his oak desk. The three monitors were off, as was his laptop.

"Your parents are looking for you," Agent Morgan said as he stood in the doorway.

"Is that your way of asking me if I spoke to my parents?" Vicky asked.

He smirked.

"You can be honest with your questions. I don't have anything to hide." All lies. She had many things to hide, but she would be more comfortable if he didn't. "Who are you?"

"The person who lives in the house that you erroneously broke into."

She dropped her eyes to her shoes, which looked older than two months; they were dirty and a little worn on the toe tips.

"You know I have cameras, right?" he asked.

"Hm. You shouldn't leave your window open then, especially if a dangerous monster lives across the street. Probably should have smothered the place in garlic a little earlier on, right?"

"Thanks for the tip, now have a seat." He headed for the love seat and moved the picture and papers over to the cluttered desk.

"I'll stand."

"Suit yourself. I don't know if it's worth asking, but do you want some coffee?" Agent Morgan asked.

She nodded. She didn't plan on drinking it—her stomach would be upset—but she preferred the smell of coffee over garlic any day. He left the room, returning the smell of brewing coffee in his absence. It didn't cover the garlicky smell, but it mixed in, making it worse.

Looking to ignore her overactive senses, Vicky surveyed the office for the second time; it had been rearranged.

Not even ten minutes later, Agent Morgan returned, two mugs in hand. He handed a bronze mug to Vicky, which she set down on the desk.

"When did you find out I was here?" Vicky asked as she studied him. His face was stern, hardened.

"That very night. Freaked my wife right out, so it was easy to get her to stay at her sister's until this is all done. Thank you for that. She doesn't like me out of her sight."

"Once what's done?" Vicky leaned against the desk as he sat on the love seat across from her.

"Now, studying to be a lawyer definitely taught you that I cannot tell you that."

She frowned, and he said, "I can help you, you know. So long as you help me."

"How?" She narrowed her eyes at him. "I don't know more than you do about her."

He sipped his coffee. "I need Patricia to help me take Randel down."

Vicky blinked, her legs going numb. "Who—her husband?"

"You catch on fast."

"What's his deal? Is he like a fraudster or—"

"You could say that, but it would only be part of it."

"Did he steal money from some trust fund? Launder money?" Randel looked like a normal man, sounded like a normal man. What crimes could he possibly commit?

"I hate to break it to you, but he is a vampire."

"No way—does Trish know?"

"I told her a couple days ago, but I don't think she believes me. I need you to help me convince her." Agent Morgan got up and headed for the desk. He opened one of the many folders and held up a photo. It was an old-timey snapshot of a man wearing a three-piece pin-striped suit. His honeyed skin was light brown against the dark background, and his thick hair hid underneath a top hat. The face matched Randel's, the man Vicky spent the better part of the day watching.

"Is this real?" she asked.

"Yes. I do not know of a world where an FBI agent would lie about something like this." He looked perplexed with a shot of annoyance. He set the folder back on the desk.

"Look, I don't know what he is or what he's up to, but I'm worried about her. He told her that he would be home for a while. It caught her off guard, like she didn't expect him to take a long break from work. And he lets the baby cry most of the day, and Trish would never do that. She wouldn't leave Darwin so upset. And then…he drove off in her new car, when he has his own SUV. Why would he do that? It's not like the car needs to go to the shop; Trish just bought it and—"

"Why didn't you go home?" Agent Morgan asked.

"What does it matter? What does that have to do with *this*?" she said, feeling herself close up. Here she was telling him something he wanted to know, and there he was, ruining it, forcing her to run back to her car or across the street to Trish's house.

"Just curious." He was looking at her like she was a prized cow. An idiot for somehow finding the woman who bit her. He was in awe.

"I can't go home like this. My family… They're better off believing that I'm gone." She couldn't say *dead*. It hurt too much.

"Did Trish tell you that?"

"No."

"You didn't think you were better off going back home?"

"Do you think I'm *stupid*? I know what's going to happen. You people told my parents I was missing because you wanted to catch me. It was a trap, and if I went home, the same thing that happened to Dr. P would happen to them. I heard you in the hospital. You already had plans for me."

"I have to do what's best for the people, and allowing a mass murderer to walk amongst us is… All I can do right now is ask for your forgiveness. I promise that nothing will happen to your family."

"Why is Dr. P dead? Is it because you guys found out that I was still alive? That he wanted to help me?"

"He wasn't going to help you."

"I don't hear you denying it…"

"You wouldn't understand."

"So, *you* had him killed?"

Nothing.

"At least tell his family! You left him there to rot."

"Not my fault that he's estranged from his family."

"And the hospital wasn't curious about him not showing up to work? He cared about his patients. He wouldn't just disappear," she growled.

"He resigned. No need for him them to ask where he is."

She shook her head, recoiling. "Wow. So-so nobody would know he was dead. How convenient."

"I don't know what you're insinuating, but someone would have found him eventually. The house would be on the market sooner than you think." He leaned in. "Maybe he should have chosen his battles more carefully."

"Why should I trust you?" Vicky said, disgusted to be standing before Agent Morgan. Regretting having shared a room with him again. Afraid, because she shoved the ball into his court. She would have been doomed if she'd gone to Dr. P's house straight from the hospital. She wondered how long the Fed's watched the house before they realized that she wasn't showing up. But Vicky opted not to ask. She settled on unpredictability, just as Morgan had.

He watched her for a minute, then huffed. "Look, it wasn't my call to have him killed. That was beyond me. Above my pay grade. If you ask me, I rather liked him. I thought he was smart and nice."

"Who told you to do it then? The president?" she said facetiously.

"Don't be stupid."

"What do you want from me then? I told you what I know."

"Help me convince her."

"How am I supposed to do that? I can't just walk up to her door!" Vicky growled.

"You let me worry about that. Until then, make yourself at home."

The Great Following

For the first time, Trish pondered the construction of a space that she had claimed as her own. No wonder Randel refused to sell the house but opted to add her to the deed. Sure, the house was paid off—he had secrets in the walls.

Randel returned to the storage room holding a familiar plastic bag. He'd taken a shower, drenched in the scent of a fake fresh spring. She heard the water running and was surprised to see him on the baby monitor screen. He'd gone into Darwin's room and offered him a bottle of milk, which he promptly took and enjoyed.

"How about a secret for a secret?" Randel asked as he moved the folding chair, opting to stand.

She sniffed, her nose nearly repaired thanks to the serum. She wanted to rub an itch away from her nostril but couldn't. Instead, her hands remained bolted to the shelf, unmoving. "What secret?"

He opened the bag and removed one of her journals. It was a standard spiral notebook with the years 1975 to 1993 written on the cover. "What are you doing?" she asked as he dropped the bag.

"I found this bag in the garage. Is this what you had in your storage unit?"

"How did you know about that?" she asked, looking for the fight in her soul, but not finding it.

"I know everything about you." He flipped the pages. "How was California? I lived on the West Coast during that time. Tracked you and your friend as you moved across the country. You played hippie for a while, right? You know, Mel approached me at the truck stop in Idaho. You were following…" He waved his hand around. "Led Zeppelin? Jimi Hendrix? I don't know. But I couldn't mistake that glossy orange hair and thin frame. She was gorgeous." He closed the notebook. "I told her I wasn't interested in buying a whore, and if I was, I'd would be interested in the girl she was with. The girl who disappeared in the cabin of a semitruck with a stranger." He laughed. "She got *so* mad—I could tell that one had a jealousy problem. But once you two hit the West Coast, I lost you. I ended up in Oregon— not too far from where I lost the scent."

He ripped a sheet from the notebook.

"No!" she shouted, the dried blood around her lips made her face feel tight. Memories and times lived on those pages. Things that she could not forget, things that she promised to pass on to Darwin if he had indeed turned out to be like his mother. And he had.

"If there was anything that Ally taught me, it was to never write anything down." He dropped the notebook on the floor and clutched the papers in his hand. He pulled a lighter out his pocket and flicked the flame, a sinister smile crossing his face.

Burning her to death wouldn't work, or at least she didn't think it would. But screeching in the storage room until her throat burned to ashes wasn't ideal either. "Wait!" Trish shouted. "What secret, what do you want?"

"What happened to Maggie?" he asked with a dry expression, as if knowing that she held the answer. As if he already *knew* what happened to Maggie.

"W-what?"

He touched the loose papers with the flame, setting them ablaze. She watched the past burn in his hand. She held a scream for her past self in her throat.

"You know…you like this room as much as I do. I watched you prep bodies for the fire pit…" He raised his brow and shook the flame out, then tossed the papers on the floor and patted them with his foot. "I watched you bring a complete stranger in the other night.

But I didn't see Maggie come in here when *she* is missing. You know Detective Woodward wants to talk to me about that?"

Trish shuddered. "What?" Things had been happening out in the world as she wallowed in her husband's prison. Things that had already found their way to her doorstep.

Randel ripped another page out of the notebook. "Yeah. Woodward's working Maggie's missing persons case. They found her friend's body in the lake on her property. Did you put him there?"

"No," she blurted, coughing on the black smoke that rose from the burning pages.

"Are you sure, because…" He balled the paper into a wad and threw it at her. She flinched when it hit her forehead. Then he set the entire notebook ablaze.

"Stop it!" she yelled.

"You sure do use the boat a lot less than you used to."

She was so caught up in the lie of Randel's existence that she forgot to go back and clean below deck.

"There was a mess, yes, like two bulls had a fight down there. And no, there aren't any cameras up there, but there are solar-operated cameras on the top deck. I know where Maggie is. I just need to know how she ended up that way."

"S-she…she was already dead."

"How, Trish? How the fuck did she end up dead?!"

He stomped the fire out and pulled out another notebook. "1924 has an entire book to itself. What happened there?" He opened it, his angry eyes scrolling over the words.

"No! Don't…don't"

He read, "'Albert gave me fruits that grow in different climates, all natural of course. I didn't feel sick when I ate—'"

"Maggie was bitten! Okay. S-she was bitten by a girl named Vicky!" Trish shouted.

Randel stopped reading and closed the notebook. His brow dragged, disappointed.

"Yeah, Vicky…turned her by accident and…and she wouldn't leave me alone. She found our house; she destroyed the Jeep…she'd been a problem. So I told her to drink Maggie and promised to help get rid of her body."

He dropped his hands to his sides; the notebook worth more than gold slid onto the floor. "Bullshit."

"What?"

"Bullshit. I don't believe you."

"I'm telling the truth!"

"When would she have done that? Huh? Bianca told the police that you hired Maggie to watch our kid that night. She was here with *Darwin*, and she left here alone that night; her keys and phone are at her house. Her brother said she looked *hurt*. Stop me when I'm wrong! Tell me that my ears and eyes are liars!"

Trish looked around, searching for an answer. Anything to get her out of her proverbial corner. There was nothing.

"You are just like the others. You don't take the time to see what you are! What's right in front of you. And because you were so sloppy, I gotta say, you are making this harder than it needs to be. And you are *such* a bad liar. No wonder you steer clear of people. It's not because they're in danger. You have more control around them than you think. It's because they'll find you out! How many times have you been found out? Don't lie."

More than three or four times, she thought, but kept it to herself. She needed to keep him talking. *Mel and Victor and Albert and Barbie and Vicky.* The list was longer than she wanted to admit.

"Fine, I'll tell you first. I've been found out maybe like, hmm, out of the hundreds of years that I have been able to ride the wave, I've been found out *maybe* three times. Once when someone walked in on me while I was draining their wife. And before you go on judging me, he didn't get out of there alive. I could have ran that town into the ground." Randel snickered.

Don't forget about the agent across the street, she thought.

"Then there was the time when the police caught me in D.C. in 1888. I got a little ahead of my skis, but those politicians were so easy to trap. Especially when they were out looking for a good time. The authorities took the fucking bracelet and locked me away while they decided how they were going to deal with a real vampire. They didn't know how strong I was, damn near walked right out the front door after bending some bars and sliding through. Naturally, the sun tore me a new asshole, and after a few wrong turns, I found myself in Hopkins, West Virginia."

Her stomach clenched as she gasped.

"I had to feed on the sheep and livestock at night and rest up in the day, because I was so weak. But before I could heal, I was burned out of the cave where I'd been hiding." He crouched in front of her and ran his thick fingers over her crown; blood dried in her hair, making it stiff and dark brown. "Before those hicks found me again, I had the luxury of feeding on a young woman who was foolish enough to be outside at night. Everyone in Hopkins knew about the feral creature lurking on farms, but I guess she never heard the story."

Trish's veins went icy as Randel's dark eyes took shape in her memory. If only they were pink. If only his skin was burned and his limbs were longer and his belly was bloated with her blood. Full on her death. His warm breath and faux compassion made her believe he was like any other man, a critical misdirection.

Randel whispered, "Her blood sustained me through the lynching. And *now*, her blood will help me again."

Trish's chest caved as tears flooded her eyes. She shook her head. "No, it can't be you. You—"

"Yeah. I turned you. So, it was no surprise when I got that list of names from Ally, and you were on there. Well, I didn't know it was you until it was time to track you down. I've always been a few steps away, my love." He winked. "You could never get too far from me."

Trish sobbed, stumbling on her memories as she searched for him. Other than that night in her family's coop, there was nothing.

"Now, I'll ask again. Are you sure you want to stick with your story about Vicky killing Maggie?"

Trish said nothing.

Randel sighed, then picked up the baby monitor, chair, and bag. He switched the light off and left her alone in the dark.

CHAPTER 33

Pita

It felt like forever when Randel opened the door and switched the light on. Trish's eyes burned, forcing her to wince. The feeling had begun to return to her hands, and the pain throbbed in her palms as she continued working the stake. Her healing hands worked against her efforts to break free as the ring began closing the wounds around the obstruction. But she said nothing, hid the pain.

Randel shoved someone inside and slammed the door shut. He remained outside. Pita crashed into the wall and fell onto the floor.

She got on her hands and knees and shouted, "What are you doing? Let me out of here, you asshole!" She got on her feet, then stopped and looked at Trish. Fury was replaced with repulsion and fright.

"Oh, oh… What?" She shook her head and said, "No. No. I—" She raced back to the door and slammed her hand onto it. She cried like a child who was stuck in a room with a hungry monster. "Please!" A guttural shriek. "Let me out!" She smacked the door again.

"No one can hear you," Trish said.

Pita shuddered and her hands balled into fists.

"Pita," Trish said.

"No!" She banged on the door. "Let me out of here! I swear I won't say anything. Please! Help me!" she cried.

"Pita."

"No!" she shouted. "I-I don't want to talk to you!"

"Pita, you have to help me get out of here."

"No!" She shook her head, her tanned skin blanching.

"You have to help me get loose." Trish's lip shivered as she pleaded. "Pita, please."

"What? Why? Why should I help you?"

Where is this all coming from? Trish thought. Her heart ached for Pita, but Trish couldn't defend what she didn't know. Pita was acting like she was stuck in a prison with rattlesnakes, not her best friend. "Pita—"

She must have registered the quizzical look on Trish's face, because she said, "No! You lied to me all this time. You...you're a fucking *killer!*"

"No, no. Randel, he's...."

"A killer just like you! He told me everything!"

"Whatever he told you isn't true."

"Stop *lying* to me!"

"I'm not—"

"You know what happened to Dr. Webb? You killed him! Gabby is torn up about it. She saw you! You were the woman that she told the police about! You destroyed an entire community, *Trish!* You traumatized those poor kids! You did that. My niece will never be the same; Gabby is broken because she didn't talk him out of leaving with you! You know that? How many more people have you destroyed? You're a killer. You're a *monster.*" She huffed, tears running her mascara, soaking her face.

How did Randel find out about Toby? Trish thought. *Is there a tracker on the Jeep?* The thought of him watching her like a moving dot on a screen made her insides crawl. *No,* she rebutted. *He doesn't know about Toby, he just knows that I was out the night that massacre happened.* "How did he know about that?" Trish asked. "How did he know about Gabby and Toby?"

Pita wiped tears from her face. "Because I told him about it when he called me over. He said you were depressed, and that you wouldn't come out the bathroom, so I rushed over and..." Her face fell. "I told him about what had been going on and how everyone is down right now because..." She cried.

"It wasn't me, Pita. It was Randel. He's the killer. He did that. He-he followed me when he found out I was having an affair, and then he killed Toby and everyone else in that house." Trish nearly held her breath, waiting for the lie to settle into the narrative.

Pita slowly shook her head. She spoke low, words loaded with exhaustion. "Just stop. Just… Randel was out of town, Trish. You were the last person anyone saw with Tobias Webb that night." She looked up and down the door and then leaned against it. She sat down.

The women stared at one another.

"What else did he tell you?" Trish asked.

Pita moved her wet eyes away from Trish. Her best friend was tense, not trusting, and wanting not to talk for the first time. She was usually so open about everything. But now? She pinned herself so close to the door that she could have disappeared inside it.

"Pi—"

"I told you what he said," she snapped. "Is it true?"

"No. He's lying."

"He showed me proof that you were in Miller that night."

"What did he show you, Pita?"

"He tracked your phone and Jeep."

Shit, Trish thought. How had she been so complacent for so long?

"He told me how you don't eat any food and then—and then I thought about it, and…*he's right*. You don't. You don't ever eat *anything*. He told me that you had Darwin in the bathroom because you have an arrest warrant. You *used* me, and you've been doing it for a long time."

That's new. Not the part about Pita being useful but… "Did he show you a warrant?"

"No."

"And you believe him?"

Pita's face crumpled in disgust. "Trish, he showed me the *teeth*."

Teeth? "What teeth?"

"The jar! Your teeth."

Trish went quiet. She felt the color drain from her face. "Pita, look at me."

She didn't.

Trish whimpered, "Please look at me. Look at what he did to me. My son is in there with him. *Darwin* is in danger, Pita."

Pita sighed.

"I am not a threat to you. I am the one who's bolted down in the storage room. But Randel is walking around. He put you in here."

"He is just as bad as you."

Trish raised her brow. "How so?"

"When were you going to tell me?"

"Probably never," Trish admitted. "But I promise, I would never hurt you."

"Yeah well, *he* is going to hurt me. And if I let you out, he said you will kill me because that is the only way you'll heal."

That wasn't a lie. Trish did need healing, even with the ring. But if she was going to get Darwin and deal with Randel, she would need all the strength she could get, fast. "I will never hurt you. You have to believe me."

"So, it's true then."

"I didn't say that."

"I can't—I want my kids. I want my husband. I want to go home," Pita declared, Trish losing her.

"I can get us both out of here if you help."

"Why should I trust you if all you do is lie?!"

"Please, lower your voice, okay? There are cameras."

Pita's wild eyes darted around. "Where?"

"I don't know where. But they are here. They are all over the house. When he had them put up the other day, he only put them up outside. But there were cameras in the house this entire time."

"He was *watching* you?" Pita trailed off, probably thinking back on all of the deeply personal conversations they'd had. "That's sick."

Trish ignored the question. It was too complicated to put into thoughts, let alone words. "Listen, Pita. I can get us out of here. You just need to help me get loose. All right? I swear, I will not hurt you. And I will not let him hurt you either."

"How did you live with him all this time, and not know what he was?" She sucked in a sharp breath. "No wonder he's always gone. He'd been hiding his life…just like you."

"It's not—"

"You always need me to take Darwin at weird times. Is that when you go out and kill people? Huh? Haven't I helped you enough already?"

"Please help me this one last time. I promise you will leave here and get to your family. I just want my son. I think Randel wants to hurt him."

Pita shook her head.

"If you let me out of here, I will tell you everything. You can turn me in to the police. I know you care about Darwin. You helped me deliver him. He loves you, Pita. And outside of all the lies, you know one thing is true: I *love* my son, and I would move mountains for him. Now please. Help me help us. Help me save Darwin."

CHAPTER 34

Red Fingers

Randel opened the door, leading with words, "I—"

The words caught in his throat when Trish slashed the pointy end of the stake like a dagger, aiming for his head. He dodged the blow, making Trish stagger.

"I was hoping you two would make up!" Randel said. He jammed his shoulder into her belly. She fell back into the tool cabinet, sucking in the air that he knocked out of her. Randel went for Pita, who was standing in the corner, out of the way as she and Trish had planned. Pita swung punches at the closing gap between them.

"No!" she shouted between grunts.

Randel laughed, allowing some of her blows to land on his chest and chin. "I always thought you were cute."

Trish jumped on his back, her forearm around his neck. He grabbed her hair and bent over, flipping her. She crashed into the shelving unit, knocking over the tote boxes that burst open. Winter clothes and holiday decorations fell to the floor.

"Help!" Pita snatched the stake from the floor and screamed as she ran into the garage.

Randel huffed as he stomped Trish's leg; it snapped at the knee. She squealed as a thunderous pang hissed through her body. "I'll be right back," he said.

Randel ran out into the garage and slammed the door behind him.

"Run, Pita!" Trish's throat went raw as she cried out. "Get my son and run!"

She planted her hands against the floor, pulled her lame leg and sapped body until she reached the door. She grabbed the doorknob and pulled herself up.

A large thud shook the house, jolting Trish as her bloody hands slipped from the doorknob, sending her to the floor.

"Pita!" she called. "Darwin!"

The silence was deafening. No screams, no cries.

"Pita! Darwin!" She pawed at the door then smacked it.

"Ahhhh," a guttural cry as she used the handle again to pull herself to her feet.

"Pita! Answer me!"

The doorknob moved, and she let go, falling back to the floor. She scooted back, making room.

The door opened and Randel stood before her. His hands were coated in blood that was not his, but that of a human. Pita's blood. The stake leaked onto the floor—the thick blood formed a viscous pool. "I planned on letting her go if you agreed to finally tell me the truth. But no, you recruited her to attack me and now… Did you really think that was going to work?" He threw the stake into the garage. The garage door responded with a metallic *thunk*. He slammed the door closed, shutting them inside the storage room.

He flexed his shoulder; it cracked. "Did Darwin bite Maggie?" he asked in a small voice.

Trish spit at his jeans.

"Hm. So, yes?" He raised a brow.

"I don't know what the fuck you're talking about," she said.

He smiled, then bared his teeth as his face went crooked as invisible hell fire crackled around them. Her gut tightened and her leg throbbed. She felt naked under his manic glare, prey to his wicked plans. Without warning, he grabbed her arm. He pulled, lifting her up from the floor. She slipped on her blood, hands shaking from blood loss and mutilation. The holes had started to close, but not fast enough. She tried pulling herself away by throwing her shoulders back, but when her footing failed, her wrists screamed.

Randel shook her, popping her shoulders, her brain crashing into her skull. The room spun, brown melted into metal, melted into the blood splatter on the walls and floor. Melted into his wide eyes, tawny skin, broad shoulders.

She screamed.

"Has he had blood yet?" Randel asked.

Why? Why does it matter so much? It's like he... Dread encompassed her being. Agent Morgan had told her that there were other women who Randel married; they turned up dead or missing. He also told Trish that Randel's children had gone missing. *He was so desperate for Ally's names...names of other vampires.*

"Did he—"

"No!" she shouted.

"When will you learn that you can't lie to me?" He moved his right hand up her left wrist, gripped her ring finger and bent it back. He studied the ring as he always had with intense adoration. "I always thought it was stupid that you put the serum in a ring. I mean, what if somebody steals it? Huh? Or what if they ripped your finger off?" He pulled her finger back, ripping tendons.

A guttural growl as Trish tried to scream, "No!"

"What? I can't hear you! No one can fucking hear you! Is...he... *ready?*"

"No!" she shouted. "Please, Randel! Don't hurt him."

He leaned into her face and whispered, "You are such a bad liar." Randel snatched her finger, snapping bone, and tearing skin. The ring was detached, her finger in his hand. Blood spewed from the new hole. She screamed, holding her wrist and thrashing as the transition took hold.

PART 5

Red

CHAPTER 35

The Ancient One

Darwin stared at Randel as if he were a stranger—the same look he'd given him since Randel had picked him up from his bed and took him down to the living room. He sat Darwin on his lap and bounced him on his knee.

"I wish you could talk to me, Darwin," Randel said. Pita's fresh blood barely covered the smell of bleach. Randel hadn't used it, hadn't needed to. But Trish may have.

"Ewwww," Darwin said with more joy than Randel had seen out of him in days, his stern expression slowly falling into a trusting one.

"I look different, huh?" Randel said, chuckling at the puzzled child. He'd never seen his father as he was: twenty-two with long thick black hair, a smooth face with a chiseled chin. Randel was thinner, his arms too small to wield a musket, even though they had. And they did well, until they didn't.

Darwin cocked his head and smiled, seemingly finding a familiar face inside Randel's eternal dark eyes.

"That's my boy. You know I'm missing a tooth?" Randel stuck a bloody finger into his cheek and pulled it back, exposing the missing molar that housed a golden filling. The filling was full of homemade serum that he was due to run out of. "One more use, and I'm done," he said, unhooking his cheek.

Darwin watched his fingers, hypnotized.

"You remember Pita? She cooked for your dad tonight. It tasted good too. Would you like some?"

Darwin ignored the question as he usually did. He only watched his father's fingers dance in the air; Pita's blood provided a gory glove.

"She must have really cared about you for her to run all the way into your room to get you instead of running out of the door. I mean, that's what I would have done. But I guess she wanted to take you away from me. Just like your mom would if she ever got out. I can't let that happen. You know that, right?"

"Mm," Darwin grunted, reaching for Randel's fingers, only for him to raise them out of reach.

"I used to have people who cared about me, an entire tribe. I always wondered why they sold us out to the settlers. Offering up our strongest to fight a war that wasn't ours in exchange for keeping *all* our land." He chuckled. "That turned out to be a crock of shit. If only they could see how things turned out." He shrugged. "I guess Pita did the same thing. And just like my tribe, she bit off more than she could chew."

He lowered his fingers again, and Darwin grabbed Randel's thumb.

"I forget about the tribe sometimes; I haven't seen them since the war. Since the colonists talked us into grabbing muskets and pushing their king off our land. I can't say that I was surprised that our land was destroyed and taken away in the process. Lucky for me, I wasn't there. No…I was hiding in a cave with nowhere else to fall back to. I entered the lair of the Ancient One, running away once gun fire was traded, and I watched my brothers and uncles fall face down into the mud we were promised well before the land became grass."

Darwin pulled Randel's thumb toward his mouth. Randel pulled it away. Slobber leaked from the boy's lips. He kicked his feet, agitated.

"The elders always told us to steer clear of the cave. That there was an agreement with this thing… A monster lived there, or so they said. I didn't know if it was true or not, but an ancient myth was less scary than gunshots and cannons. Men in coats on horses with weapons. I didn't have a choice but to enter the wet, cold, dark place. At least until the cannonballs stopped flying. With all of the sacrifices my people made to the Ancient One, I thought I'd be welcomed, offered refuge. But instead, something slammed into my body. My bones snapped in my ears, every last one of them. Before I could pass out, before I could come to, my blood was stolen. The Ancient One's mouth was cold on my neck as she slurped. Her silky hair covered my face, blinding me to her features. My body vibrated with every ounce of blood that she'd stolen. As every inch of my life was taken."

Darwin groaned, grabbing Randel's thumb again. Randel pulled it away and rubbed the boy's face.

"One of those cannonballs hit the cave's entrance, and the rubble came down on us. The hardened rocky mouth shattered, speckling pebbles, moss and dust throughout the ancient cavern. I honestly thought I was dead. With her cold breath going warm, her teeth buried deep in my neck…" Randel swallowed and his throat tightened. His son's eyes glazed, taken by wonder, simmering in want as he glared at Randel's red fingers. "I thought our collective corpses belonged to the war, but her body protected me; her gray withered face shrieked, forcing me to share in her agony as she let off her bite, and stared me in the face. Those pink irises pierced the dankness of the moist space as it settled to the ground. She took rocky walls and stray sunrays that ate the back of her head and back. She screamed for so long and I held my breath as her blood flooded my face. Then her blood turned into ashes. The foul paste forming on my face didn't harden, didn't flow. It clumped and crept into all my orifices. The sun's fire ate her inside out, but the front of her face stayed intact, staring at me. Jealous, afraid…aware. I passed out right there, lost in a cavern full of blood and broken bodies. When I finally woke, it was night out, and the ruckus of war had dragged on to the west. I was different when I pulled myself out of the wedged space."

Darwin's fangs slid past his gums, pointy and thick. Magnificent and new. He cooed.

Randel smiled, his heart leapt, vindicated. "You're ready, Darwin." He hugged Darwin, who fussed in return, expectant of something that was never given or paid out.

Randel sniffed, tears welling in his eyes. "My son, I promise you will be rewarded. You're so different from the others. And I knew it." He pulled Darwin away and smiled. New plans formed. An easier way forward presented itself. "You will—"

A slinking sound from the foyer caught Randel's attention, a movement that he could not pinpoint. The noise was too small to be Trish, no way she'd gotten out.

The doorbell rang.

Randel set Darwin on the floor where he rushed over to his toys, griping the entire way. Randel headed for the door; his eyes caught on the black tape over the hole that Trish put through it.

He tilted his head. *It staying that way*, he thought, deciding that it would be better to abandon the house entirely. It would be seized eventually, just as other properties he'd owned through the decades.

He looked through the peephole. A misplaced blinding blackness met his gaze.

What the fuck?

He went into the office and peered out the window. The porch was empty.

Odd… Someone had been on the porch, and they'd blocked the peephole. *Hiding from me*, he thought.

He washed the blood off his hands and slid on a puffer coat, covering the mess Pita made of his shirt, neck and mouth.

He opened the door and found a note covering the peephole.

Pick Up

Randel pulled their guest's SUV into the garage, hopped in his own vehicle, and took off, leaving space for Vicky to make her move. Cloaked by the shield of night, she rose from the neighbor's shrubs. *I guess you were right, Morgan,* Vicky thought.

Two hours earlier, Morgan put on another pot of coffee and explained his plan for the fourth time. They'd adjusted it once Vicky told him what she knew about Trish and the layout of her house. Vicky had finally sat in his leather desk chair, and he took a seat on the desktop, across from her. "We're lucky. Mrs. Pepper is out for the week. She left for South Carolina to be with her sister."

"Did you have anything to do with that?"

"Ah, no. Like I said, lucky. She's lucky that her neighbors haven't cared to get ahold of her either. That woman is nosey."

"You talk to her?"

Morgan sighed. "Enough. She told me about their schedules and how Darwin hasn't gone to school. How our friend, Randel goes out of town for work, and how she suspects Trish of cheating on her husband. I almost laughed at that."

"Okay. So, the nosey neighbor is gone. What about the woman who's over there now?" Morgan had reported that someone showed up to the house at some point that afternoon.

"Ah, she's a woman who takes their kid sometimes. May even be what Patricia calls a *friend*. I have a feeling that she's not leaving that house ever again. Especially not after he gets our note."

Vicky blinked. If she'd known that delivering the invitation would get someone killed… "Are you going to help her?" she asked, perplexed by his true mission. "Aren't you supposed to serve and protect the public? I mean, what the fuck?"

Morgan snickered. "No. I'm not. In fact, the outcome of my mission is for the greater good of humanity in the long run. It always has been. The cost of humanity is way higher than one woman who trust the wrong people. If anything, she is a helpful distraction for the enemy."

"I mean, can—"

"No more questions about the stranger across the street please. We need to move on."

She hoped the woman got out alive. *Trish wouldn't let someone die with Darwin in the house. Would she?* Vicky shook her head, shaking the silly thought. *She couldn't even protect Maggie so…* She went on with the discussion. She sighed. "What about the cameras that Randel put up?" Vicky leaned forward and crossed her arms on the desk's top, waiting for the man with all the answers to speak up. Waiting for the man with all the answers to realize that he needed Vicky and Trish more than they needed him. He needed to make a deal with Vicky and she wasn't doing a damn thing without one. No way was he discarding her like he carelessly discarded the friend across the street or Dr. P.

"It won't matter if he sees you on camera," Morgan said, his expression as still as a statue. His groveling tenor steady and assured. "I'll keep him out long enough for you to get Trish and Darwin. An hour at least."

"You're so confident that he's going to leave his house to come speak with you. Like, why would he do that?" If Randel was the man that Morgan said he was, then he'd be skeptical. Vicky squirmed. The holes in Morgan's plans seemed to grow each time they went over it.

"Oh, trust me, he wants to speak with me." Agent Morgan winked.

Vicky scaled Trish's house that night, taking the queue to move the plan along to the next step. Darwin's cries grew louder when she reached the side where his room was. If she broke in, the security system would go off and the police would be right over, finding Darwin and hopefully Trish inside.

Would they? "Hmm," she mused. *Doubt it.* The Westons were monsters. The last thing they wanted was for the police to show up. If anything, Randel would get the warning and cancel his meeting with Morgan.

But if the alarms don't go off... Regardless, Darwin and Trish needed to be far away from Randel, who was exactly who Morgan said he was. He looked younger when he went to his SUV, comfortable in his vampiric form at night. He couldn't smell Vicky just like Vicky couldn't smell him. Luckily, the lady next door had gone out of town; Vicky used her front and backyard to keep watch, out of Randel's camera view.

Still, for Randel to be in his vampiric form in Trish's house while she was home... With that, Vicky rounded the front of the house, sprinted past the porch and the camera over the garage, and hopped the fence that led to the backyard She tensed, waiting for metal teeth to shred her ankles. But her feet landed softly on the freezing grass. She stepped carefully in the dark, putting a light toe forward until she reached the patio stairs. Small creaks sounded as she carried herself along, heading for the glass door. She peered at the camera over the patio. It watched her back but didn't move, unexcited by her trek. Vicky grasped the handle, and pulled it to the right, disengaging the lock that crumbled under her newfound strength. The clattering of dismantled metal pieces scattered and fell onto the tiled kitchen floor. She stepped inside, eyes already adjusted to the darkness of the kitchen and living room. The furniture was in place and the space reeked of bleach and blood. Darwin shrills sounded tired and flustered.

"Trish," Vicky called out. She stopped in the kitchen, next to the kitchen table. There were no rushing steps. No call backs for the mother of the house; only a child and visitor awaiting her arrival.

Vicky ran down the steps, heading for the bottom floor. Her knees locked as a wave of nectar washed her tongue. The savory smell of fresh blood flooded the air from a source so close, so ready to be eaten. The secret hid behind one of the three closed doors along the dark hallway. Her heart throbbed as Darwin's cries grew louder. Vicky knew where his room was. It was the first one on the right.

"Mama!" he yelled.

But it was the room that sat diagonal to his that caught her eye. Something enticing hid within its depths. Something that her teeth nearly gnashed for. She pursed her lips, calming the need to drink, tempering the want to eat.

"No," she whispered between a shaky breath. "I—I don't…" she swallowed the lump in her throat and turned, heading for a familiar room.

In the dark, Dawin was standing in bed and pulling on the oak rails that came up to his shoulders. Drool driveled from his mouth as he cried, fangs showing themselves.

"Oh no, Darwin. Are you okay? Did he hurt you—"

Vicky stopped short, tilted her chin. *Is he going to bite me?* Her inner ear rang as she contemplated. If he bit her and it felt like Maggie's bite, she, Trish, and Darwin weren't going very far. The ghost of a spoiled stomach and weak knees infiltrated Vicky's body. Anxiety clenched her gut. She sucked in a deep breath. Darwin reached for her as his crying simmered to hesitant breaths. "Ma-ma," he said.

"Okay," she said. "Okay, Darwin. We're…" She picked him up. "Please don't bite me," she whispered as he settled over her shoulder. His breathing stuttered on the tail end of a tantrum. He wrapped his arms around her neck.

"It's okay," she said as she carried him up to the kitchen. She opened the refrigerator, pulled out a pre-made glass bottle.

Vicky sighed, looked around. She heard nothing but Darwin, who was still coming down from his enraged fussing. "I'm going to set you down, all right?" Not waiting for a response, she took him into the living room and turned on a standing lamp that flooded the space in a bright yellow light. She sat him on the floor and crouched down in front of him. He looked up at her.

"Where is your mommy, Darwin?" she asked, handing him his bottle. He took it and opened his mouth, his fangs gone. He drank hungrily.

"Stay here. I'll be right back." Before he could acknowledge her, Vicky ran back down to the bloody floor, knowing that the blood didn't belong to Trish, but to an unlucky human. Vicky opened the room diagonally to Darwin's. The master bedroom was dark, the blackout shades blocking out the moonlight. Vicky flipped the light on. A woman, maybe in her early to mid-forties, lay at the foot of the king bed. A gnarly slit split her neck in half. Blood soaked the floor and her face. Her dead, wide eyes pleaded for an explanation as her long silky dark hair soaked in her fleeting life liquid.

Trish's nameless friend may have felt safe in that house full of vampires and she could have been saved had Morgan thought she was worth the time or a quick message. But she became nothing more than a casualty. Vicky shook her head, picturing her life outside of her last moments. Was she a mom? A wife? A coworker? Sibling?

"I'm sorry," she said to the body sprawled on the floor. Vicky was sorry for many things. Sorry that the woman knew Trish and Randel and Darwin. Sorry that she wasn't worth the FBI's time. Sorry that she smelled like sustenance.

Sorry, sorry…

Vicky stepped over the corpse and checked the closet and the master bathroom. "Trish?" Vicky asked. Nothing.

Vicky left the room and headed across the hall to the bathroom. Nothing there either.

"Come on, where are you?" Vicky said.

She ran back up to the living room and checked on Darwin. He was laying on the floor, chewing on a stuffy, content.

"Where is Trish?" Vicky asked, pressure wearing on her shoulders, blooming in her chest. "This house isn't that big," she sneered. "Where the hell…?" Then she snapped her fingers and headed for the garage where the Honda and SUV were parked. In passing, she saw Darwin's car seat still inside.

"Please, please be here," she said.

She cocked her head as she approached the storage room door, then slowed. She sucked in her lower lip. A barrel bolt latched the room closed on the outside—*that's new*. She didn't remember it being there before when Trish treated Vicky's bear trap wound in that very room. She undid the barrel bolt and let herself inside.

"Vicky!" Trish's call sounded hoarse and tired. Etched with pain.

"What happened?" Vicky asked, near tears. She rubbed the wall, searching for the light.

"Vicky," Trish said though exasperated breaths.

Once the light flooded the space, Vicky opened her mouth to speak, but the words didn't come for the monster who had turned her. Trish's nose and lips were plumped purple and dry with blood. Wet stringy black hair matted to her face. Her robe barely clung to her body as her bruised shoulders and legs were exposed. Scentless blood coated the ragged flesh, bloodied tendons and broken bones that outlined the quarter sized holes in either hand. Her ring finger was missing, leaving a gory stump amongst the remaining fingers in her left hand. She looked frail and pale. Not fair-skinned and thicker in the legs. Her form took Vicky back to the night they met, and the vulnerable being was ripe for revenge.

Once Trish got onto her shaking knees, Vicky stepped away. *Leave her*, Steve's voice. *Leave her and the kid—turn them over to the police. Tell Morgan that the FBI already has them.*

"Where's Darwin?" Trish asked as she limped for the door.

"He's…he's fine," Vicky said.

"Randel?"

"He's gone. But he won't be gone long. We need to go, now."

Darwin cried.

"I'm coming, baby," Trish said, having made her way into the garage. Her lame leg refused her advances once she reached the parked cars. She went down on her knees and wailed. "Please, please Vicky. Help me get to my son."

***

"Where are you taking us?" Trish asked from the back seat. She cuddled with Darwin as they lay there, their bug-out bags on the floor in front of them. She hadn't spoken to Vicky much since the garage. There was only the bloodcurdling scream when she found Pita dead in her bedroom. Even in Trish's physical state, she didn't lick or drink the blood of the woman on the floor. Instead, she cried and whispered regrets.

"Somewhere safe," Vicky said. They rode in the Buick Century, which was surprisingly strong for what she paid for it. The old farmer deserved more money for it, and Vicky saw herself riding the thing until the wheels fell off. She didn't need to worry too much about the tabs. As Agent Morgan agreed, he'd get her legit tabs and a new identity for her help. She was happy to have gotten the hard part out of the way. The hard part for her at least.

"You trust the agent?" Trish asked. Vicky looked in the rearview mirror, barely seeing her. She helped Trish slide into Randel's navy blue snow suit and a black poof ball hat. She wrapped her mangled hands with socks and took several iron pills before packing the rest. Darwin wore the same onesie he wore when Vicky showed up. He fell asleep in his mother's arms instantly.

"Who do you think got Randel out of the house? You should be thanking Morgan."

"I don't trust him," Trish said sheepishly.

"I don't trust anyone," Vicky declared. "But it looks like we don't have a choice."

"Hm," Trish said. "He's out with Randel; he could detain him on the spot. Why wouldn't he do the same thing to us?"

"I—" Stumped, Vicky went quiet. Even though Agent Morgan promised her safety and expressed his need for Trish's help with Randel, he never gave explicit details. He was the same man who planned on disappearing Vicky and telling her parents that she had died in the hospital. *Why wouldn't he detain Randel on the spot?* Steve's voice.

"So I ask again, where are we going?"

"Some hotel on the outskirts of town. He said it was safe."

"No," Trish said.

"Where else are we—"

"I said no!" she shouted. She coughed, clearing her throat. "Take us somewhere else," she said.

"Like where?!"

"Figure something out! I had a storage unit, but you know what happened there."

Vicky huffed. They couldn't aimlessly drive around; she'd get pulled over for her shady plates and be stuck explaining the vampires in the car. And in Trish's condition, she might kill the cop, making their problems exponentially worse. But she was right. Agent Morgan couldn't be fully trusted, even though their deal seemed solid.

"Why do you trust him?" Trish asked.

"We made a deal."

"Did you sign it?"

"Yes, of course I did," Vicky said, curious as to why Trish didn't ask what the deal was.

"It's invalid because their laws don't apply to us. Understand that and understand it now or you *will* get us detained."

Morgan did plan on killing me once... Who's to say he won't try that shit again? "Well, what the hell are we supposed to do?" Vicky asked.

"Figure it out."

"That's not helping!"

Trish sighed. "Where did you go when you left the marina? You didn't go straight to Agent Morgan. You got this car from somewhere else..."

Mr. Wroth's dying place. "I— We can't go there."

"Where and why?" Trish sounded stern that time, less tired.

"Industry Row. Where the refinery is."

"A lot of abandoned buildings over there," Trish said matter-of-factly.

"Yeah. Lots."

"Is that where you got this car?"

Vicky said nothing. Going to the old farmer's house was out of the question. Trish wasn't going to drain him, and they were not commandeering his house to hide from her crazed husband or the thirsty FBI. Vicky waited for the idea to die in the silence.

"Why can't we go to Industry Row? It sounds safer than the trap you're walking us into."

"Because it's just not a good idea." *Mr. Wroth's blood may still be wet on the warehouse floor.*

"Sounds like you have a choice to make then," Trish said before falling silent, cuddling with her snoring baby.

Bars and Diners

"I see you didn't bother getting dressed," Morgan said as he dumped sugar into his coffee. "If I didn't know what you were, I'd think you were insane, walking around with a long sleeve t-shirt and a pair of jeans in this freezing weather." Morgan looked across the booth. "You look thin and pale."

"And I see your love for out of the way diners hasn't changed," Randel said. He fiddled with a napkin and peered out the window. The night was vast on the highway, where a cluster of cars sped by every few minutes. The bright lights of the tall windows of Moore's Café glowed on the parking lot where three semi-trucks parked, their owners either at the counter or resting. The raw smell of body odor, maple syrup, popping bacon, and coffee overpowered the blood circulating through the patrons' bodies. And as before, Agent Morgan reeked of mint that overpowered his addiction to coffee. The faintly polished blemishes on his teeth said as much.

"No, it hasn't. Neither has my propensity to not trust you," Morgan said.

Randel glared across the table, their booth small and unassuming to the couple of patrons and servers. He wanted to snatch that dated black fedora off Morgan's bald head and shove it down his throat. The agent looked much older than he had before. The wrinkles on his forehead and around his brown eyes deepened, and his waist gained several inches. His dark skin seemed creased, permanently making room for Agent Morgan's signature scowl. He was a maggot to a corpse, up Randel's ass at the worst times. But his negging had to stop before it grew into something unwieldy. "What do you want?"

"You know, when I saw you last—"

"Portland, 1996," Randel recited. "I was working in a dive bar and setting up punk rock shows. How could I forget?"

"Yes, that's correct. You looked good with that sky-high mohawk, patchy denim vest, and holey jeans."

Randel snickered, nostalgia filling him with brief comfort before it welted into discontent. "Hell, I even got around on a skateboard."

"Yeah, I know. When I met you at the bar, I told you that your days were numbered. And then you disappeared."

"Anyone with a brain would do just that if the FBI came around with threats. Trust me, I didn't need that bartending gig *that* bad."

"Have you ever wondered why I didn't arrest you then and there?"

"Because you found Sophia's body rotting in a barrel in the bayou and you could not find—"

"The twins. *Your* twins."

Randel sighed. "Right. Is that what this is about? You finally finding me after all this time?"

"Why'd you flee?"

Randel shifted and put an arm over the top of the booth. "If the government is onto you, flee. Everyone knows that."

"Everyone who is guilty," Morgan said, his tone growing combative.

"Huh," Randel said. "So, all right. You finally found me. Now what?"

"The murders in Miller last week," Morgan started.

"Had nothing to do with me," Randel said, only having seen the news talk about it nonstop for almost a week, and gathering more context clues from Trish's Jeep tracker. He hoped Pita would lay into her, giving Trish a reason to get the woman to set her free just for Trish to drink her. It would have been fun to watch the exchange on camera. But instead, they worked in tandem, and the show wasn't fun anymore.

"I know it wasn't you. Your wife told me as much."

"Ah. You know, I'm only just learning about how *big* her mouth is? I can't get her to open up any other time, but it seems like you cracked the code. Good for you!" Randel tapped his thick fingers against the table. *So she already knew. The garlic soup, her subtle panic that morning…*

"Randel, if anything happens to Patricia…"

"Yeah, yeah, yeah, I know. She's your witness for a private prosecutor, private trial, and a federal judge who will help you figure out what to do with me. God, see, this is why I *love* America. Even a monster has rights." Randel shook his head. His prosecutor and judge were the knives that government scientists would use to slice him open. His capture was Morgan's grant application for said experiments. Randel was well aware of this, but he wanted Morgan to deny it. He didn't. "Did you finally convince your superiors that I was worth the budget?"

Morgan raised a brow.

"Whoa, is that a smile I see on that wrinkled face?"

"Not yet." Randel followed Morgan's glare as he looked out the window. Even though there were no nondescript vehicles parked out there, not even the car Morgan arrived in, Randel was sure that backup was a whisper away. "You could plead out. Come with me now," Morgan said.

"You say that like I'm actually getting a trial? It's more fun to make you catch me, more fun to think of you pleading with your boss about how I am the guy that they lost so long ago."

"1888."

"Yeah." Randel shifted in the booth, leaned forward. "Do you still have my bracelet?"

"No. And its not like you need it anymore. I'm sure Sophia served her purpose. Now, if only we knew where the kids ended up…" Morgan searched Randel's face.

Randel raised a brow to this. "You know damn well that my families—all two of them, both of which were in existence well before you graced the FBI with your wonderful presence—did not, and still do not, have the same rights as humans. You would have killed them as soon as you got them into custody. So, let's not pretend like they mattered."

"You know why they matter." Morgan clenched his jaw.

"Oh, did I strike a nerve?" Randel scoffed, chuckled.

"They matter because…"

"…I'm *still* alive."

They sat in silence.

"If that's all you have, then I need to get going," Randel said. "You're not going to slap cuffs on me here, because I will ask why I'm under arrest, and you'll have to say." Randel chuckled. "I can hear you now: *Because you are a murderous vampire from the year of our lord 1807—at least that's what we think anyway—and you are responsible for many many murders. You even kill other vampires,* which isn't a crime at all, but whatever. Just like the death penalty. We're killing you because you kill others. Humans are so fucked up."

Morgan blinked.

"So, you got nothing, just as I expected." Randel sat back and crossed his arms. His heart slammed into his chest. The agent had come out to play. "But I mean, I can give you someone else. Take Trish and *Victoria Scott.*"

Morgan tensed.

"Ah, so you *know* Victoria was turned. I only know because she's been hanging around my house a lot since I was out of town. Did some face recognition shit, and there was her missing persons poster. She's been missing for two months. Attacked on one of my wife's infamous yoga nights. I can give you leads on all these yoga nights, and I guarantee you'd fare better with closing a load of new cases than trying to figure out who killed what vampire way back when. Why waste time solving that crime, when you can solve crimes where humans were affected? I'm sure that's what your superiors have been saying to you. You take Trish and Victoria off the street, and you don't have to worry about finding them in a barrel."

"And Darwin?"

Randel's son's name sounded foul coming from Morgan, the pissant human who acted as the authority. He pried in Randel's affairs as if he owned them. Randel could kill the entire diner, drain Morgan, and be on his way before the FBI showed up. But to what end? He clenched his jaw, Trish's naggy words plaguing his recent memory: *They make the laws. They have the numbers. They are the main beings.* "I love my son," Randel said. "He's staying with me."

"Until he goes missing too."

Randel tsked. "My kids don't go missing."

"Then where are they?"

Randel stood up from the table, narrowly avoiding bumping into the server who whisked by with a platter full of pancakes.

"Watch yourself," Morgan spat, remaining seated. "And have the decency to use your serum next time. Don't want anyone to recognize you, do you? Unless you're all out of serum."

Randel raised a brow as ancient sweetness coursed through his gums and cheeks. "I—" Randel stopped. He wanted to ask the agent if he had his jug, his life, his juice, his serum that had been hidden in the RV for years, undisturbed. Did he know the Bares and more importantly, did he know what had happened to them by playing such a dangerous game? What were the risks of taking Morgan and ripping his toes and fingers off until he confessed, until he forced the FBI to give that jug back? *It doesn't matter anymore. Move on.* Randel scoffed. "Leave a note when you're ready for me to give the information I promised. If you were smart, you would play hero and take it."

"I'll think about it," Agent Morgan said, sipping his coffee.

CHAPTER 38

Claims

Trish sat on the floor near the desk, Darwin still asleep in her arms. Vicky sat near the door across from them; it led to the lobby. The space was dark, but Vicky's cell phone flashlight offered little light for their temporary office space. The warehouse reeked of old paint, dusty drywall, and standing water; she couldn't pinpoint how long it'd been vacant; she only knew that it sat in the shadow of an oil refinery that sprouted up in Lakeshore over a year ago, and that it was due to open soon. A pet project of Vicky's, Trish wanted to ask how she felt about her planned protest falling through, or if she ever thought she'd hide near there, using the area for cover. No. Trish had a more pressing question.

"How's the bite?" Trish asked. Last time she saw Vicky, she'd fallen violently ill and was offended by the mere mention of seasickness. Trish spent a lot of time on boats in her earlier days, wooing sailors and fishermen off the coast of Maryland. She ended up on boats often and was never struck by motion sickness. Vicky couldn't blame vampirism for her subtle illness. But a fangless bite was another thing entirely.

"It's fine," she said, avoiding eye contact as she scribbled something in a spiral notebook. Her words felt shy and protective.

"How long were you sick? You look better now. Was it the bite?"

Vicky looked at Trish, blinked. "Yeah. I got better that night when I left."

"Hm. Did you find more iron pills or—"

Vicky narrowed her eyes. "What does it matter?"

"It doesn't." A bite from a half (*or quarter?*) vampire seemed to be enough to make a full vampire sick. Vomiting, shaky limbs, sweaty skin. All Vicky's symptoms seemed to vanish, and she didn't care to share how it was possible. Trish's heart sank. With everything they'd gone through, trust was nonexistent. She could tell from the cold distance between her and Vicky in that very room. She could see it all over the bleak expression on Vicky's face.

"You thought about leaving me, didn't you?" Trish asked. "You thought I belonged in that storage room, right?"

"Yeah," Vicky said pointedly. "Yeah, I did. I thought maybe the world was better off with you stuck in your own house, held prisoner by your own husband who is somehow worse than you…"

"Huh. What made you change your mind?"

"Because you changed yours," Vicky said, eyes back on her written words. "And because I don't have anyone else."

Trish frowned. "I don't understand. Do you really need anyone else? Morgan made a deal with you. You could have gone to that motel or wherever the hell he wanted us to be, but you didn't. You could be back in Detroit by now…or not." Trish raised a brow.

"You wanted to kill me at first. You said it yourself; I was supposed to be dead. Remember that? And I don't know if you changed your mind because you didn't know how to kill me or maybe you felt guilty, but…you helped me. You…helped me more than anyone else. You know exactly what it's like to be like this. Nobody else can feel it. Taste it. Be it…but you can. You make me feel like I'm not crazy, even though I am."

Trish drew her head back. "Crazy or primal?"

"No, no…crazy." Vicky looked at Trish. "Steve delivers my consciousness sometimes. I don't know why. I don't know how to make it stop." She sucked in a breath. "But I know he's dead and that his body is with the FBI or whatever. But I feel him. His breath on my face. His voice in my ears. But the things he says…it's what I'm thinking." Her voice grew heavy as tears raced down her cheeks. "Will he ever go away? I mean, will I ever own my own thoughts again?"

"No. It took years for Mel to leave my mind. Her laugh and her dreams and motivations somehow merged with mine. So after I killed her, after I beat her to death with my bare hands, after I dumped her in one of her boyfriend's whisky barrels in a landfill, she walked beside me just like she had all those years, all those concerts, and communes, and truck stops, and bars, and…" Trish cleared her throat. "She was my best friend because she was the easiest human to be around, until she wasn't. Until she got suspicious. Until she figured it was easier to torture me and leave the house that we bought together than to continue with a stable life that I talked a nomad, a travelling hippie, a gypsy, to embrace. She started hating me, and originally, the plan was to make my death look like an overdose. But when she took my ring off, the plans changed…I woke up and murdered my best friend. It never stops hurting. The voices never leave. They force us to keep a toe in our humanity. And I'm sorry that Steve gets to be yours…"

Vicky sighed. "And that's why I let you out. That's why we didn't go to Morgan. That's why we're here together. You know me… nobody else does."

"Hm." Trish said. She shifted a little, another burning question surging. "What did Agent Morgan offer you?"

"What?" Vicky asked, worry dragging her expression.

"What did he offer you?"

"Immunity…for the both of us."

"And you believed him?" Trish asked, wondering if the girl listened to anything Trish had told her over the past week. Wondering how Vicky's run in with Steve didn't teach her anything: humans could not be trusted.

"What?" Her face crumpled. "L-like you believed Randel?" Vicky asked, her icy glare staring daggers into Trish.

"That's different!" Trish spat. Vicky had no right to speak on something that she didn't understand.

"Sure. Well, I told Agent Morgan that something was wrong because your husband left Darwin crying for hours." She nodded. "I was going to go into your house on my own because Randel was going to leave eventually, right? But Morgan came to me first. Said I was *fucked* if I didn't help him. See, if you had handled your husband or stopped trusting humans like you trusted Mel, then me and Agent Morgan wouldn't have talked. I would have gone straight to you. In fact, *Pita* wouldn't have her throat slit. But..." she looked Trish up and down, "Randel had been handling you *pretty* good."

"Fuck you," Trish said, placing herself back into that storage room, her hands bolted to the counter, her body shaken and weak, her finger and ring violently ripped from her body by someone she trusted, someone she loved. Her eyes as she watched Pita's lifeless body as Vicky gathered the bug out bags. Her voice as she cried for the mother, wife and nurse who would never see life again. No more calls. No more laughs. No more café meet ups. "Don't you *dare* bring Pita into this. You have no idea what she meant to me and my son."

"Whatever, Trish. I didn't work with the FBI to just get you out of your house, I did it for Darwin. Just like I didn't deserve to be turned into *this*, he didn't either. He didn't choose—"

"Don't talk about my son. Look..." Trish rotated her neck and huffed, retargeting her fury. "I appreciate what you did, but you should never trust the Feds. You understand? They do not have you or Darwin's safety on their list of priorities. They don't care about you. Hear me? We are monsters to them."

Vicky smacked her lips. "Okay, Trish. Fine. But it looks like the monsters are just as bad as the Feds! Your finger is gone! A monster did that to you! A monster killed Pita! Don't you see that? Morgan wanted to help us deal with him, deal with your husband who you let manipulate you! Who you had a kid with. Randel kills vampires! You said that was impossible. But it's not. He would've killed you if me and Morgan left you in that house!"

Trish scoffed. "Morgan is *no* hero. Do you want to know why he asked you to break into my house? Wonder why he didn't send a team in to get us? Or better yet, wonder why he, himself, did not come in and get me? They're scared, Vicky! Scared of causing a spectacle, letting normal people know that vampires exist, scared of us smelling them coming, and scared of being killed. That's why. You let him use you—"

"To help you! Am I missing something, because it—"

A thunderous metallic ruckus from the warehouse.

Trish stood, holding Darwin close. She looked around, her chest pumping. Then she saw it: a place to hide Darwin.

"What the hell was that?" Vicky asked as she, too, got to her feet.

"I thought you said this place was abandoned!" Trish whispered.

"It is!" Vicky hissed. "But I also didn't want to come here! I told you that." She set her notebook next to her backpack and went out into the lobby.

Trish wrapped Darwin in clothes that she'd had in her own bag: a black sweater and three pastel cotton shirts. She tucked him underneath the desk, an alcove that faced the wall, hidden away from the door. She handed him a bottle that she filled with water.

"I'll be right back," she whispered before giving him a kiss on the forehead. He sighed in response, still asleep, ignorant to the disturbance.

Trish ran into the lobby and stopped short at the beginning of a hallway, the streetlights on the street casting a dim glow in the space. At the end of the dim hallway was an entrance, the word *Warehouse* was scrolled in bulky black letters just overhead.

Randel blocked the passage, standing over Vicky who lay on the floor unmoving.

"Randel…leave her alone," Trish said in a small voice. Her palms throbbed, reminding her of her holey hands that had yet to fully heal under her bandages, and the gap between her extremities that will forever remain empty.

Randel looked up at her, his eyes red, his claws exposed. Blue veins pressed against his thin tan skin. His silky hair was wild and mad, strands falling over his face.

"Why?" he asked. "You jealous?"

"Leave her out of this."

Randel knelt, got a closer look at Vicky. "I guess I was wrong about you. Here I was thinking you hated everyone. Thinking that if not for me and Darwin, you would still be the Loner Killer, slashing and draining bodies for the rest of your days. But look at you… You went out and made a friend after all. Good for you." He stood up. "Where is my son?"

Trish swallowed the lump in her throat.

"Oh, come on, Trish," he said, stepping over Vicky, inching toward Trish.

She stepped back. "Stay back!" She put a hand up.

"Stay back? Me? But you love me, don't you? You certainly don't think that I will let you keep my son away from me. That's fucking insane. Especially because I worked so hard for him. Harder than you did, that's for sure. I put in *years*. Years of hunting you down. Years of trying and trying until the pregnancy took. Years and years. It's time to cash in."

"You're not sacrificing our son," she cried. "I know that's what the kids are for. You asked if Darwin killed Maggie over and over again. Morgan didn't know what happened to your kids. They found one of your wives, but your kids were never seen again. And the names. The names that Ally had. The name you *told* me about..." Trish wavered. *Once a season. Once a season, then no more because the serum runs out...until you make more.*

"No, no, no." Randel wagged his finger, his pointy claw waving. "Darwin is not a sacrifice; he's more of an—"

"Ingredient," she whispered, her eyes blurred with tears. "I can't let you do that to him. You run out, you run out, that's it."

"Yes, I am, Trish. Yes, I am, and you nor Morgan nor *Vicky* will stop me."

"You'll have to kill me."

Randel dropped his head, then he charged, slamming his shoulder into her gut. She spit out a harsh breath as her back slammed into the wall. She smashed the bottoms of her fists into his back and shoulders, breaking his hold on her waist. She grabbed his hair and lifted her knee, slamming it into his nose, again, again, and again. Randel's head thrashed back, his nostrils flared as blood trickled. Losing her grip, she reached for his shirt again. Randel threw an uppercut into her chin. Her teeth clacked as she fell back into the wall. Then he grabbed her neck and lifted. She kicked, feet slamming into his shins as she coughed and croaked, searching for breath. He threw her and she came down on her shoulder, sliding across the lobby's dusty tile floor.

She went to get on her feet, managed to sit up right as her lungs greedily sucked up air. But Randel was on her, a small jar in his hand, the smell of sulfur so pungent in the air that she fought to hold her breath; her swollen throat wouldn't allow it. He grabbed her hair and pulled her head back, making her look at the ceiling. His knees and legs locked her arms and shoulders in place.

"You're lucky I don't have a full barrel," he said, before pouring the stinky chemical on her face. It stung, clogging her nose. She opened her mouth and screamed as her face burned, small knives tearing her skin apart, the heat killing the nerves in her cheeks.

Darwin screamed. "Momma!"

"One minute, bud," Randel said, as he dropped Trish's hair. She patted at her face, trying to wash the chemical away from her nose and mouth, trying to find her way to Darwin. But her legs refused to move, and her arms and hands followed suit, falling to her sides. She lay on the floor, floundering like a fish out of water. Her breaths went shallow and her extremities ignited in a pulsing pang. The chemical slinked its way into the back of her throat, forcing her to choke. She used her last movements to turn her neck. Sulfur infringed on all senses.

Randel stood over Vicky as she grunted, coming to. He forced her on her back and sat across her lap. He used his knees to pin her arms to her sides.

"Get off me!" Vicky yelled, kicking her legs, kneeing him in the back.

"You don't need those," he muttered. "You might as well be wearing a badge."

"Ahh!" A throaty shrill from Vicky. Her head moved with his violent pulling and thrusting. He yanked and yanked, and she screamed and screamed. Her head fell to the floor as he held up her fang like a trophy.

Ultraviolet

The morning sounds dragged Trish back into consciousness, the wind applied pressure to her broiling face. The concrete floor beneath her was smooth and painted light gray, and the roll-up door was half-open, allowing the elements in, making way for the sun. The snowsuit that she escaped in had been pulled off, leaving her bare down to her cheekies and bra.

Trish grimaced when she motioned for her body to move, but nothing happened. The tight skin on her face threatened to tear if she talked or screamed. Her bones stewed in the chemical that invaded her body. Sulfur plagued her every breath and sunrays crept through the opening.

"Mmm," she grunted, moving her head against her body's wishes, setting her nerve endings ablaze. Vicky lay a few feet away, her bloody mouth against the floor, her battered face and head in the path of the oncoming sun. She, too, was stripped down to her black boy shorts and bra. "Hmmmm," Trish gurgled through her strained throat, willing Vicky to wake. Vicky's chest didn't rise or fall. She didn't move or complain. There was nothing.

Yellow ate the floor as the clouds moved, welcoming another morning, seeing another day. *No, no,* Trish thought, her cries stuck in her head. The sun licked Vicky's bare foot before it found Trish's leg. She squealed in her throat, her face restrained by the chemical burns. The rays moved up her thighs, clawed at her flesh, chewed up her blood. Death smelled like brimstone and felt like fire.

Darwin, she thought. Randel had done this to her. Not only torture, mutilation, chemical and sun burns. He killed her by taking her son. *My poor baby*, she sobbed, her tear ducts not frozen in shock, allowing grief as the sun crawled up Vicky's legs.

The door flung up and quickly fell down, the abrupt opening making way for the sun to flash Trish's face. The sun split the chemical welts open, leaving Trish's face wet once the door was fully closed.

Randel had returned to pour more DMSO on her face or to carry her out to the sun. Trish braced herself, baring teeth at what was to come.

But Randel wasn't the man looking down at her with panic engraved in all his features. Agent Morgan's mahogany face dragged with worry as he looked around with a phone against his ear. "I need backup, quick!"

"I'm— Shit," he said as he hurried off.

Trish's face leaked and pain stabbed her thoughts. Her eyes fluttered to a close. Darwin smiled, living in her best thoughts. His dark hair and tawny skin. His hatred of blankets and love for toy trucks. His baby jabber and his curious gaze. His small fangs and blood on his lips.

Salt

Vicky's eyes shot open, a biting odor crawling up her nostrils. She sat up quickly, a soft mattress underneath her.

"Ugh!" she exclaimed, entangled in throwing hands and ripping claws. Blood saw her dying, and Randel was the administrator. "Wha—what?" she shouted, swinging her arms as the bloody lake of her dreams unhanded her, pushed her to the surface.

"It's okay, Victoria," a familiar voice with a face that could have been Daddy's twenty years into the future. "You're okay."

"What the hell is that?" she said, holding her nose. Her nostrils stung and her eyes watered.

"Salts to wake, blood to heal, chemicals to kill," he recited. "You people aren't the only ones that have access to an alchemist's pantry."

"I—I… Ahh!" she shrieked as pain ignited in her gums, head, and legs. Randel's hands. His fists came down hard on her face right after she tasted his flavorless skin as he forced her mouth open and ripped her fangs out. His weight nearly crushed her pelvis as he sat on her, his face young with red eyes full of old fury. He ripped and snatched, destroying her mouth.

"Here, here," Agent Morgan said. He handed her a burgundy jug, the savory smell of life liquids overtaking her need to scream and run—she was still dressed to do so, the black jogging suit still intact. But she wasn't running with a damaged body. Her head throbbed maddeningly as her mouth cramped with what felt like twenty rotted-out teeth. Her hips were numb, slowing her movements after her shocked revival. She took the blood and downed it like water in the desert.

Morgan stepped back. His once-white collared shirt was covered in blood. The room around them fell into itself, spinning, unrecognizable. Vicky stopped drinking and wiped her mouth with the back of her hand. "Where am I?"

"You are in the hotel room that I told you to come to. What the hell, Victoria?!" Morgan shouted as if his investigation were more important than the burns on her feet and legs, the gaping holes in her gums, or the sharp pain in her face and head. She looked around. "Where is—"

"She's in the bathtub, soaking in ice. She's not awake yet." Agent Morgan's nostrils flared. "You flaked on our deal!" he shouted.

She took another sip.

"Why?" he asked.

"We weren't sure if we could trust you. If this was an ambush."

"Well, looks like you walked right into one. He put trackers in their bags! He found you and took the kid!"

Darwin. Poor Darwin. Vicky teared up, hating her position, wondering what Trish would do once she woke up.

"Dammit! We can't proceed until Trish wakes up. We need her for the next phase—we need both of you for the next phase."

"Why? What the fuck is this next phase that you keep saying? I don't know what that is." Her ribs ached and her lungs tensed. She coughed.

Morgan sighed. "He hasn't left for Deedum yet. He knows I have eyes on him. But as soon as he takes off, starts heading that direction… You better hope it isn't too late for the kid or I swear you and her," he pointed to the bathroom, "will go down. I *swear* to you!"

"Just use the salt to wake her up."

"So that she can attack me?! The sun ate large portions of her skin. She needs to heal enough for me to wake her up without her being in too much pain. Do you understand that? I guess not, because all of this could have been avoided had you stuck with the plan!"

"I'm sorry!" Vicky said. "Okay! I'm…" She set the jug on the nightstand and went to stand up, but her legs buckled, sending her to the floor. Pangs throbbed in her knees. "Ahh!"

"Oh for…" Morgan rushed over, put her arm over his shoulder. "You gotta help me here! It was hard enough putting your damn clothes back on and lugging you out of the warehouse!" he said as he lifted. Using the mattress, she pulled herself up, and Morgan pushed her onto the bed. "Hurry up and drink the whole thing," he demanded. He handed her the jug.

"I can wake her up, Morgan."

"No! You need to drink that and get your strength back, fast. We are moving on to the next phase as soon as she wakes up."

"She will wake up if Darwin is—"

"Darwin!" Trish shouted, her call echoing in the bathroom. Morgan rushed over to a sack that had been sitting on a desk. He pulled out another jug full of blood.

"Drink!" he told Vicky, before disappearing into the bathroom.

CHAPTER 41

Cold Slab

This is the next phase, Trish thought as she lay across the leather back seat of a nondescript Lincoln with windows tinted on all sides. Morgan chewed on several pieces of minty gum, and Vicky stared longingly at the passenger window.

Trish's head finally cleared, pulling her past the need to rip the agent's face off when he came rushing into the bathroom—her body buried in chipped ice cubes in a too-small hotel tub. Before she opened her eyes, before dragging herself toward consciousness, Trish walked through the wilderness of her mind; red snow poured on her face as she drank it. She smiled, drenched in the comfort of knowing her personal place remained unchanged: the black trees swayed in the wind, mounds of red snow coated the ground, so soft against the bottoms of her feet, and the mountainous peaks lasted forever, outlining a dark sky with clouds packed with blood. The aches eased and her bones felt new, her skin smooth. The wisping wind blew, washing her in calm, the small sounds of creaking branches and clattering icicles accompanying her stroll. The soft clanging quickened, ringing. The piercing sound grew to a shrill, forcing her to cup her ears. She swiveled around, searching the private landscape for the disturbance. The black tree trunks remained unchanged. The juicy clouds wept. But the easy landscape's voice changed as nature's calls deteriorated into incoherent yelling. Someone's screaming. No. Shouting. Someone shouted their pain, their suffering rolling through the mountain pass and through the woods, their blood falling from the sky, their offerings for her to heal. No. Not their offering. Trish squeezed her eyes shut, her head throbbing. No. Not shouting. Trish dropped to her knees, misplacing snow, distorting red. Crying. A baby's cry. Darwin's cry. She woke with a stir, finding Morgan offering her a much-needed drink and a dire mission: get her son back.

The last two hours in the government-issued vehicle felt like a lifetime as Morgan drove across the state, following Randel by twenty minutes. Trish wasn't convinced that it was the smartest idea: trusting the FBI and going into a fight with no weapons, no blueprints. The plan was sure not to work. But the FBI had all the confidence in the world because they had their secret weapon. They'd had it since they found out Randel married and had another child. They'd had it as soon as they found Toby, Barbie, Tay, and Danny. *And Chad and Vicky and Mel and Johnny and…and…* She shook her head, a migraine inching into her temples. Regardless of what they planned, there was only one reason for her cooperation: they knew where her son was. She'd deal with thwarting Morgan's shitty proposal once she got her son back.

"We paid the Bares to allow us to take free reign over Randel's RV," Morgan said. "We retrieved the serum batch that he had in there. We needed to make sure he was all out, desperate, possibly forcing an error while he was confined to the night… Make it easier to keep up with him and limit his feeding schedule."

"Or to force him to kill *my son* sooner than later," Trish said.

"No. Not at all, Patricia. He uses kids when they are older. The first one was six and the twins were five. I didn't know he was going to take Darwin, and we really don't know *why* he did. We expected for him to run out of serum way before he could…" He paused, cleared his throat. "We'll get Darwin back," he assured.

Randel took Darwin because he's ready, she thought, not looking to answer for Maggie's disappearance. She wasn't sure if Morgan knew about that or if he knew that Darwin's first drink had primed him, making him *ready.*

Refusing to feed the human's knowledge base, she changed the subject.

"Was that DMSO that he threw on me? The chemical that you found one of his wives sopping in?"

"Yes,'" he said, eyes still on the road. "I smelled it as I drew in on the warehouse. It's pungent and very deadly to your kind. You're lucky he didn't have more; it's really hard to get barrels nowadays."

"Don't get any ideas," Vicky said as she looked out the passenger window. Trish felt her there, but didn't have the words safe enough to say around Morgan. Vicky must've felt the same; she hadn't said a word since Trish came to in the hotel room.

"No games here," Morgan said. "I'm happy you all recovered, even if it's just enough."

To that, neither woman spoke. The ice bath and gallon of blood healed Trish's cracked ribs, sun and chemical burns. The iron pills took care of the rest. Trish's face was still raw, shedding dead skin—she swept flakes off her snowsuit bottoms and onto the floor—and her chest ached when she breathed in too hard, or at all. She was one finger down, and the holes in her hands had closed, leaving new birthmarks. She'd wrapped them with a single layer of gauze. She glared at her knees, still smelling remnants of Randel's aftershave and body wash on the snowsuit that he used to shovel and salt theirs and Mrs. Peppers' walkways and driveways. Back when he was her husband and the father of her miracle baby. Back when she was all right with her heart beating for him and that her moves were made to avoid breaking his. Back when she lay in his arms and kissed him softly on the lips. *Back when...back when...* Her eyes moistened for the lost times and the times that were no more and never were. She could rip the suit off, but it had protected her until it hadn't. She wished Morgan hadn't found the snowsuit in the warehouse.

"If you came to the hotel," Morgan said, "then this would not be happening. We had a trap set for him. All you had to do was follow directions."

Here he goes with this we *stuff,* Trish thought. Her baby was in danger, and all Morgan cared about was his *we. And if* we *had indeed showed up, we would have been caught in the same trap.*

"How did you find us?" Vicky asked. "I imagine you put a tracker somewhere, but it wasn't on Randel's car."

"What makes you think that?" Morgan asked, a smirk on his face.

"Because it took you a while to find us."

"I guess that means you can answer your own question then."

Trish knew the answer. Vicky parked several blocks away, forcing them to walk to the warehouse because it was abandoned and it needed to appear as such. Randel found them because at some point in their fucked-up union, he put a tracker in the seam of the bag that Trish thought was a secret; he found them straight away. Agent Morgan was in the right neighborhood, just unsure of the exact location. She pictured him running up to several warehouses, kicking in doors with his long legs and penny loafers before finding the oddly ajar warehouse roll-up door. The sneaky tracker he put on Vicky's car only did half of the job.

"You knew I wasn't going to the hotel," Vicky said.

"Maybe you were, maybe you weren't. And you didn't. If I hadn't found you, you'd be skin soup in an abandoned warehouse."

To that, Vicky said nothing.

***

The small house sat on a massive slab of land, and it looked empty; all the lights were out. But Randel's SUV sat in the driveway, gleaming in the moonlight.

"The Bares have been MIA for about a week," Morgan said. "Randel must've been really angry when he found his serum gone."

"You must have known he was going to freak out on them," Vicky said, dismayed.

Bingo, Trish thought. Vicky was finally getting it. "What are we waiting on?" she asked, bouncing her knee. Morgan's agenda was the only thing keeping her in the car. She couldn't afford to be shot by *we* if they were in the area waiting, and if she knew anything about cops or the government, everything was a team effort.

"I expected for him to work in the RV when we set everything up. It's where his lab usually is, but he's doing it in the house. They clocked him moving new equipment inside before he returned to Lakeshore."

"Okay, tell them to stand down. I'm going to get Darwin," Trish said.

"Wait, wait. *All* of us are going," Morgan said.

Trish raised a brow. "You're going in too? Alone?" she asked.

"No. There's you and Vicky and me. That's three people." He pulled a handgun from his holster. "I don't know the layout of the house, but I do know it isn't very big. If he is prepping, then he must be in the kitchen."

Lies, Trish thought. *He knows the layout of the house. If he didn't, he wouldn't have his job.* But she let him go on.

"I'm not sure where he'll drain—" Morgan averted his eyes, thinking of a better term to describe her child's pending fate. But he stopped there, and Trish's heart fluttered. "Just remember what we talked about Patricia. We only have one shot at this…"

Vicky looked over her shoulder. A quizzical gaze crossed her face.

Trish looked away. "*We ran many experiments on the trace evidence that we have. There is only one way to end this, and we'll have everything we need once we reach Deedum.*" Morgan had said as Trish drank blood and swallowed iron pills, her body immersed in ice.

"Let's go. I'll take the front, and you two take the back door. It's right off the kitchen."

"Of course." Vicky sighed.

Hush

Vicky followed close on Trish's heels as they headed around the side of the small brick house that was consumed by a large plot of land with an old RV off to the side, maybe fifty yards away. The dry grass crackled, obliterated by careful feet. The crickets' songs were all encompassing, but not as alarming as their advance.

Vicky waited for Trish to protest Agent Morgan's plan. Waited for her to declare it off the table, or, at the very least, tell Vicky what it was. She hadn't been in the bathroom when they shared a hushed conversation, and Vicky couldn't hear them over the booming exhaust fan that Morgan switched on once Trish woke up. Trish hadn't even protested the jugs of blood, the ice bath, or them ending up in the very hotel room that she'd warned against. Judging by the strength of her gait, and the consciousness of her swift movements, she was suddenly all in on Morgan.

Trish came to an abrupt stop at the back door, a white light shining bright above it. The holey screen was worn, and small dents covered the dusty white fiberglass.

"What was Morgan talking about?" Vicky whispered, stopping next to Trish.

"Doesn't matter," Trish said. She tilted her chin and glared at the door. Her eyes narrowed.

"Do you hear something?" Vicky asked, not hearing anything.

Trish put her hand up, requiring silence.

The crickets' voices filled the space, nearly ringing in Vicky's ears. A light breeze rolled across the baren land, playing in the twilight.

Trish reached for the knob and turned. She huffed. "It's locked," she said as she kept turning it, her arm straining.

As Trish began their break-in, Vicky wondered just how close Morgan was to the Bares, the people who had been pretending to be Trish's mother- and father-in-law for years. Did the FBI have the keys to their house? Did the Bares participate willingly? Either way, Morgan held his plans close to his chest. He only told them what he wanted from them, skimping on the details as appropriate. For instance, he knew a lot about their morphology and habits, but they didn't know anything about him other than his first and last name. His house wasn't even his house. She imagined Morgan standing by in the Bares' living room, waiting for her and Trish to bust the door down, pulling Randel's attention so that he could make a sneak attack on all of them…lock all the monsters away, including the baby.

Is Morgan using us as bait? She wasn't sure of the plan he and Trish concocted, but Vicky's theory made more and more sense. Why wouldn't Morgan show up at the back door alongside them? Morgan didn't plan on getting his hands dirty at all. He wanted them all, and he had them all in the same place. Frowning, Vicky raised her hand, ready to tap Trish on the shoulder, tell her to abort mission and regroup, scratch out whatever Morgan's plan was and make their own.

Then the lock crumbled, metal busting loud enough for anyone in that very room to hear. Hand still on the knob, Trish stood so still that Vicky thought she had frozen in time. Then she wondered if Randel had been inside at all; he'd no doubt heard them coming if he were.

But the door wasn't snatched open from the other side. No hurried footsteps rushed for them. There was nothing but a creeping sulfuric odor.

Trish let them into a dim kitchen, the light over the stove offering a small glimpse of the space. A pot of days old spaghetti sat on the stovetop, a thin crusty layer of the sauce clung to the sides of the once shiny silver dish. The counters were congested with dirty bowls, plates, and silverware, and the small wooden kitchen table was cluttered with mail, magazines, napkins, and screws—the junk drawer was the surface of that table.

Trish had ventured on to the knife block on the counter, hidden within the cacophony of dishware. Several of the knives were missing, but the biggest one, the butcher knife, was there. She pulled the knife, the metallic whisper filling the space as the weapon scratched wood.

Vicky looked around, not having much luck in finding a weapon of her own. She opted for the cast-iron skillet with a layer of bacon grease evenly spread across the surface.

They stopped again. The mumbling noises of a familiar voice spoke easily underneath the blaring exhaust. It wasn't just any type of HVAC—it reminded Vicky of the fume hood in her chemistry lab class. The kind that discarded poisonous fumes. The sounds roared beneath them.

No wonder he couldn't hear us. She cringed. The sulfuric smell made sense—Randel was mixing something down there. She only hoped that the worst of Darwin's fate was listening to his psychotic father talk him to tears. But Darwin wasn't crying. The child made no sounds.

Trish made it to a doorway and peered inside. She nodded sideways, beckoning Vicky to come along, possibly finding the stairs.

"Where is Morgan?" Vicky mouthed, not seeing or smelling him at all. He smelled like mint in the car, which she appreciated more than the garlic, but found it annoyingly strong. But spending time with him made her realize that he did things like that on purpose. Just like he ditched them in Randel's lair on purpose. She spun around, not seeing him anywhere. She headed for the hallway, which was just past Trish, but Trish grabbed Vicky's arm, stopping her.

"Where the fuck is he?" Vicky mouthed.

Trish shrugged, flustered. "Come on," she whispered, before letting Vicky's arm go. She stepped forward, heading down the steps.

CHAPTER 43

Ingredients

"All my kids are different, one way or another," Randel said. He was facing a bright fume hood, wearing a rubber apron and jeans. His back was bare. The rest of the basement outside of his workspace was dim. A long wooden table took up the space in the middle. On it was a host of glassware, knives, jars full of fresh blood and tools. Then there was a metal tub, big enough to bathe a baby.

Trish stood in the middle of the staircase, stealing glances of the space as she used the wall as cover. Vicky stood behind her, holding the skillet, ready to swing.

"They all changed when we least expected it—their mothers didn't know what to do. Sophia was beside herself. She would've fallen into some kind of depression or mania if I waited any longer to drown her in that barrel. But Mary? She went along with it, thinking that we would keep each other's crimes secret forever." Randel chuckled. "She was stupid."

Trish looked again, finally finding Darwin. He was locked in a large dog kennel. He sat there watching his dad play with stinky chemicals. His face appeared nonplused, wondering where he was and why his father was speaking to him that way. Not understanding what the mad man was saying or what he intended to do.

"The first kid, Sarah, was six when she showed up at the apartment covered in blood. See, I would send her to the park on her own and see what she was like when she came back home. She was a smart kid—looked just like me, like all my kids."

Trish cringed at that.

"Sarah didn't talk to strangers. She didn't make friends. She just played by herself. But one day, her frilly dark hair and pink dress changed colors. They were dark red with blood that belonged to a man who thought he could take her away from the park." Randel snickered. "He regretted that up until he woke up in a bush and attacked people on the street. I mean, the man would jump on people and tear their faces off—he mutilated eight people before the Duluth police shot him clean in the head. Put him right down…sorry bastard. It was 1873, so naturally, they thought somebody voodooed him…turned him into Satan's puppet or something—a lot like your friend Maggie." He looked at Darwin. "You did that, buddy, just like Sarah had all those years ago. After the attack, Sarah came home with blood all on her mouth and clothes and hair… I was like, 'Damn, girl! Did you swim in it?' She didn't cry or say anything; she treated the situation like she just drank a cup of milk. No guess work there."

Trish took another step, clearing the wall.

"Now the twins, they were my favorites. See, Sophia knew what I was, and I had no idea that she had gotten wise. She tried to dump my own DMSO into *my* bath." He laughed. "I drowned her in that very vat that she stole from, and force-fed the neighbor to the twins. They were five, and I had no more time to wait." He stopped, his gaze lingering on a thought. "I loved those kids. They lasted for a *very long* time. Still would have them today if your dumb-ass grandparents didn't throw them out." He shrugged. "Oh well."

Trish moved slowly, each nervous step carrying her to the bottom of the staircase.

"And look, this isn't personal, son. I mean it, I think you're a great kid. But you have to know that you serve a greater purpose. That's something to be proud of." Randel chuckled.

Trish cringed as hate bloomed in her chest. She clutched the knife's handle as she walked on her toes.

"When you drank your *Maggie*, you activated something in your blood, something that this old man needs to keep going for another hundred years. Your activated blood, flax seed extract, and coffee grounds. That's it...that's all it takes—well, not including the solvents, catalyst, filters and...am I boring you?"

Darwin stared blankly. Randel shrugged. "Fine. I guess we'll just sit here in silence until I get this going."

Clearing the bottom step, Trish approached him from behind. She raised the knife level with his neck.

Randel hummed an amusing song as her steps grew heavier; her heart pounded louder.

"Momma!" Darwin shouted.

Trish's eyes widened as she caught a glimpse of herself. Pale, sunken cheeks, dark around the eyes. The small mirror stationed inside the hood, next to the Bunsen burner and beakers varying in size, peered back at her. Her ring was also there, glistening in the private light.

Randel spun around as Trish brought the knife down, embedding it in his shoulder.

"You should be dead!" he roared, his claws growing as he pawed at her face. She flew into the wall and fell to the floor. Pain ignited in her cheek as the open slits leaked blood.

Vicky met him just past the table where she swung the skillet, but he grabbed it, tussling for it. Vicky pulled, as did Randel. He twisted it, and Vicky's arm snapped. She screamed as he snatched it and slammed it against her head—a resounding *bong* echoed throughout the basement. She crashed into the steps and slid down to the floor.

Trish used the table to help her to her feet, then she leaped on his back as he went for Vicky. He spun around as she grabbed the knife, and pulled, fighting to take it from his shoulder. But he grabbed her hair and flung her away, her scalp screaming once he let her go. She slid across the table, and belly flopped at the base of the fume hood. A cramp shot through her chest once it met the hard floor. Randel stomped over, brought his foot down on her back, pinning her there. He stomped, and her chest exploded in crippling pangs. He stomped, and her lungs screamed. He stomped, and she spit out blood. She kicked her legs, tried to turn on her side, tried to fight off the next blow. Tried… tried….

"Momma! No!" Darwin's small, pained voice.

"Vicky," Trish cried. "Help! Hel—"

He stomped again.

"Momma!" Darwin's scream dug into her ears,

Randel growled and stomped again.

"V-V-Vicky!"

Firey shots cracked the chaos, and Randel stopped. Heavy breath and shock filled the basement. Trish turned on her side and Randel stepped back, turned toward the steps. Morgan stood on the staircase, the barrel of his pistol aimed at Randel. He fired three more shots, and Randel fell to his knees, then onto his side, collapsing on Trish.

"Vicky, you all, right?" Morgan asked.

"No," she said between grunts, holding her head. The skillet had split her skin, leaving a nasty leaky gash on the side of her face.

Agent Morgan went the rest of the way down the steps. "Here, help me get her out from under him."

Vicky held onto her lame arm and limped over. Using her good arm, she helped Morgan release the weight off Trish's side. It felt like an elephant had been lifted off her bones—her body shook with pain with every breath. They laid Randel next to her.

"Do it, Trish," Morgan demanded. "He's going to get up if you don't."

"Do what?" Vicky asked. "Let's get Darwin and go!" She limped over to the cage and Darwin reached for her, crying for her attention.

Trish looked at Randel, the angry holes in his chest filling with blood, spilling onto the floor. His chest wasn't rising or falling underneath the rubber apron. An untrained eye would think he was dead. But Morgan was right. Just as she got up on the dining room table to face Albert, and just like she was rejuvenated after Barbie's shotgun blow, and just like she survived Mel and Tucker's assault, Randel would rise again, more desperate than ever.

"Trish!" Morgan shouted.

Hands against the floor, Trish pulled herself up the length of Randel's body. She searched his face, finding the being who killed her all those years ago. But he wasn't beaten. He wasn't burned. He had a chiseled chin, sunken eyes and cheeks. Full lips and black, silky hair. Beige skin that was once honeyed. He was in his early twenties, hungry and lost in a time that did not belong to him, over two hundred years off course. Breaths staggered, she peered over her shoulder at their son. Shock and sorrow registered on his small face.

"Trish?" Vicky asked sheepishly. She crouched next to Darwin, ready to pull him out of the cage. They both looked on, hungry for guidance. Needing next steps. Hopeful that Trish could fix this.

And she could.

Trish blinked, failing to stop the tears from falling. She coughed, spraying blood on Randel's cheek. "I love you, Darwin," she said. "I would do anything for you."

"Do it before he gets up!" Morgan said.

"Do *what*?" Vicky asked, flustered.

"Thank you, Vicky. I—You—I trust you. And I care about you. I am so sorry for what I did to you; I hope you can forgive me someday."

"What? I-I do forgive you, Trish. You're not getting rid of me; don't you get that? You-you're my only friend. You and him." She looked at Darwin.

A wry smile. "That means a lot to me. P-please take care of him," Trish said.

"Why are you saying that?" Vicky asked, exasperated. "No. Trish, let's get out of here. Now!" She gave Morgan the side eye.

"I don't want Darwin to see this."

Giving up on her inquiry, Vicky promptly pulled Darwin out the cage. He cried, reaching for Trish, but Vicky held him with one arm. "You don't wanna leave?" Vicky's eyes pleaded. "We need you…"

Trish eyed the monster that she married, the man that she protected and respected enough to hide her secrets away from his perfect life.

"How could you be so fucked up?" she asked him with a shaken throat.

"Remember our *deal*, Trish," Agent Morgan reminded her.

"*We tested Randel's stash against the blood that was drawn from Vicky at the hospital. The serum temporarily alters the cells that make you a vampire. But when we tested Vicky's blood against your and Randel's trace evidence from the many crime scenes you left behind…*"

Trish's fangs slid from her gums as she lifted Randel's head, his eyelids moving, threatening to open.

"*…full on cellular destruction,*" Agent Morgan had said earlier when he helped her out of the ice bath, her body numb but refreshed. "*Looks like you have a choice to make.*"

Sweet venom soaked her tongue as she sank her fangs into Randel's neck. Stale sour blood flooded her mouth.

Blood for Blood

"Trish!" Vicky shouted, having looked over her shoulder as she rocked Darwin, quieting him down. Trish's back arched as she drank Randel in. He lazily batted at her chest and shoulders, failing to push her away. Trish sucked in a breath, teeth and fangs still buried in Randel's neck.

"N-no!" Randel mustered up before gurgling on what could have been his own blood.

Trish pinned his arm down, taking him, drinking faster. Her arms shook, as if all of her power rested in eating him whole.

Vicky turned away and sobbed into Darwin's hair. Maggie's bite was enough to make Vicky feel like she was dying, and she would have if she hadn't drained Mr. Wroth. Agent Morgan's incessant demand for Trish to drink Randel made the ugly truth clear.

Randel howled a guttural cry that shook the basement, his strength sinking into the floor.

Trish coughed, wet choking sounds erupted from her mouth. But her fangs stayed deep inside Randel's neck. She didn't stop. She drank. Drank for Randel's wives, drank for Randel's kids. Drank for Darwin. Drank for the madness to stop. Drank to end her own suffering.

The minutes rolled by, and the monsters before Vicky changed.

Randel's heaving chest slowed, then stilled. His hands gave up on pushing his reaper away. He lay still, eyes plastered to the ceiling.

Trish pulled her mouth from his neck and rolled over, laying on her back next to him.

Agent Morgan backed away and pulled out his phone. "Stay here," he said to Vicky, then headed up the steps.

Vicky carried Darwin over to where his parents lay. The surface of Randel's eyes looked uneven, bubbling like boiling water. His veins pressed against the underside of his beige skin, blue tunnels coursing with venom that he was meant to secrete, not take in. The holes in his chest had stopped bleeding, with no blood to be released. He wouldn't have the son that he intended to get. Instead, he got the mother.

Vicky grimaced as she crouched next to Trish. Her arm throbbing and still, while her head leaked and a migraine surfaced.

Trish looked at Darwin with red eyes, her breaths shallow. "I-I'm," she sputtered; blood spewed from her mouth.

"Don't talk," Vicky said. "Just…"

"N-no," Trish said. She lifted her hand and rubbed Darwin's hair.

"Momma?" he asked.

"Y-yes, baby?"

"Ew," he quipped. Then he smiled, reached for her.

Trish shook her head and smiled back. "I love you," she said. "B-be good, o-okay?"

Darwin responded with baby jabber, something that Vicky couldn't understand. But Trish must have, because she nodded. She looked at Vicky.

"Th-thank y-y—"

"Stop, Trish." Vicky couldn't bear for her to suffer any longer.

Seriousness crossed her pained face. "T-the ring." Trish peered at the hood. "P-put it on and e-e-eat once a season. Y-you can go in the s-un without burning. You can- you'll age slow-slowly. That's- how I—Take it o-off to eat. You have to…"

"Okay," Vicky said, all the pieces falling together. But Vicky lived without the serum for so long that she didn't think she needed it. But there was no harm in having that work of magic on hand. Vicky could sit in the sun and age, albeit only on the surface—something was better than nothing. Trish went on, her throat straining around desperate words. "G-get o-out of here. He-he—" She pressed her bloody lips together and threw her eyes to the ceiling. Vicky followed suit.

Morgan. Trish didn't trust him, and neither did Vicky. There was no way he would let Darwin and Vicky walk out of there. He'd probably get a raise for capturing two old vampires and locking up two new ones. Trish must have known that. That's why she played ball until hers and Randel's end, for Vicky and Darwin to have another chance. Vicky's heart lurched. Trish wanted them to take on the world with her by their side and Randel on their heels. But the authorities would always be there.

Vicky looked back at Trish. She watched Vicky with a cold, dead gaze.

Eight years later

"Yes. Mrs. Scott, we are doing everything we can to find Victoria," Pete said. "Her missing persons case is still open and active." He stood in his office surrounded by glass walls. The bustle of the headquarters teemed with new hires and returning ones. Suits and skirts answered tip lines, held meetings, and typed up reports with him in the center.

"God bless you, Agent Morgan. I really appreciate all your work—I just don't want you to forget about my baby," the woman said, her voice raspier each time she made her monthly call to his office.

"No, ma'am, I understand. I'll let you know as soon as we get some credible leads."

After they hung up, Pete headed for his desk. Three monitors adorned the sleek cherry oak surface, his priority cases showcased on each one. The one to the far left was an ad for a house in Detroit. The tenants ended up abducted or mangled in the basement. The second one was an overview of a six-hundred-page manifesto and recipe book by a woman who lived in the underbelly of Bayou Country, and the third screen showed a map of the United States, red dots marking places of interest. The spots were predominant in the spaces between major cities throughout the top half of the country, from Michigan to Montana. "I will find you. And when I do, I will make you disappear for the last time," he recited.

Trish knew it was the end of the line: the FBI had her surrounded, and there was no way Pete was allowing any of them to leave his sight again. But Darwin and Vicky snuck out the back door, ran across the land, and dove into the forest while the agents on hand stood out front, listening to Pete's instructions.

I guess she didn't trust me after all. Smart girl.

Vicky's spree started that very evening when she killed a man in a cabin and stole some supplies and his truck just to get Darwin out of the cold. It didn't stop there according to the hundred or so dots on his screen. *I guess those fangs grew back in…*

Although she and the kid had gotten away, much of Pete's job was to clean up the mess that the investigation into Randel and Trish had left behind. Not only did he keep Vicky's parents believing that she was never seen again after leaving the hospital, but nuance was also required to close the book on some loose ends.

They found the Bares on their own land; boot imprints forever bruised Mr. Bare's flattened skull and all the bones in Mrs. Bare's neck were deteriorated to nothing. Morgan grimaced, having archived those crime scene photos, he opted to remember the spunky, highly transactional couple as they were in life. Although they were unethically cremated, their families still questioned the official cause of death of carbon monoxide poisoning.

Dr. P's death was the simplest to close as it was ruled as a break-in gone wrong. The story spent a few days in the news cycle with the FBI taking over the manhunt for the nonexistent killer. Peter tsked. *Everyone can't be a hero.*

Pita's family was the hardest to deal with, as Pete had to confess that Randel had indeed killed her and that the couple died in a murder suicide in their own home. The child was reported missing. Missing because someone would call it in, inadvertently helping with the Vicky investigation. Missing because no one knew where he was and they never would if they didn't work for the FBI.

Neither he nor Maggie would ever be found no matter how many private investigators the Poloskis threw at either case. Pete had to dedicate an entire team to throwing the hounds off the scent—Maggie's parents were relentless with too much time and money to blow.

Either way, Pete was sure the Westons were responsible for Maggie's disappearance. That and the boy they found in Bronze Lake. But with Randel and Trish gone, the attacks spread beyond the Midwest, occurring across regions, all of them temperate with nice long winters. Pete wondered if Vicky was eating for herself or if Darwin shared her meals.

It explained where the ring went…one of the things missing from the evidence catalog.

"Hm," he said, mistakenly imagining what it was like for Darwin, the halfling.

Pete leaned back in his cushy leather chair. One of the dots on his screen was Kimmel Wroth, a senior manager from Bigman's Refinery. Vicky tossed his body into a swampy area near the refinery, prompting them to postpone the opening for a few months.

He chuckled. The girl sure was clever. But not clever enough. A camera picked up a shadowy figure with the same stature and build of Victoria Scott. Pete laughed. "Ohhh, Victoria…" he sang.

Even though Pete's joints hurt when he bent his fingers to tap on the keyboard too hard, he couldn't live without his cases. Sometimes, it shook his soul to close any of them, signifying the end of a hunt. For that, he thanked Vicky for sneaking out of the house that night.

A new email came in with the subject line: *Another One.*

He opened it to find another flyer. There was a man with long oily hair and ivory skin. He smiled at the camera, his cheeks red. He was a bigger guy, wearing a denim jacket and a yellow shirt. His name was Robert Shay, and his bloodless corpse was found in an illegal tent on a wildlife preserve. He'd been missing from Dewberry, Montana for three months. Pete went back to his map and placed a dot on that very spot. He refined the view, focusing on the trail that started in West Michigan, *Kimmel Wroth*, and ended in Montana.

"Hello, Vicky and Darwin. Can't wait to catch up."

He replied to the email:

I'm on my way.

EXCERPT FROM
NETTED -
THE BEGINNING

CHAPTER 1

Sully lifted his heavy eyelids. The blue luminescent light stung, making him squint. He grunted, bringing life to his sore throat. His mouth felt like he'd sucked down a jar of cotton balls. He went to move his arms to wipe the crust from his eyes, much like he'd done every morning throughout his forty-seven years of life.

The belligerent clinging of metal sounded as chains smacked the chair's steel arms while they held his wrists down.

He shifted his shoulders and met a sheer resistance. An extended grip spanned the length of his chest, crinkling his dingy black t-shirt underneath it. Chains wrapped him so tight, he felt the chill from the links deep in his lungs and heart. He went to move his legs and found his ankles in a similar condition: pressed hard against the chair's steel legs.

A migraine split his brain, causing him to utter a harsh grunt. This was worse than a tequila hangover from that time he dropped off supplies in El Centro. It was even worse than the time he flew into the grassy null off I-64 outside of Louisville, lodging his sleeping face into the thick steering wheel of his rig. This discomfort was a new pain that left his head, from his temples up to his forehead, feeling like aching, useless mush.

Breathing hard, he peered forward with wide eyes. A camera stared back into his face as it sat on a tripod. The dark lens gleamed in the harsh light.

Sweat trickled down his forehead as he tried moving his fingers, but they sat stiff, purple and bulged at the tips as if blood stopped flowing past his bound wrists hours ago.

"Help!" he wailed. He cleared his throat to loosen the thick grogginess in his tone.

His heart dropped when a door to his right swung in, allowing a figure to enter.

The figure approached and stood between Sully and the camera before crouching. The only thing Sully could make of the man kneeling before him was the sweater taut against his wide chest and broad shoulders. The cursive letters on his right peck read: Father Paul. A black ski mask hid his face.

"Please…buddy…" Sully cleared his throat again. The stale taste of sleeper's breath coated his mouth. "You gotta help me. I don't know where I am…where my rig is…"

The man only stared; his dark eyes scolded Sully from behind a pair of thick goggles.

Sully passed the stranger a peculiar glare as he tried recollecting thoughts from the past few hours. How'd he get here? The last thing he remembered was the motel room off I 94, a big slab of a road. He and his rig were on the way to The Windy City to drop off some car parts from Albany. He'd made perfect timing, nearly setting a record. There was more than enough time to stop two hours west of the Motor City at a dive, Pete's Grill.

While sitting at the bar, a beaver, Pam, approached him at the bar. Her thick lips and cherry-red hair left him stiffened below the belt. The way that red dress hugged her curvy body made him want to explore what laid underneath it. She was a queen, the type to be his significant other and deep down, he'd hoped to ask her to take on the road with him. She'd be a beautiful passenger seat cover for the old dog. A worthy companion for a man who only knew the road and planned to live out his days riding it. But it wasn't only because of her youthful face and gentle smile. It was the noteworthy conversation; she knew a lot about rigs and trailers. Trucks and tires. More than your typical lot lizard.

After they had a few draft beers, he remembered taking her for a ride up the road about fifty miles and stopping at the Go Go Inn, her idea. Soon after they'd entered the room, Sully complained about how the ugly floral décor looked like baby-sized cockroaches resting on the mattress and curtains before something heavy pummeled the back of his skull. He recalled falling face-first into the scratchy, dingy carpet. The smell of mildew stuffed his senses before the room blurred and his eyes shut.

Now, there was a blinking red light from a camera, bugging his retinas and intensifying his headache. With every shallow breath, the throbbing in his chest hitched, stuffing a sickening ball in his gut.

"Where am I?" he cried.

Father Paul continued to stare up at him.

The black window across from them, just behind the camera, took on a rectangular gleam. There was a TV mounted to the wall behind him. A red skull spun in its center.

Sully tried shifting his weight by rocking side to side. Or at least he thought he was. The chair underneath him stood still. Dizzy with exhaustion, panic riddled his nerves. "Answer me!" Tears fell down his face.

Father Paul's eyes lit up as if pleased to hear another man beg.

The screen behind Sully went black. Then a short phrase popped up in bold letters. They appeared blurry as tears clouded his sight.

He wished he'd read it. But as he batted his eyelids and squinted hard, the words disappeared.

Father Paul stood straight, towering about six feet over Sully, and swaggered over to an oak bookcase.

Sully watched in horror as Father Paul swiped up a rip saw from the top shelf and walked back over with an urgent stride in his step.

Sully fidgeted and shook. Through exasperated breaths, he said, "Wait, wait, *wait*! Please don't. Uh... I'm sorry for whatever I did! Please, just don't—"

Father Paul pressed the saw's teeth onto the bridge of Sully's nose.

Sully sobbed and stammered. "P—p-please!" he said.

Father Paul took a handful of Sully's thick hair and yanked his head back. Sully's scalp screamed as his hairline burned. He tried turning his neck and shaking his head, but Father's Paul's grip only tightened.

Start the Netted Trilogy today:

Dale and Jessica find themselves caught in the web of Father Paul—a predator who orchestrates terror for an audience that craves blood. Trapped and desperate, they must make impossible choices while sadistic viewers watch and bet on their fate.

But escape is only the beginning of the nightmare.

mybook.to/Nettedebook

Sign up for updates from K.T. Rose:
https://www.kyrobooks.com/subscribe-1

MORE FROM K.T. ROSE

The Trish Vampire Series Book 1
Blood
Hunger. Desperation. Terror. A mother's love knows
no bounds - neither does her appetite.
https://mybook.to/trishblood

The Trish Vampire Series Book 2
Monster
Blood. Family. Secrets. In the quiet suburbs, a mother's darkest
instincts threaten to unravel the very foundation of her world.
https://mybook.to/trishmonster

The Trish Vampire Series Book 3
Watcher
Trish's worst nightmare has come true—her secrets are unraveling.
https://mybook.to/trishwatcher

Trinity of Horror- Macabre Tales Volume 1
When suspicion meets desperation, the inner
demons of desperate souls ignite.
https://mybook.to/3hs5FUT

Netted- A Serial Killer Thriller and Fast-Paced
Suspense Series Box Set Books 1-3
https://mybook.to/1D0ntJP

**Netted- A Serial Killer Thriller and Fast-Paced Suspense Book 1
The Beginning**
*Can Dale and Jessica escape Father Paul, the
dark web's most sadistic cult leader?*
https://mybook.to/asJQ6Yo

**Netted- A Serial Killer Thriller and Fast-Paced Suspense Book 2
Inside Out**
Is it possible to escape a cult that feeds on fear?
https://mybook.to/bKRr

**Netted- A Serial Killer Thriller and Fast-Paced Suspense Book 3
The Crash**
When time runs out, bodies will fall.
https://mybook.to/aeMfHJ

Trinity of Horror- Macabre Tales Volume 2
A normal summer day…drenched in blood.
https://mybook.to/Fqsg

**The Haunting of Gallagher Hotel- A Chilling
Haunted House Horror Novel**
Pride and greed infect the soul, trapping the dead in Gallagher Hotel.
https://mybook.to/FbYFj

Stay connected with K.T. Rose by visiting:
https://www.kyrobooks.com/subscribe-1

www.ingramcontent.com/pod-product-compliance
Lightning Source LLC
Chambersburg PA
CBHW060306310726

48976CB00007B/2233